Murder to Music

Murder to Music

Musical Mysteries from
Ellery Queen's Mystery Magazine
and *Alfred Hitchcock Mystery Magazine*

Edited by
CYNTHIA MANSON and
KATHLEEN HALLIGAN

Carroll & Graf Publishers, Inc.
New York

Introduction copyright © 1997 by Cynthia Manson and Kathleen Halligan

First Carroll & Graf edition 1997
Carroll & Graf Publishers, Inc.
260 Fifth Avenue
New York, NY 10001

Library of Congress Cataloging-in-Publication Data

Murder to music : musical mysteries from Ellery Queen's mystery
  magazine and Alfred Hitchcock mystery magazine / edited by Cynthia
  Manson and Kathleen Halligan.—1st Carroll & Graf ed.
     p. cm.
  ISBN 0-7867-0406-3 (cloth)
  1. Detective and mystery stories, American.   2. Detective and
mystery stories, English.   3. Musical Fiction.   I. Manson, Cynthia,
II. Halligan, Kathleen.   III. Ellery Queen's mystery magazine.
IV. Alfred Hitchcock's mystery magazine.
PS648.D4M883   1997
813'.067208367—dc21   97-517
                                                               CIP

Manufactured in the United States of America

The acknowledgments on the following page constitute an extension of this
copyright page.

Contents

Murder to Music

Introduction

We have gathered together a collection of mystery stories in which music plays a key role. Among our maestros of mystery are authors such as Agatha Christie, Cornell Woolrich, Lillian de la Torre, and others.

The author's compositions of character and plot are as diverse as their choice of musical texts. Opera, jazz and blues, rock 'n' roll, country and western, as well as classical selections, set the stage for murder and mayhem. Edward D. Hoch's undercover agent Jeffery Rand pursues a case backstage at the opera. Lynne Barrett's colorful Elvis impersonator undergoes a marked change while on a road tour. Agatha Christie's tale stars Mme. Paula Nazorkoff, the quintessential opera diva, while Charlotte Hinger spotlights a country-western singer whose glory is soon to fade.

On a different note, we have John Lutz's private eye Nudger trailing a blues singer in the jazz clubs of New Orleans and Doug Allyn's gumshoe tracking down a record company's unpaid royalties for an angry client. Linda Haldeman's libretto represents a dark tale for fans of *Tosca*, while Michael Underwood describes the drama of a Wagner fan who becomes a suspect in a murder case.

For music and mystery lovers alike this collection will strike a particularly enjoyable chord.

Swan Song

by Agatha Christie

*I*t was eleven o'clock on a May morning in London. Mr. Cowan was looking out of the window; behind him was the somewhat ornate splendour of a sitting room in a suite at the Ritz Hotel. The suite in question had been reserved for Mme. Paula Nazorkoff, the famous operatic star, who had just arrived in London. Mr. Cowan, who was Madame's principal man of business, was awaiting an interview with the lady. He turned his head suddenly as the door opened, but it was only Miss Read, Mme. Nazorkoff's secretary, a pale girl with an efficient manner.

"Oh, so it's you, my dear," said Mr. Cowan. "Madame not up yet, eh?"

Miss Read shook her head.

"She told me to come round at ten o'clock," Mr. Cowan said. "I have been waiting an hour."

He displayed neither resentment nor surprise. Mr. Cowan was indeed accustomed to the vagaries of the artistic temperament. He was a tall man, clean-shaven, with a frame rather too well covered, and clothes that were rather too faultless. His hair was very black and shining, and his teeth were aggressively white. When he spoke, he had a way of slurring his "s's" which was not quite a lisp, but came perilously near to it. At that minute a door at the other side of the room opened, and a trim French girl hurried through.

"Madame getting up?" inquired Cowan hopefully. "Tell us the news, Elise."

Elise immediately elevated both hands to heaven.

"Madame she is like seventeen devils this morning; nothing pleases her! The beautiful yellow roses which monsieur sent to her last night, she says they are all very well for New York, but that it is imbécile to send them to her in London. In London, she says, red roses are the only things possible, and straightaway she opens the door and precipitates the yellow roses into the passage, where they descend upon a monsieur, très comme il faut, a military gentleman, I think, and he is justly indignant, that one!"

Cowan raised his eyebrows, but displayed no other signs of emotion. Then he took from his pocket a small memorandum book and pencilled in it the words "red roses."

Elise hurried out through the other door, and Cowan turned once more to the window. Vera Read sat down at the desk and began opening letters and sorting them. Ten minutes passed in silence, and then the door of the bedroom burst open, and Paula Nazorkoff flamed into the room. Her immediate effect upon it was to make it seem smaller; Vera Read appeared more colourless, and Cowan retreated into a mere figure in the background.

"Ah, ha! My children," said the prima donna. "Am I not punctual?"

She was a tall woman, and for a singer not unduly fat. Her arms and legs were still slender, and her neck was a beautiful column. Her hair, which was coiled in a great roll halfway down her neck, was of a dark, glowing red. If it owned some at least of its colour to henna, the result was none the less effective. She was not a young woman, forty at least, but the lines of her face were still lovely, though the skin was loosened and wrinkled round the flashing, dark eyes. She had the laugh of a child, the digestion of an ostrich, and the temper of a fiend, and she was acknowledged to be the greatest dramatic soprano of her day. She turned directly upon Cowan.

"Have you done as I asked you? Have you taken that abominable English piano away and thrown it into the Thames?"

"I have got another for you," said Cowan, and gestured toward where it stood in the corner.

Nazorkoff rushed across to it and lifted the lid.

"An Erard," she said; "that is better. Now let us see."

The beautiful soprano voice rang out in an arpeggio, then it ran lightly up and down the scale twice, then took a soft little run up to a high note, held it, its volume swelling louder and louder, then softened again till it died away in nothingness.

"Ah!" said Paula Nazorkoff in naïve satisfaction. "What a beautiful voice I have! Even in London I have a beautiful voice."

"That is so," agreed Cowan in hearty congratulation. "And you bet London is going to fall for you all right, just as New York did."

"You think so?" queried the singer.

There was a slight smile on her lips, and it was evident that for her the question was a mere commonplace.

"Sure thing," said Cowan.

Paula Nazorkoff closed the piano lid down and walked across to the table with that slow undulating walk that proved so effective on the stage.

"Well, well," she said, "let us get to business. You have all the arrangements there, my friend?"

Cowan took some papers out of the portfolio he had laid on a chair.

"Nothing has been altered much," he remarked. "You will sing five times at Covent Garden, three times in *Tosca*, twice in *Aïda*."

"*Aïda*! Pah," said the prima donna, "it will be unutterable boredom. *Tosca*, that is different."

"Ah, yes," said Cowan. "*Tosca* is your part."

Paula Nazorkoff drew herself up.

"I am the greatest Tosca in the world," she said simply.

"That is so," agreed Cowan. "No one can touch you."

"Roscari will sing 'Scarpia,' I suppose?"

Cowan nodded.

"And Emile Lippi."

"What?" shrieked Nazorkoff. "Lippi—that hideous little barking frog, croak—croak—croak. I will not sing with him. I will bite him. I will scratch his face."

"Now, now," said Cowan soothingly.

"He does not sing, I tell you, he is a mongrel dog who barks."

"Well, we'll see; we'll see," said Cowan.

He was too wise ever to argue with temperamental singers.

"The Cavaradossi?" demanded Nazorkoff.

"The American tenor, Hensdale."

The other nodded.

"He is a nice little boy; he sings prettily."

"And Barrère is to sing it once, I believe."

"He is an artist," said Madame generously. "But to let that croaking frog Lippi be Scarpia! Bah—I'll not sing with him."

"You leave it to me," said Cowan soothingly.

He cleared his throat and took up a fresh set of papers.

"I am arranging for a special concert at the Albert Hall."

Nazorkoff made a grimace.

"I know, I know," said Cowan; "but everybody does it."

"I will be good," said Nazorkoff, "and it will be filled to the ceiling, and I shall have much money. *Ecco!*"

Again Cowan shuffled papers.

"Now here is quite a different proposition," he said, "from Lady Rustonbury. She wants you to go down and sing."

"Rustonbury?"

The prima donna's brow contracted as if in the effort to recollect something.

"I have read the name lately, very lately. It is a town—or a village, isn't it?"

"That's right, pretty little place in Hertfordshire. As for Lord Rustonbury's place, Rustonbury Castle, it's a real dandy old feudal seat, ghosts and family pictures, and secret staircases, and a slap-up private theatre. Rolling in money they are, and always giving some private show. She suggests that we give a complete opera, preferably *Butterfly.*"

"*Butterfly?*"

Cowan nodded.

"And they are prepared to pay. We'll have to square Covent Garden, of course, but even after that it will be well worth your while financially. In all probability, royalty will be present. It will be a slap-up advertisement."

Madame raised her still beautiful chin.

"Do I need advertisement?" she demanded proudly.

"You can't have too much of a good thing," said Cowan, unabashed.

"Rustonbury," murmured the singer; "where did I see—"

She sprang up suddenly and, running to the center table, began turning over the pages of an illustrated paper which lay there. There was a sudden pause as her hand stopped, hovering over one of the pages, then she let the periodical slip to the floor and returned slowly to her seat. With one of her swift changes of mood, she seemed now an entirely different personality. Her manner was very quiet, almost austere.

"Make all arrangements for Rustonbury. I would like to sing there, but there is one condition—the opera must be *Tosca*."

Cowan looked doubtful.

"That will be rather difficult—for a private show, you know, scenery and all that."

"*Tosca* or nothing."

Cowan looked at her very closely. What he saw seemed to convince him; he gave a brief nod and rose to his feet.

"I will see what I can arrange," he said quietly.

Nazorkoff rose too. She seemed more anxious than was usual, with her, to explain her decision.

"It is my greatest role, Cowan. I can sing that part as no other woman has ever sung it."

"It is a fine part," said Cowan. "Jeritza made a great hit in it last year."

"Jeritza?" cried the other, a flush mounting in her cheeks. She proceeded to give him at great length her opinion of Jeritza.

Cowan, who was used to listening to singers' opinions of other singers, abstracted his attention till the tirade was over; he then said obstinately:

"Anyway, she sings 'Vissi D'Arte' lying on her stomach."

"And why not?" demanded Nazorkoff. "What is there to prevent her? I will sing it on my back with my legs waving in the air."

Cowan shook his head with perfect seriousness.

"I don't believe that would go down any," he informed her. "All the same, that sort of thing takes on, you know."

"No one can sing 'Vissi D'Arte' as I can," said Nazorkoff confidently. "I sing it in the voice of the convent—as the good nuns taught me to sing years and years ago. In the voice of a choir boy or an angel, without feeling, without passion."

"I know," said Cowan heartily. "I have heard you; you are wonderful."

"That is art," said the prima donna, "to pay the price, to suffer, to endure, and in the end not only to have all knowledge, but also the power to go back, right back to the beginning and recapture the lost beauty of the heart of a child."

Cowan looked at her curiously. She was staring past him with a strange, blank look in her eyes, and something about that look of hers gave him a creepy feeling. Her lips just parted, and she whispered a few words softly to herself. He only just caught them.

"At last," she murmured. "At last—after all these years."

II

Lady Rustonbury was both an ambitious and an artistic woman; she ran the two qualities in harness with complete success. She had the good fortune to have a husband who cared for neither ambition nor art and who therefore did not hamper her in any way. The Earl of Rustonbury was a large, square man, with an interest in horseflesh and in nothing else. He admired his wife, and was proud of her, and was glad that his great wealth enabled her to indulge all her schemes. The private theatre had been built less than a hundred years ago by his grandfather. It was Lady Rustonbury's chief toy—she had already given an Ibsen drama in it, and a play of the ultra new school, all divorce and drugs, also a poetical fantasy with Cubist scenery. The forthcoming performance of Tosca had created widespread interest. Lady Rustonbury was entertaining a very distinguished house party for it, and all London that counted was motoring down to attend.

Mme. Nazorkoff and her company had arrived just before luncheon. The new young American tenor, Hensdale, was to sing "Cavaradossi," and Roscari, the famous Italian baritone, was to be Scarpia. The expense of the production had been enormous, but nobody cared about that. Paula Nazorkoff was in the best of humours; she was charming, gracious, her most delightful and cosmopolitan self. Cowan was agreeably surprised, and prayed that this state of things might continue.

After luncheon the company went out to the theatre and inspected the scenery and various appointments. The orchestra was under the direction of Mr. Samuel Ridge, one of England's most famous conductors. Everything seemed to be going without a hitch, and strangely enough, that fact worried Mr. Cowan. He was more at home in an atmosphere of trouble; this unusual peace disturbed him.

"Everything is going a darned sight too smoothly," murmured Mr. Cowan to himself. "Madame is like a cat that has been fed on cream. It's too good to last; something is bound to happen."

Perhaps as the result of his long contact with the operatic world, Mr. Cowan had developed the sixth sense, certainly his prognostications were justified. It was just before seven o'clock that evening when the French maid, Elise, came running to him in great distress.

"Ah, Mr. Cowan, come quickly; I beg of you come quickly."

"What's the matter?" demanded Cowan anxiously. "Madame got her back up about anything—ructions, eh, is that it?"

"No, no, it is not Madame; it is Signor Roscari. He is ill; he is dying!"

"Dying? Oh, come now."

Cowan hurried after her as she led the way to the stricken Italian's bedroom. The little man was lying on his bed, or rather jerking himself all over it in a series of contortions that would have been humorous had they been less grave. Paula Nazorkoff was bending over him; she greeted Cowan imperiously.

"Ah! There you are. Our poor Roscari, he suffers horribly. Doubtless he has eaten something."

"I am dying," groaned the little man. "The pain—it is terrible. Ow!"

He contorted himself again, clasping both hands to his stomach, and rolling about on the bed.

"We must send for a doctor," said Cowan.

Paula arrested him as he was about to move to the door.

"The doctor is already on his way; he will do all that can be done for the poor suffering one, that is arranged for, but never, never will Roscari be able to sing tonight."

"I shall never sing again; I am dying," groaned the Italian.

"No, no, you are not dying," said Paula. "It is but an indigestion, but all the same, impossible that you should sing."

"I have been poisoned."

"Yes, it is the ptomaine without doubt," said Paula. "Stay with him, Elise, till the doctor comes."

The singer swept Cowan with her from the room.

"What are we to do?" she demanded.

Cowan shook his head hopelessly. The hour was so far advanced that it would not be possible to get anyone from London to take Roscari's place. Lady Rustonbury, who had just been informed of her guest's illness, came hurrying along the corridor to join them. Her principal concern, like Paula Nazorkoff's, was the success of *Tosca*.

"If there were only someone near at hand," groaned the prima donna.

"Ah!" Lady Rustonbury gave a sudden cry. "Of course! Bréon."

"Bréon?"

"Yes, Edouard Bréon, you know, the famous French baritone. He lives near here. There was a picture of his house in this week's *Country Homes*. He is the very man."

"It is an answer from heaven," cried Nazorkoff. "Bréon as Scarpia, I remember him well, it was one of his greatest rôles. But he has retired, has he not?"

"I will get him," said Lady Rustonbury. "Leave it to me."

And being a woman of decision, she straightway ordered out the Hispano Suiza. Ten minutes later, M. Edouard Bréon's country retreat was invaded by an agitated countess. Lady Rustonbury, once she had

made her mind up, was a very determined woman, and doubtless
M. Bréon realized that there was nothing for it but to submit. Also,
it must be confessed, he had a weakness for countesses. Himself a
man of very humble origin, he had climbed to the top of his profession, and had consorted on equal terms with dukes and princes,
and the fact never failed to gratify him. Yet, since his retirement to
this old-world English spot, he had known discontent. He missed
the life of adulation and applause, and the English county had not
been as prompt to recognize him as he thought they should have
been. So he was greatly flattered and charmed by Lady Rustonbury's
request.

"I will do my poor best," he said, smiling. "As you know, I have
not sung in public for a long time now. I do not even take pupils,
only one or two as a great favour. But there—since Signor Roscari
is unfortunately indisposed—"

"It was a terrible blow," said Lady Rustonbury.

"Not that he is really a singer," said Bréon.

He told her at some length why this was so. There had been, it
seemed, no baritone of distinction since Edouard Bréon retired.

"Mme. Nazorkoff is singing 'Tosca,'" said Lady Rustonbury.
"You know her, I dare say?"

"I have never met her," said Bréon. "I heard her sing once in
New York. A great artist—she has a sense of drama."

Lady Rustonbury felt relieved—one never knew with these singers—they had such queer jealousies and antipathies.

She reentered the hall at the castle some twenty minutes later
waving a triumphant hand.

"I have got him," she cried, laughing. "Dear M. Bréon has really
been too kind. I shall never forget it."

Everyone crowded round the Frenchman, and their gratitude and
appreciation were as incense to him. Edouard Bréon, though now
close on sixty, was still a fine-looking man, big and dark, with a
magnetic personality.

"Let me see," said Lady Rustonbury. "Where is Madame—? Oh!
There she is."

Paula Nazorkoff had taken no part in the general welcoming of
the Frenchman. She had remained quietly sitting in a high oak chair

in the shadow of the fireplace. There was, of course, no fire, for the evening was a warm one and the singer was slowly fanning herself with an immense palm-leaf fan. So aloof and detached was she, that Lady Rustonbury feared she had taken offence.

"M. Bréon." She led him up to the singer. "You have never yet met Madame Nazorkoff, you say."

With a last wave, almost a flourish, of the palm leaf, Paula Nazorkoff laid it down and stretched out her hand to the Frenchman. He took it and bowed low over it, and a faint sigh escaped from the prima donna's lips.

"Madame," said Bréon, "we have never sung together. That is the penalty of my age! But Fate has been kind to me, and come to my rescue."

Paula laughed softly.

"You are too kind, M. Bréon. When I was still but a poor little unknown singer, I sat at your feet. Your Rigoletto—what art, what perfection! No one could touch you."

"Alas!" said Bréon, pretending to sigh. "My day is over. Scarpia, Rigoletto, Radamès, Sharpless, how many times have I not sung them, and now—no more!"

"Yes—tonight."

"True, madame—I forgot. Tonight."

"You have sung with many 'Toscas,' " said Nazorkoff arrogantly, "but never with me!"

The Frenchman bowed.

"It will be an honour," he said softly. "It is a great part, madame."

"It needs not only a singer, but an actress," put in Lady Rustonbury.

"That is true," Bréon agreed. "I remember when I was a young man in Italy, going to a little out-of-the-way theatre in Milan. My seat cost me only a couple of lira, but I heard as good singing that night as I have heard in the Metropolitan Opera House in New York. Quite a young girl sang 'Tosca'; she sang it like an angel. Never shall I forget her voice in 'Vissi D'Arte,' the clearness of it, the purity. But the dramatic force, that was lacking."

Nazorkoff nodded.

"That comes later," she said quietly.

"True. This young girl—Bianca Capelli her name was—I interested myself in her career. Through me she had the chance of big engagements, but she was foolish—regrettably foolish."

He shrugged his shoulders.

"How was she foolish?"

It was Lady Rustonbury's twenty-four-year-old daughter, Blanche Amery, who spoke—a slender girl with wide blue eyes.

The Frenchman turned to her at once politely.

"Alas! Mademoiselle, she had embroiled herself with some low fellow, a ruffian, a member of the Camorra. He got into trouble with the police, was condemned to death; she came to me begging me to do something to save her lover."

Blanche Amery was staring at him.

"And did you?" she asked breathlessly.

"Me, mademoiselle, what could I do? A stranger in the country."

"You might have had influence?" suggested Nazorkoff in her low, vibrant voice.

"If I had, I doubt whether I should have exerted it. The man was not worth it. I did what I could for the girl."

He smiled a little, and his smile suddenly struck the English girl as having something peculiarly disagreeable about it. She felt that, at that moment, his words fell far short of representing his thoughts.

"You did what you could," said Nazorkoff. "That was kind of you, and she was grateful, eh?"

The Frenchman shrugged his shoulders.

"The man was executed," he said, "and the girl entered a convent. Eh, voilà! The world has lost a singer."

Nazorkoff gave a low laugh.

"We Russians are more fickle," she said lightly.

Blanche Amery happened to be watching Cowan just as the singer spoke, and she saw his quick look of astonishment, and his lips that half opened and then shut tight in obedience to some warning glance from Paula.

The butler appeared in the doorway.

"Dinner," said Lady Rustonbury, rising. "You poor things, I am so sorry for you. It must be dreadful always to have to starve yourself before singing. But there will be a very good supper afterwards."

"We shall look forward to it," said Paula Nazorkoff. She laughed softly. "Afterwards!"

III

Inside the theatre, the first act of *Tosca* had just drawn to a close. The audience stirred, spoke to each other. The royalties, charming and gracious, sat in the three velvet chairs in the front row. Everyone was whispering and murmuring to each other; there was a general feeling that in the first act Nazorkoff had hardly lived up to her great reputation. Most of the audience did not realize that in this the singer showed her art; in the first act she was saving her voice and herself. She made of La Tosca a light, frivolous figure, toying with love, coquettishly jealous and exacting. Bréon, though the glory of his voice was past its prime, still struck a magnificent figure as the cynical Scarpia. There was no hint of the decrepit roué in his conception of the part. He made of Scarpia a handsome, almost benign figure, with just a hint of the subtle malevolence that underlay the outward seeming. In the last passage, with the organ and the procession, when Scarpia stands lost in thought, gloating over his plan to secure Tosca, Bréon had displayed a wonderful art. Now the curtain rose upon the second act, the scene in Scarpia's apartments.

This time, when Tosca entered, the art of Nazorkoff at once became apparent. Here was a woman in deadly terror playing her part with the assurance of a fine actress. Her easy greeting of Scarpia, her nonchalance, her smiling replies to him! In this scene, Paula Nazorkoff acted with her eyes; she carried herself with deadly quietness, with an impassive, smiling face. Only her eyes that kept darting glances at Scarpia betrayed her true feelings. And so the story went on, the torture scene, the breaking down of Tosca's composure, and her utter abandonment when she fell at Scarpia's feet imploring him vainly for mercy. Old Lord Leconmere, a connoisseur of music, moved appreciatively, and a foreign ambassador sitting next to him murmured:

"She surpasses herself, Nazorkoff, tonight. There is no other woman on the stage who can let herself go as she does."

Leconmere nodded.

And now Scarpia has named his price, and Tosca, horrified, flies from him to the window. Then comes the beat of drums from afar, and Tosca flings herself wearily down on the sofa. Scarpia, standing over her, recites how his people are raising up the gallows—and then silence, and again the far-off beat of drums. Nazorkoff lay prone on the sofa, her head hanging downwards almost touching the floor, masked by her hair. Then, in exquisite contrast to the passion and stress of the last twenty minutes, her voice rang out, high and clear, the voice, as she had told Cowan, of a choir boy or an angel.

"Vissi d'arte, vissi d'amore, no feci mai male ad anima vival. Con man furtiva quante miserie conobbi, aiu-tai."

It was the voice of a wondering, puzzled child. Then she is once more kneeling and imploring, till the instant when Spoletta enters. Tosca, exhausted, gives in, and Scarpia utters his fateful words of double-edged meaning. Spoletta departs once more. Then comes the dramatic moment when Tosca, raising a glass of wine in her trembling hand, catches sight of the knife on the table and slips it behind her.

Bréon rose up, handsome, saturnine, inflamed with passion. *"Tosca, finalmente mia!"* The lightning stab with the knife, and Tosca's hiss of vengeance:

"Questo e il baccio di Tosca!" ("It is thus that Tosca kisses.")

Never had Nazorkoff shown such an appreciation of Tosca's act of vengeance. That last fierce whispered *"Muori dannato,"* and then in a strange, quiet voice that filled the theatre:

"Or gli perdono!" ("Now I forgive him!")

The soft death tune began as Tosca set about her ceremonial, placing the candles each side of his head, the crucifix on his breast, her last pause in the doorway looking back, the roll of distant drums, and the curtain fell.

This time real enthusiasm broke out in the audience, but it was short-lived. Someone hurried out from behind the wings and spoke to Lord Rustonbury. He rose, and after a minute or two's consultation, turned and beckoned to Sir Donald Calthorp, who was an eminent physician. Almost immediately the truth spread through the audience. Something had happened; an accident; someone was badly hurt. One of the singers appeared before the curtain and explained that M. Bréon had unfortunately met with an accident—the opera could not proceed. Again the rumour went round, Bréon had been stabbed, Nazorkoff had lost her head, she had lived in her part so completely that she had actually stabbed the man who was acting with her. Lord Leconmere, talking to his ambassador friend, felt a touch on his arm, and turned to look into Blanche Amery's eyes.

"It was not an accident," the girl was saying. "I am sure it was not an accident. Didn't you hear, just before dinner, that story he was telling about the girl in Italy? That girl was Paula Nazorkoff. Just after, she said something about being Russian, and I saw Mr. Cowan look amazed. She may have taken a Russian name, but he knows well enough that she is Italian."

"My dear Blanche," said Lord Leconmere.

"I tell you I am sure of it. She had a picture paper in her bedroom opened at the page showing M. Bréon in his English country home. She knew before she came down here. I believe she gave something to that poor little Italian man to make him ill."

"But why?" cried Lord Leconmere. "Why?"

"Don't you see? It's the story of Tosca all over again. He wanted her in Italy, but she was faithful to her lover, and she went to him to try to get him to save her lover, and he pretended he would. Instead he let him die. And now at last her revenge has come. Didn't you hear the way she hissed 'I am Tosca'? And I saw Bréon's face when she said it, he knew then—he recognized her!"

In her dressing room, Paula Nazorkoff sat motionless, a white ermine cloak held round her. There was a knock at the door.

"Come in," said the prima donna.

Elise entered. She was sobbing.

"Madame, madame, he is dead! And—"

"Yes?"

"Madame, how can I tell you? There are two gentlemen of the police there; they want to speak to you."

Paula Nazorkoff rose to her full height.

"I will go to them," she said quietly.

She untwisted a collar of pearls from her neck and put them into the French girl's hands.

"Those are for you, Elise; you have been a good girl. I shall not need them now where I am going. You understand, Elise? I shall not sing 'Tosca' again."

She stood a moment by the door, her eyes sweeping over the dressing room, as though she looked back over the past thirty years of her career.

Then softly between her teeth, she murmured the last line of another opera:

"La commedia e finita!"

Shabby Little Shocker

by Linda Haldeman

Fiorenza liked to talk as she fitted the girls for their costumes, and they for the most part liked to listen. The old costumer was full of anecdotes, some familiar, some fantastic, tales of the long lost golden age when she had been a prima donna somewhere, one never found out quite where, in the Italian provinces.

"Ah, I do not like it, *signorine*, the *Tosca*," she muttered through a mouthful of straight pins, a feat that the girls of the chorus attributed to ventriloquism. "Such an ugly story. *Come brutta*. 'That shabby little shocker,' one critic has called it."

"Seems pretty tame compared to some of the movies around now," observed Alicia, leader of the alto section, raising her arms in cross fashion to allow for the fitting of a gusset.

"At least old Tosca wasn't one of those wimpy virgin sopranos, all head tones and insulted virtue. It must be a great part to play. Did you ever sing Tosca, Madam Fe?"

"*Una volta*," the old woman sighed with gusto. "I sing the Tosca once only and never again. *No davvero*. No. A terrible, terrible thing."

The girls in the chorus exchanged looks. A story. What could all this broken Italian lamentation mean but a certain prelude to a story? But not one of those minor backstage anecdotes, spun off in lyric mock English while turning hems and pinning gathers. This promised to be a major tale, a full evening of revelation made only after a good meal and much wine.

"Hey, gang, I've got an idea," someone exclaimed with unconvincing spontaneity. "Let's all go to Antonio's Trattoria tonight. All the manicotti you can eat." She waited for the others to pick up her cue and conjure some genuine enthusiasm for manicotti before she took the next step. "How about it, Madame Fe? Want to come along? My treat."

Madame Fe was a hungry old woman and a lonely one. How could she refuse? It would not be the first time she had sung for her supper.

From Antonio's they went to Alicia's apartment, a handful of girls from the chorus. The serious ones like Alicia herself, who dreamed of singing the great roles on the great stages, and the wide-eyed opera groupies, who worshipped anyone who had sung the great roles on the great stages and sighed and stammered over anyone who had sung any role on any stage. Alicia arranged them all in a circle on the floor, with Fiorenza enthroned like a bard in the center, and passed among them plastic glasses filled with cheap chianti. The night was too far gone and they had drunk too much to waste good wine.

Fiorenza arranged herself carefully, spreading her wide peasant skirt around her, a prima donna once more, for a while.

"I was good in my time," she said quietly. "But for the *Tosca* I maybe would be great. Had God blessed me with voice only, as so many He has, some day maybe I would have sung at the Met with all the other ugly sopranos. But no, He have to make me *bella, bellissima*. You believe that? Old Fiorenza a great beauty? Ah, *é vero, é vero*. They love me, the men, before ever I open my mouth. *Capito?* I was like la Tosca in those day, exploding with the love and the art. I could even act, and singers in those day was not expected to act. Macero, he was my Cavaradossi, he couldn't act the far end of the horse. You know il Macero, no? Vincente Macero, *primo tenore assoluto*.

He look like the *grosso* wine barrel, stand on the middle of the stage like it is the concert hall and just bellow out. His *amori* and his *maledizioni* all sound same. Ah, but such a *bello* bellow!" Fiorenza giggled at her clumsy bilingual pun. "And so good a lover, barrel belly and all." She giggled again, catching the startled look of one of the groupies, a first soprano with a promising D natural. "Ah, *si, mia cara*, I made love with il Macero. I made love with all my tenors. It is good for the performance. Not that I advise it for you, *carissime*." She held her glass out for a refill. "I tell you this tale, this 'shabby little shocker,' as a warning. If God grant you to sing la Tosca, do not forget that you only play. The opera she is a strange art; she is just the show, but so great a show. Sometimes she is like the great fearsome rite calling up the pagan gods of old. And that is dangerous to do. The wise men, they disturb not these things but let them sleep. La Tosca, she was not the first to kill and die because of the art. We come of a long line. And I was so like Floria Tosca in those day. I killed through the power and wiles of those wicked old gods, and I carry their curse.

"It was Macero's fault, you know. If God have granted him a smaller belly and a larger brain, we maybe all have could be spared. Ah, the tenors, *care*, beware of them.

"He was a dreadful man, Macero. I was young and full of art and ambition. He was, how is it, center age, and oh so temperamental. All the time he fight with director, fight with maestro, fight with the baritone, everybody he fight with but me. Me he make love with, not much the difference.

"It was last week of rehearsal. Macero he is throwing the fits. He said how the baritone roughed him so much in the second act. I don't know what he expect from Scarpia, head of secret police, interrogating a rebeller. But I say Macero pay no thought to the drama. He liked to watch me, though, in that scene. Everybody watched me, even in rehearsal. I was so great a Tosca. Never forget that thing. I was so beautiful, so *furiosa*, forced to give my body to that weasel Scarpia to save my lover. And I sing the '*Vissi d'Arte*,' lying on my belly on the stage. They give me *brave* even at rehearsal, I am so good. Then I take the knife from the table. This production I am to back up into the table and touch the knife like by accident. That was not easy to do without the looking, staring all the time at Scarpia with such hate and watching the prompter out of the edge of the eye. Opera, it is not the easy art, *care*. Sometimes I get so excited that I stabbed the poor lad hard enough to hurt, though the knife was of course the stage trick. Did he complain I am rough? Oh no. All the complaining that the production could hold was complained by my dear Macero. He drove that poor young man away. Macero said, 'He goes or I go.' He was Macero. So the baritone went. But for that the baritone went I could have sing Tosca at La Scala and later also the Metropolitan, and now would I be singing benefit concerts at the Carnegie Hall instead of sewing the flounces on the chorus girls. You have more wine, *per favore? Grazie.*

"He was an American, the *nuovo* Scarpia. A wild sort of person, very tall and thin with a such long face and a such long nose. Not a pretty fellow this, but so very an actor. I do not meet him but for shake hands before we rehearse. He scared me when he came on stage. You know the scene—the sacristan and choirboys are mischiefing around the church, and old Scarpia comes and everything stops all at the once. It did. Everything did. Not just on stage, everywhere. I have the scene at the end of the act where he talks so kind while he be's so cruel. I almost couldn't sing I am so terrified. When the maestro laid down his baton he took one breath and shook like the wet dog, and the evil was gone. Then this baritone he walked back to me with a so dear little boy smile on his long face.

" '*Bravissima, madama.* You are a great singer and a great actress.' And he kissed my hand. Then he leaned down (he is so tall) and whispered, 'Who's the soufflé playing Cavaradossi? I've seen ripe tomatoes with more expression.'

"I try hard not to giggle. 'That is the great Macero himself. You must treat him with respect, or he will get you fired.'

"He laughed. It was not pleasant. 'He better not tangle with me. I'll dip him in batter and fry him in lard. But enough of him, and I do mean enough. You and I must be better acquainted. I'm Dirk McCready. You are?'

" 'Fiorenza Palmieri.'

" 'Fiorenza?' He laughed, pleasant this time. 'No, rather Fierenza, my little Italian wildcat.'

"Imagine that. He tried to make the Italian pun. And he is an Irishman from Chicago. It was not good Italian, but I do not tell him that.

" 'Have dinner with me tonight, Fierenza *mia*,' he said. 'To work well together we must get to know each other better.'

"Macero is expecting me to go with him, naturally, but before I could explain this, the tenor he come to us, scowling mightily.

" 'Could I interrupt this little convention?' he asked rather nastily. 'I need you, Fiorenza. *Presto!*'

"I went with him as he expected, but I could feel the American's eyes following us, not smiling. As I suspect, Macero was not needing anything, he just wanted to get me away from that Dirk McCready. I mocked him for his jealousy, and we quarreled. Just like Tosca and Cavaradossi. As we took our places for the second act, I tell Dirk yes for dinner, in the hope a bit that Macero would carry his anger onto the stage. But alas, he was stiff and woodlike as always. He alone in all that place have no feel to Dirk's so evil Scarpia. Poor *babbo*, he was a so ridiculous figure, like the great wheel of cheese on elegant banquet table. By end of rehearsal I have lost all respect to him as the artist and as the man. That was bad. It made the final act so hard. All that passion and joy, I really had to work at it. In my deepdown heart I was glad for Scarpia's—what you say—two-cross. It is not the easy scene for acting. Think on it; the actress has to pretend to be pretending that she thinks her lover is being shooted, but she thinks it is not true bullets, what you call, blanks. Then he does not get up, and she knows that dead Scarpia is still doing his evils and that her lover is really shooted dead with really bullets. Oh, the irony. It is not shabby; it is so lovely.

" 'You know what my deep-down heart said?' I asked Dirk that night as we ate the steak and drank the much wine. 'I wished there were for real bullets in those guns.'

"He laughed that laugh I did not like.

" '*Madama*, your wish is my command. Nothing is beyond the power and wiles of Scarpia.'

"I laughed too, playing the game. 'And what should we do for a tenor for the second night?'

" 'Train a hyena with a high C,' he said.

"We laughed a lot and drank a lot the wine. And somehow we ended the evening at his hotel. And we were lovers, *care*. Never had I made the love with a baritone before. It was most good.

"But not for the opera. In the opera I am suppose to hate the baritone and love the tenor. Ah, what a struggle there was in my deepdown heart. Nothing, *care*, to touch the struggle between my rival lovers.

"Ah, my eyes wetten even now to remember Macero, *poverino*. He was not match for my clever Dirk. It is a knife, like a stiletto, no? this Dirk. And such a one was he, my baritone lover, clever as Scarpia but not so evil. How he teased my poor dumb *tenore*. You know how it is those tenors have such ringing head tone. There is no brain up there to interfere with the resonance. Ha, ha. I joke."

The girls sitting around the old diva laughed a trifle stiffly. Alicia pulled another half gallon of wine out of the refrigerator. "Did you dump the empty-headed tenor?" she prodded.

"Oh, no. I could not bring my heart to do that. I loved him, you see. He was so the little child inside. I could not bear the second act, though I always watched it. How I hated Dirk when he was the Scarpia, like I think that Tosca hated him, with something else, too. Something of sex maybe. When I took that knife onstage, I in truth wanted to kill him for being so cruel and so smug when he is Scarpia, and being so hard on poor Macero when he is Dirk.

"Everything came out for bad, as it must soon or after, at the dress rehearsal. Dirk, that wicked one, came to my dressing room before the second act when I am in only my unspeakables. I tell him this is against rules backstage. It is for bad luck. He but laughed.

" 'What for do we need rules, you and I,' he said. 'We break all the rules.' And he my dresser sent away. 'I dress you myself, Fierenza *mia*. This Scarpia gets everything he's after, even his Tosca.' And he dressed me in the red velvet gown of my costume as no performer have ever been dressed. That is how I am loving him even as I am hating him. There are men like that, cruel, charming men that treat women so, like the street ladies, and women find strange pleasure in them. It is in such a way that I loved Dirk McCready.

"When he had fastened my gown with many wicked caresses and arranged my wig, he took the cameo on black ribbon and tied it around my neck. I stood before the mirror, he behind me. I could see reflected his face over my shoulder. It was a very Scarpia face. Slowly he tightened the black ribbon around my neck.

" 'You are still seeing (only he used another word, not so nice as "seeing") Winnie-the-Pooh?'

"I never know why he called Macero by that name, but I knew that is who he meant. The ribbon was so tight I could not speak. The door opened all on the sudden. Behold Macero, very red in the face.

" '*Assassino!* Get you out of here,' he shouted. 'You do not belong in this place. You do all the wicked you want onstage. When curtain is down you leave this *donna mia* alone.'

" 'Donna you-a? Not by a lot,' Dirk speak very quiet but very cruel. 'You got no claim on this rare jewel. You are the little man.' Only that is not how he really says. I cannot say to young ladies the word he used *in vero*. Poor Macero, no one ever talk to him in this manner.

"Macero scream at him. 'You are bastard. I kill you!'

"Now Macero he was the big man, and when he ran at Dirk, I bob out of the way. I think I'm screaming then because Dirk is jumping back to my dressing table and grabbing the dressmaker scissor. Macero hold hard his wrist to make him drop it, then they roll on the floor hitting and punching.

"It took the stage manager and the director and two stagehands to pull them apart. They both had got bloody faces, very ugly. The director scowled at all of us, even me, as if it is my fault that men fight over me.

" 'I have no care,' say the director, 'what you do in your privacies. But it is no to be carried into theater. We have a show to put on tomorrow, and nothing matter before that. *Capito?* You three ones stay away from each the other except when you are on stage together. If it is not so, I will see that none of you never sing on any stage in Italy, in the world maybe.'

"Oh, how terrible a threat, terrible because like a curse it came to pass. Dirk broke free from the stagehands and shook off himself, all cool and contempt, you know. Macero, he could not go cool. The stagehands they pulled him out of the room.

" 'I kill you, bastard,' he called, blood running down his poor fat chin.

" 'We see who kills who,' Dirk called back over his shoulder as he went to his dressing room. 'Not to worry,' he say to the director. 'The show will go on, yours and mine.'

"It was not a pretty scene, I tell you. And the rehearsal as it continued was not pretty, either. Scarpia got very rough with Cavaradossi during the interrogation, and Cavaradossi at the *'Vittoria!'* took himself Baron Scarpia by the shoulders and shaked him. The director screamed *'Basta!'* and leaped up onto stage. 'What you doing? You crazy? Nobody dare touch this man. He is most powerful man in Rome. You do not try for to act, Macero. Just you sing, *capito?* Go on now, maestro.'

"By end of that rehearsal I was one nervous wreck and just went home. I not want to go out with anybody. I stand those two bad boys together and try to make them have the peace. When they will not, at least I make them promise to stay away from each other.

" 'For you, *bellissima,* I do anything,' said my baritone. 'You I promise that I will not speak to or touch this bloated leech again for not just tonight but for the rest of his putrid life, however long that may be. Your wish is my command.' Then made he a deep bow and kiss my hand, and off he went, smiling just a little, how Scarpia smile when he make the trick with the shooting.

" 'Now you go home as well,' I told Macero, 'and make not more trouble.'

" 'I go then, *cara.* For you I go home. But I will have the *vendetta.* How he say—not to worry. The show she will go on. Not a word to the laughing hyena, not a blow. But he will pay, fear you not. *Buona notte.'*

"Can you imagine the night I spent? And I with an opening night before me. But what they say about the show is so true, especially of the opera. When I went to the theater, all did seem to be well. They were both there already and in their dressing rooms, and there was not trouble. Still I am nervous. When I come on in the first act to meet my lover at the church, he give me a most strange smile, like we are in a plot together. That made me so nervous I am missing my cue, and the prompter nearly jump out of his box to get me back in tempo. But cover it I did. I was an artist, *in vero*. But the Scarpia as he exit after the scene with the fan leaned close to me and whisper, 'Your wish is my command.'

"All the intermission I stay in my dressing room trying to call back my character. After all, I am Floria Tosca, the great actress. I am brave and strong. What happen on stage is all that matters this night. I must forget all else. So I tell myself, and so I believe. I went on in the second act with free mind, and I played well. Those two also were playing straight, and it was a good act. Even poor Macero was not so wooden. I sang the *'Vissi d'Arte'* and meant it, and as triumphing Scarpia came to claim me I backed up to that dining table and touched the knife, just where it was to be. That is always a bad moment. One must pray that the property mistress have not slip up. It was there and I grabbed the handle. I never looked at it, that stage knife with the collapsing blade. I play the scene, and I am Tosca. I raised the knife and struck his chest, shouting the line about Tosca's kiss. Something was wrong. The blade do not collapse. I don't understand. Dirk make such a strange sound, like nothing he do in rehearsal, and I pull the knife out. But I don't scream. I am, so to say, in the shock. Dirk is gasping, holding onto me with such a strong grip. His face is close to me, very white.

"He cries, *'Aiuto! Muoio!'* right on cue and manages in the five and a half beat rest he has to whisper to me, 'Do the scene.' Then he cry, *'Succorso'* perfect in tempo. What an artist. We do the scene, just so. And were we magnificent! No one knew except the poor prompter, who dropped the baton when he see blood and lose his place. But we needed not the prompter. It was our scene, and we played it. It is a blessedly short scene. I am standing over him, snarling, *'Muouri, dannato!'* and watching him die. He sighs and then lies still as he is suppose to, but the blood is going all over the place. This scene cannot be hurried. It must be done with the music. I put the candles by him and the crucifix on the chest. Then I tippytoe out as the orchestra rises to its final chord. I could hear the applause as I collapsed into Macero's fat arms. He is there, watching. Quickly I recovered and pulled away from him. Now I knew.

" 'You. You do this terrible thing. You come here early and put a real knife on property table. This is your vendetta, wicked one.'

"He is smiling but not happy. 'He has ruined all with his show-go-on. I meant to destroy him, not make him the legend. Now will they tell his story wherever this opera is played. But at least I save you from him.'

" 'You make me a murderer. Go from me!'

"I hurried back onstage. Dirk was struggling, trying to get up. He gripped onto the director as he had gripped me.

" 'Hospital all right,' he gasped, 'but not police. Don't stop the show. It must go on. Promise me. Promise.'

"Then he saw me. 'Ah, *fierenza mia*, you are a great diva. Kiss me while I can still feel your lips. We play one great scene together, don't we?'

"I kissed him. Already his lips were cold. 'Play the last act well, my love. It will be a great triumph, yours and mine. You will see.'

"The ambulance came to take him away, though we all knew he was dying. He held hard my hand.

" 'We have much fun together,' he whispered. 'Don't forget what once I said. Your wish is my command. Still is.'

"Then they carried him off, and I—I never saw him again. The third act curtain was delayed somewhat so that the stagehands could clean up some the blood, but the show goes on. The director asked me was I all right. I could not more than nod, I was so whelmed over. He asked Macero the same, and he said he never felt the better. Ah, how I understand la Tosca when she sing '*Vissi d'Arte.*' Here must I be a great actress indeed, singing joyous love duets with my lover's killer, setting aside my grief for later. I was good. I was very good, for Dirk would have me so. Macero was better than usual, crowing in the triumph of his vendetta. For Scarpia is dead, and he is glad. And that is how he is supposed to sing it. From the upstage I watched his bravado before the firing squad, and I made again the curse I gave at rehearsal. May the bullets be real. It was only then that I understood what Dirk was meaning, 'Your wish is my command.'

"Could I have stop it, you ask? There might have been time had I have screamed out and stop the show. But I have promise Dirk. And—and in those few measures before the shots I knew I did not want to stop it. Don't you see, *carissime*, how beautiful it is, like a great tragedy that must be played out? Dead Scarpia reaching out for his vendetta. Never has there been such a night in all time of theater. You have more the wine?"

Alicia, struggling back to reality as from a dream, shook her head. "Sorry. We're all out. But—but what happened to you?"

"I go to the prison for twenty years. No Italian judge would hang me, of course. But all were sure I am the murderer of both. I do not tell them otherwise. To what purpose? My professional life, and so my life, was over after such a scandal. And I feel in my deepdown heart that I am the culprit in vero. They kill for me; they die for me; they get their inspiration from me. There is a comfort of sorts in that. And I have the easy time in prison, for the governor, a very Scarpia himself, kept me well, and I sang recitals for his parties. Always I sang for him the 'Vissi d'Arte.' Always I looked just at him, but he never let on if he understood. By the time I am let out, the scandal is over and all have forgotten, but all have forgotten me as well, and my voice is no longer so great. That is why I come to this country and make costumes for the great divas and" (she smiled with foggy graciousness) "the piccole divezze. But now the wine is gone, and my story is done. I go."

"It's very late," Alicia said. "Why don't you let us call a cab or just sleep here until someone can walk you home?"

"Oh, no," The old woman rose with surprising agility for her age and state of intoxication. "Always I walk alone. That is best. Buona notte."

And she floated off into the night like a theater wraith.

Stella Bringanza was singing her first Lucia, and she was nervous, struggling with a minor bronchial infection and the inexperienced performer's fear of the critic and the fan.

"You are shaking, ma petite," her dresser murmured as she carefully arranged the Lammermoor tartan around her pale shoulders. "A great artist must forget personal fear before her art. And you are going to be a great artist."

"You think so?" Stella whispered. "I don't know if I'm ready for a part like this. Vocally I think I'm okay. But I don't know how to play the role. It's so far from real life. I mean who would really marry a man she didn't like just because she was gullible enough to believe her conniving brother's lies about her true lover? And then instead of running off with her lover she goes crazy and stabs her husband on the wedding night. That's freaky. I can't relate to that.''

"Ah, no, *ma chère*. You are so young." Her dresser, a veteran of the French stage, sighed. "Such things do happen, even in these free times. I know. But that is another story, and no one for your young ears. Come, I will show you how I did the Mad Scene when I was young and had so lovely the upper register.''

"You sang Lucia?" Stella exclaimed. "I never knew that.''

"It was so very long ago, *ma chère*. Everyone has forget now. I was after so long in the hospital mental. I sing it only once, the *Lucia*. But it was so great a performance. But that is another story. I tell you one day. Not now. Now you must go out and make your own history. The tenor awaits you.''

The Sultans of Soul
by Doug Allyn

*P*apa Henry's Hickory Hut serves the best barbeque in the city of Detroit, bar none. Ribs to die for. The Hut is just a storefront diner, booths along one wall, a scarred Formica counter and backless chrome stools. Ah, but behind the counter, shielded by a spattered Plexiglas screen, is an honest to Jesus barbeque pit. You can watch your order revolve on the rotisserie, kissed by flames and hickory smoke, while homebaked hoecakes warm on the grill. High cholesterol? Probably. But since the Hut's on the rough side of Eight Mile, keeping your veins intact is a more pressing worry than having them clogged.

I'd ordered a late breakfast at Papa's, and was sipping coffee, waiting, when a white Cadillac limo ghosted to the curb out front. The chauffeur, a uniformed black the size of a small building, popped an umbrella against the April drizzle, and opened the back door. An elderly black gentleman eased slowly out. The chauffeur watched, wooden, offering no help.

The old man looked exotic, like a Nigerian diplomat. An orange patterned kente-cloth cap, a Kuppenheimer's continental-cut black suit, hand-tailored to a tee. He had café au lait skin, a spray of coppery freckles across the bridge of his nose, a metallic gray Malcolm X goatee. Dark, intense hawk's eyes.

He'd have stood six feet plus upright, but he was pain-hunched into a question mark, using a silver-headed bamboo cane for support. I guessed him to be fiftyish. Fifty isn't old for most people. It was for this guy.

He moved like he'd been wounded at Gettysburg. Step, lean, step, lean. The gait was familiar. Sickle cell anemia, very late in the game. I grew up around it down home. This old man had lasted longer than most. But it was coming for him now. And he was coming for me, sizing me up all the way. I was easy enough to spot. As usual, I was the only white face in the Hut.

It took him a month to limp the dozen paces back to my booth. He stopped in front of my table, leaning on the cane, wobbly as a foundered horse. "You'd be Axton, right? From the detective agency up the street?" he asked, his voice a low rasp. Black velvet.

"Yes, sir. Something I can do for you?"

"For openers, you can speak up. I don't hear too well. My name's Mack, Varnell Mack."

"R. B. Axton," I said, offering my hand. He ignored it. "Would you care to sit down, Mr. Mack?"

"No thanks, too damn hard to get up again, and I won't be here long. I'm into a few things around Detroit, mostly real estate, own some rental units. Willis Tyrone, the guy that owns them pawns down in the ward? Willis tells me you're good at collectin' money folks ain't altogether sure they owe."

"I make collections sometimes," I said cautiously, "but I don't do evictions."

"Neither do I," Mack said, "that's the problem." A spasm took his breath for a moment. His knuckles locked on the cane and a faint sheen of moisture beaded on his forehead. "I believe I will sit down after all," he said, swallowing. He drew a silk handkerchief from his breast pocket, flicked the dust off the bench across from me, then casually replaced the handkerchief in his pocket with a flip of his wrist. A perfect fleur-de-lis. I was impressed. I can barely manage to knot a necktie.

"See, I had this old gentleman livin' in one of my buildin's,"

Mack said, easing into the booth. "Used to be a helluva singer 'round Detroit back in the fifties, early sixties, even cut a few records. Horace DeWitt. Ever hear of him?"

"Can't say I have, but I'm not from Detroit originally."

"Knew that the minute you opened your mouth. Where you from, boy? Alabama?"

"No, sir, Mississippi. A little town called Noxapater."

"They teach you to call blacks 'sir' down there, did they?"

"They taught me to be polite to my elders," I said evenly. "And to watch my mouth around strangers. You were saying about Mr. DeWitt?"

"I used to write tunes, sing backup in Horace's group. Called ourselves the Sultans of Soul."

"No kidding? I remember the group. From when I was a kid, down home. I've still got one of your songs on an oldies tape. 'Motor City . . . something?'"

" 'Motor City Mama.' I wrote that one. Our last single. Cracked the top twenty on the race charts in sixty-one. Never made no money off it, record company folded right after, but it got us a name so we could make a few bucks doin' shows. Then things petered out, the group busted up. I went into real estate, did all right for myself. Helped out Horace some, last few years, with rent and such. He had a stroke a few months back, had to move to a rest home. One of them welfare places. I offered to help, but he wouldn't take it. He's flat busted, cain't even afford a TV in his room."

"Sorry to hear it," I said.

"Maybe you shouldn't be," Mack said. "Might be somethin' in it for you. Thing is, I still hear 'Motor City Mama' on the radio sometimes. So I figure somebody must owe the Sultans some money. I want you to collect it."

"Collect it?" I echoed.

"That's what you do, ain't it?"

"I, ahm . . . Look, Mr. Mack, what I do is skip-traces mostly. People who light out owing other people money. I hunt 'em up, talk 'em into doin' the right thing."

"So?"

"So, for openers, who do you expect me to collect from?"

"That's your problem. If I knew who owed Horace, I wouldn't hafta hire you. I'd see to it myself."

"You can't be serious."

"Boy, I never joke about money."

"All right then, straight up. Even if I could find somebody who'd admit to owing the Sultans some royalties or whatever, it probably wouldn't amount to beans. And I don't work cheap."

"Two-fifty a day, Willis told me," Mack said, snaking an envelope out of an inner pocket, tossing it on the table. "Here's a week in advance. Fifteen hundred. You need more, my number's on the envelope. But I expect to see some results."

I left the envelope where it was. "Mr. Mack, I really don't think I can help you. I wouldn't even know where to start."

"Willis gave me your card," Mack said, using the cane to lever himself to his feet. "R. B. Axton, private investigations. That makes you some kinda detective, right?"

"Yes, sir, but—"

"So maybe you oughta try earnin' your fee. Investigate or whatever. Look, I know it'd be cheaper to just lay the damn money on Horace. He won't take it. He was a dynamite singer once. And people are still listenin' to his music. He shouldn't oughta go out broke like this. It ain't right."

"No, sir," I said, "I suppose it isn't."

"All right then," he said grimly. "You find out who owes the Sultans some money. And you get it. How much don't matter, but you get Horace somethin', understand?"

I picked up the envelope, intending to give it back to him. But I didn't. There was something in his eyes. Dark fire. Anger perhaps, and pain. It cost him a lot just to walk in here. More than money. I put the envelope in my pocket. "I'll look into it," I said. "I can't promise anything."

"Banks don't cash promises anyway," Mack said, turning, and limping slowly toward the door. Step, lean, step, lean. "Call me when you got somethin'."

"Yes, sir," I said. He didn't look back.

* * *

Finding a place to start looking wasn't all that tough. The cassette tray in my car. I did have the Sultans of Soul on tape. "Motor City Mama." There was no information on the cassette itself. It was a bootleg compilation from Rock 'n Soul Recollections, on south Livernois.

R&S isn't the usual secondhand record shop with records piled around like orphaned children. The shop's a renovated theater, complete with bulletproof box office, which, considering its location, is probably prudent. The walls are crammed floor to ceiling with poster art, larger-than-life shots of Michigan music monsters, Smokey Robinson, Bob Seger, The Temps, Stevie Wonder. The bins are immaculate, every last 45 lovingly encased in cellophane, cross-referenced and catalogued like Egyptian antiquities.

All this regimentation is a reflection of the owner/manager, Cal, a wizened little guy with a watermelon paunch and a tam permanently attached to his oversized pate. I don't recall his last name, if I ever heard it, but he knows mine. Not just because I'm a good customer, but because he remembers everything about everything. He knows every record he has in stock, and probably every record he's *ever* had in stock.

On the downside, he's compulsive, wears the same outfit every day: green slacks, frayed white shirt, navy cardigan clinched with a safety pin. His hands look like lizard-skin gloves because he washes them forty times a day. Still, if I wanted to know about the Sultans, Cal was the person to ask.

"You've got to be kidding," he said.

"Hey, I should think you'd be flattered. I thought you knew everything about those old groups."

"I do know about their records," he said, irritated. "The Sultans cut three forty-fives and one album, all out of print. But as to who owns the rights to their music now? Hell, there were a million penny-ante record labels back then, and the royalty rights were swapped around like baseball cards. Most of the forty-fives were cut in fly-by-night studios owned by the mob—"

"Whoa up. Mob? You mean organized crime?"

"Absolutely. In the fifties and early sixties radio play was still segregated. Damn few stations would air black music, so the only market for it was jukeboxes. And most of the jukes and vending machines in Detroit were mob controlled."

"Terrific."

"The bottom line is, if you want to find somebody who might owe the Sultans a few bucks, you're probably looking for some small-time hood who once owned a few jukes and a two-bit recording studio and went out of the record business before you were born."

"But I still hear 'Motor City Mama' on the radio sometimes."

"Local deejays play it because of the title, but Detroit's probably the only town in the country where it's aired. Wanna try muscling a few nickels out of Wheelz or WRIF?"

"Fat chance. What label did the Sultans record for?"

"That at least I can tell you," he said, flipping through a stack of albums. "None of their stuff has been reissued, even on a collection. The Sultans just weren't big enough. . . . Here we go, the Sultans of Soul, 'Motor City Mama.' "

He passed me the album. The cover photo was a blurred action shot, four black guys in gold lamé jackets doing splits behind the lead singer, a beefy stud with conked hair. Mack appeared to be the tall guy on the left, but the picture had faded. So had Mack. I flipped the album over. "Black Catz?" I read. "What can you tell me about it?"

"Not much," Cal said. "It was a local label, defunct since . . ." He frowned, then shook his head slowly, his face gradually creasing into a ghost of a smile.

"I knew it," I said. "You do know something, right?"

"Nothing that'll help you, I'm afraid," he said. "But I did come across a Black Catz reissue recently. Not the Sultans though. Millie Jump and the Jacks."

"Never heard of them."

"Maybe you don't remember the Jacks, but you should remember Millicent. Soul singer who had a few hits in the sixties, then tried Hollywood and bombed? The Jacks was her original group, until she dumped 'em to marry the label owner and use his money to go solo."

"Wait a minute, you mean Millicent's husband, Sol Katz, was the original owner of Black Catz?"

"That's right," Cal said. "You know him?"

"I not only know him, I've worked for him."

"Worked for Sol?" Cal said, squinting at me from beneath his tam. "Doing what? Kneecaps with a baseball bat?"

"Actually I didn't exactly work for Sol. His daughter, Desirée, was an opening act for Was Not Was at the Auburn Hills Palace. I was her bodyguard."

"I would have thought Sol had bodyguards to spare."

"He wanted somebody who knew the local music scene. Most of his guys are from L.A."

"And it didn't bother you, working for a hood?"

"I—heard rumors about Sol, but in this business you hear smoke about everybody. Hell, half the guys in the biz pretend to be hoods just to spook the competition."

"Sol Katz isn't pretending, Ax, he's the real thing. His old man was an enforcer for the Purple Gang back in the thirties. Sol took to the family business like The Godfather Part II."

"I thought he was from L.A.?"

"He went out there awhile after the Purples ran him out of Detroit for marrying Millie. Having a black mistress in those days was one thing, but marriage? Not in his set. Besides, Millie figured she was ready for the bright lights. She was a fair singer, but never quite good enough to make it big, even with Sol's money. How's the daughter, whatsername, Desirée?"

"About the same, not bad, not gangbusters. I think Millie and Sol want her to make it more than she wants it herself. They've got her cutting an album of classic soul stuff out at the Studio Seven complex. What label was the reissue on?"

"Studio Seven, which means Sol may still own the rights to the Black Catz library. Including the Sultans. Lucky you. You going to try to collect?"

"That's what I'm being paid for."

"Hope you're getting enough to cover hospitalization. By the way, who is paying you? I thought the Sultans were all playing harps these days."

"They nearly are. Horace DeWitt, the lead singer, is in a rest home and the guy who hired me, Varnell Mack, looks like an AWOL from intensive care."

"I probably have them mixed up with another group. There were so many in those days," he said softly, glancing around the displays, filled with CDs, albums, tapes. And raw talent. And Soul. "So many. You know, it might not matter much to world peace, but it'd be nice if you could squeeze a few bucks out of Sol for the Sultans. Just for the damn principle of the thing."

"Principles?" I said. "In this business?"

Actually, principle was all I had going for me. Mack hadn't given me as much as a faded IOU to work with. In the music biz, sometimes deals with *very* serious money involved are done with a handshake or a phone call. I occasionally get hired to collect on oral contracts, but usually folks know in their heart of hearts that they owe the money. This was different.

Technically, Sol Katz probably didn't owe the Sultans dime one. Hell, after all these years he might not even remember who they were. Whatever deal they'd had, they'd lived with it for nearly thirty years, so if Sol told me to take a hike, I'd walk. Assuming my knees were still functional. Still, I figured I had a small chance. Mobster or no, a guy who'd risk his neck to marry the woman he loved must have a heart, right?

Right. So why did I keep remembering every story I'd ever heard about the Purple Gang? Two-to-a-box coffins, the shooters at the St. Valentine's Day Massacre, the gang that pushed Capone out of Detroit . . .

I shook it off. Ancient history, all of it. Then again, so were the Sultans of Soul.

The Studio 7 building is a spanking new concrete castle just off Gratiot Avenue, in the equally new city of Eastpointe, née East Detroit. The locals rechristened the town, trying to shed its Murder City East image.

Funny, it had never occurred to me what a fortress Sol's studio complex was. I'd called ahead to let Desi know I was coming, but

I still had to identify myself to a uniformed guard at the parking lot gate when I drove in, and to a second guard at the front door, then get clearance from a body-by-steroids male receptionist to use the elevator. There was nothing unusual about the stiff security arrangements. In a town where gunslingers will hold you up in broad daylight to steal your car, paranoia is an entirely rational state of mind.

Still, knowing Sol was a born-to-the-purple mobster made all the guards and guns seem a lot more sinister. It was like finding out your lover and your best friend were once lovers. You can't help revising all previous data.

The recording studios are on the fourth floor of the complex. The rooms are carpeted floor to ceiling in earth-tone textured saxony, and subdivided into a half-dozen Plexiglas booths which separate the musicians and singers on the rare occasions when two people actually tape at the same time. Nowadays most tracks are cut solo to avoid crosstalk and achieve maximal clarity. State-of-the-art digital recording, as sterile as a test-tube conception. And even less fun.

Roddy Rothstein, Sol's head of security, was leaning against the wall outside the studio door. He looks like an aging surfer: bleached hair, china-blue eyes, a thin scar that droops his left eyelid. He was wearing jeans, snakeskin boots, and an L.A. Raiders jacket that didn't quite conceal the Browning nine millimeter in his shoulder holster. He gave me a hard, thousand-yard stare. Nothing personal. Roddy looks at everybody like a lizard eyeing a fly.

"Hey, Ax, what's doin'?"

"Small stuff. Is Mr. Katz in?"

"Everybody's in but me," Roddy grumbled. "The music biz. Life in the fast lane."

"Beats honest work," I said.

"How would you know? Go ahead, green light's on."

Even with Roddy's okay and the warning light in the hall showing green, I still eased the door open cautiously. At five hundred bucks an hour, you never barge into a studio. But it was okay. They were in the middle of a sound check. Desi was wearing headsets in a sound-isolation booth. Recording company promos always shave a decade or so off performers' ages, but in her Pistons T-shirt and bullet-riddled jeans, Desi really did look like a high-school dropout, dark, slender, drop-dead gorgeous. If she ever learns to sing as good as she looks . . . She gave me a grin and flipped me the fickle finger. I waved back.

Millie and Sol were chewing on the engineer about clarity. Interracial couples aren't unusual in Detroit, but Sol and Millie were an especially handsome pair. Sol, slender, dapper, with steel-grey hair, grey eyes, fashionably blasé in a pearl-grey Armani jacket over a teal polo shirt. Millie was probably a few pounds heavier than in her Millicent days, but she wore it well. Voluptuous, in deceptively casual jogging togs that probably cost more than my car. Sol left the argument to give Millie the last word and strolled over. The Godfather II? Maybe. Maybe so.

"Axton," he nodded, "how are you doin'? Glad you dropped by. Desi was going to call you. She's going to do some charity shows for AIDS next month, Cleveland and Buffalo. I'd like you to handle security if you're free."

"I'll be free," I said. "If you still want me. This, ahm, this isn't a social call, Mr. Katz. It's business."

"What kind of business?" Millie said, waving the engineer back to his booth. I felt sorry for him. Millie can be a hard lady to be on the wrong side of. A tough woman in a tough trade.

"It's a bit complicated, but basically, somebody hired me to, uhm . . . to collect an old debt."

"What kind of debt?" Sol said evenly. "Who am I supposed to owe?"

"I'm not sure you owe anybody, Mr. Katz. Look, let me lay this thing on you straight up. Do you recall a group that recorded for you back in the early sixties called the Sultans of Soul?"

"The Sultans?" Millie echoed. "Sure. We did a few shows together at the Warfield and the Broadway Capitol."

"Do you remember Varnell Mack?" I asked.

She shot a sharp glance at Sol, then back at me. "I remember him. Tall, with a goatee?"

"He's not so tall now," I said. "To make a long story short, Mr. Mack says Horace DeWitt, the Sultans' lead singer, is down and out. In a rest home."

"I heard," Sol said coolly. "So?"

"So Mr. Mack is hoping you can see your way clear to . . . help Mr. DeWitt out. For auld lang syne."

"Just Horace?" Sol frowned. "Or would Varnell be wanting a taste, too?"

"No, sir, Mr. Mack seems to be doing quite well. New Caddy and a chauffeur, in fact."

"Good for him," Sol said evenly. "Did he say anything about my trying to contact him?"

"He didn't mention it. Why?"

"Nothing heavy," Millie put in, a shade too casually. "We've been thinking of calling Desi's new album *Motor City Mama*, so we need Varnell's permission to use the song. We had Roddy ask around, but nobody seemed to know what happened to him."

"He said he quit the business years ago, went into real estate," I said.

Sol shrugged. "Well, if all Mack wants is a few bucks for Horace, maybe we can work something out. Tell you what, Ax, bring Varnell by the club tonight. Tenish? We'll have a few drinks, talk it over."

"Fine by me. I'll have to check with Mr. Mack, of course."

"Do that, and get back to me. Meantime, if you don't mind, we're gettin' ready to roll tape."

"No problem. I'll be in touch. And thanks."

I stopped at the first 7-Eleven I came to and used the drive-by phone in the lot to call Varnell Mack. He answered on a car phone; I could hear the traffic noise in the background. I tried to tell him what I had, but he cut me off.

"Boy, I can't hear worth a damn over this thing. You got news for me?"

"Yes, sir."

"Then meet me at that rib joint down from your office. Twenty minutes?"

"I'll be there."

Mack's Cadillac limo was parked illegally in front of Papa Henry's, motor running. His chauffeur was behind the wheel, his huge hands tapping out rhythm to the thump of the Caddy's sound system. Mack was sitting in a front window booth facing the street. Not a spot I would have chosen, but then I don't need a cane to get around either. At least, not yet. I slid into the booth. Mack was warming his hands around a cup of tea. I gave him a quick rundown on what I'd turned up.

"Ol' Sol's still in the business and livin' fat city?" he said, showing a thin smile. "And still with Millie? I'll be damned. Who woulda figured it after all this time?"

"It hasn't really been so long," I said.

"Been a lifetime for some people," Mack said, glancing out the flyspecked window at the street. A posse car cruised slowly past, a blacked-out Monte Carlo low rider. Mack didn't notice it. He was looking beyond to . . . somewhere else.

"Millie remembered you," I said.

"A lotta woman, Millie. Smart, too. Smart enough to marry money, and stick to it."

"Maybe it wasn't like that," I said.

"No?" the old man said, annoyed. "Know a lot about it, do you, boy? You married?"

"I was. Once."

"Once oughta be enough for people, one way or another. You know, Willis told me you were sharp, Axton, but I'll tell you the God's truth, when I laid that money on you, I thought I was kissin' it goodbye, I truly did. You did okay."

"I haven't actually done anything yet," I said.

"How do you figure?"

"You hired me to collect some money for the Sultans. Sol said he was willing to work something out about the rights to 'Motor City Mama.' He didn't actually say he'd pay or how much."

"Don't worry 'bout it." Mack smiled grimly. "The important thing is, he's willin' to talk. This ain't really about money, you know? It's about doin' the right thing. So whatever Sol's willin' to pay, it'll be enough." He used his cane to lever himself painfully out of the booth. "I'll pick you up here at nine-thirty."

"Right," I said absently. The posse car was coming by again, probably checking out Mack's Cadillac. I watched it pass, then realized what was bothering me wasn't the car, it was something above it, something glinting from the roof of the building across the street. For a split second I froze, half-expecting gunfire. But the flash was too bright to be metal. And it wasn't moving. Mack was eyeing me oddly.

"Anythin' wrong?"

"Nope," I said, "not a thing. I'll see you tonight." I waited in the booth while he limped out to the Caddy and climbed in. As the car drifted away from the curb, a man stood up on the roof of the building opposite. With a minicam. He photographed Mack's car as it made a left onto Eight Mile.

I slipped out the back door of Papa Henry's into the alley, trotted down to the end of the block, and walked quickly to the corner, keeping close to the building. The man on the roof was gone.

Damn! I sprinted across the street, dodging traffic, and dashed down the alley. A blue Honda Civic was parked in a turnout, halfway down. It had to be his. Nobody parks in an alley in this part of town.

I heard a clank of metal from above and flattened against the wall. Someone was coming down the fire escape, moving quickly. A slender black man in U of D sweats and granny glasses, toting a black canvas shoulder bag. I waited until he was halfway down the last set of firestairs, then stepped out, blocking the path to his car.

"Nice day for it," I said.

He froze. "For what?"

"Taking pictures. That's what you were doing, right? Of me and the man I was with?"

He hesitated a split second, then shrugged. "If you walk away from me right now, maybe you can stay out of this thing."

"What thing?"

"An official Metro narcotics investigation."

"Narcotics investigation? Of who? Me? Papa Henry? You'll have to do better than that."

"I'm warning you, you're interfering in—"

"Save the smoke," I interrupted. "If you're a cop, show me some tin, and I'm gone."

"Fair enough," he said coolly. He unzipped the canvas bag, took

out a packet, and flipped it toward me. I half-turned to catch it, and
he vaulted the rail and hit the ground running. He only had me by
two steps and the bag on his shoulder must have slowed him, but
he was still too fast for me.

"Heeelllp!" he shouted as we pounded down the alley. "The
maaan! The maaan!"

It worked. I broke off the chase a few feet from the alley mouth.
There was no way a white guy could chase a black man down Eight
Mile without attracting an unfriendly crowd, and we both knew it.
He cut a hard right when he hit the street and disappeared. I turned
and trotted back to his car.

The packet he'd tossed at me was useless, a brochure for camera
film from a shop on Woodward. I considered breaking into the car,
but decided against it. For openers, I wasn't certain it was his car.
But I was fairly sure that he'd been filming Mack and me. We were
the only ones sitting in the windows; he'd photographed the Caddy
as it pulled away, and stopped shooting when it was gone.

A narcotics investigation? Possible. God knows, there are enough
of 'em in this town. But if he was a cop, why not just show me
some ID? Or a .38? No narc would work an alley off Eight Mile
unarmed. And if he wasn't a cop, then what was he?

I was getting an uneasy sense of blundering through a roomful
of spiderwebs. The only reason I could think of for someone to film
me talking to Mack was that one of us was being set up for something. I've ticked off a few folks over the years, but none I could
think of who'd bother with a cameraman. Not in a town where you
can buy a hit for fifty bucks. Or less.

That left Mack. Was he mixed up in the drug scene? Maybe,
though the drug trade'd be a rough game for somebody who can
barely walk. Besides, he hadn't asked me to do anything illegal. He
hired me to collect money for the Sultans from persons unknown.

Or had he? All I really knew about Mack was what he told me.
Millie remembered him, and Sol too. From the old days. This whole
thing kept coming back to that. The old days. And the Sultans of
Soul.

And Horace DeWitt. And since in a way I was actually working
for DeWitt, maybe it was time I met the Sultans' leader. Besides, I'd

been hearing "Motor City Mama" since I was a tad. It would be interesting to finally meet the face behind the voice.

I've acquired a modest reputation in music circles for tracing skips and collecting debts. The sign on my office door says private investigations, but the truth is I don't have to do much Sherlocking. The people in this business aren't very good at hiding. And since he wasn't hiding, Horace DeWitt was easier to find than most.

Mack mentioned DeWitt had only been in the home for a few months, so he was still listed in the phone book at his old address on Montcalm, and a quick call to the post office gave me his forwarding address. Riverine Heights, in Troy.

The funk from some welfare-case warehouses will drop you to your knees a half a block away, but Riverine Heights appeared to be better than most, a modern, ten-story cinderblock tower on Wattles Road. It even had a view of River Rouge.

At the front desk, a cheery, plump blonde in nurse's whites had me sign the visitor's log, and told me I'd probably find Mr. DeWitt in the fourth-floor residents' lounge. Fourth floor. A relief. The higher you go in these places, the less mobile the patients are. The top floors are reserved for the bedridden, only a last gasp from heaven. A fourth-floor resident should be ambulatory, more or less.

It was less. The residents' lounge was a small reading room with French doors that opened out onto a balcony. Institutional green plastic chairs lined the walls, a few well-thumbed magazines lay forgotten on the bookshelves. An elderly woman in street clothes was sitting on the sofa with a patient in a robe. The woman was knitting a scarf. Her date was asleep, his mouth open, his head resting on her shoulder.

Horace DeWitt was awake at least, sitting in a wheelchair in the sunlight by the French doors. A folding card table was pulled up to his knees. He was playing solitaire.

I'd seen his picture only hours before, but I barely recognized him. The singer on the Sultans' album had been a macho stud. The old man in the chair looked like a picture from Dorian Gray's attic. The conked hair had thinned and his slacks and sports shirt hung on his shrunken frame like death-camp pajamas. The stroke had melted the right side of his face like wax in a fire, one eyelid drooped nearly closed and the corner of his mouth was turned down in a permanent scowl.

His left arm lay in his lap like deadwood, palm up, fingers curled into a claw. Still, he seemed to be dealing the cards accurately, even one-handed. And he was cheating.

"Mr. DeWitt?" I said. "My name's Axton. I've been a big fan of yours for years. Got a minute to talk?"

"I guess I can fit you into my dance card," he said, peering up at me with his good eye. "But if you want me to headline one o' them soul revues, I'll have to pass."

His words were slurred by the twisted corner of his mouth. But his voice carried me back to steamy Mississippi nights, blowing down backroads in my daddy's pickup, WLAC Nashville blaring clear and righteous on the radio. The Sultans of Soul. "I'm comin' home, Motown Mama, I just can't live without ya . . ." I think I could've picked Horace DeWitt's voice out of a Silverdome crowd howling after a Lions' touchdown.

"Fact is, in a way I'm already working for you, Mr. DeWitt," I said, squatting beside his chair. "Varnell Mack hired me to try to collect some back royalties for the Sultans."

"Did he now?" DeWitt said, cocking his head, looking me over. "What's he got against you?"

"Nothing I know of, why?"

" 'Cause the last guy I heard of tried to squeeze a nickel outa Sol Katz wound up tryna backstroke 'cross Lake St. Clair draggin' a hunert pounds o' loggin' chain."

"Maybe I'll have better luck. I can't promise anything, but I think there's a fair chance we'll shake a few bucks loose."

"Uh-huh," he said, turning to his game. "The check's in the mail, right? So what you want from me?"

"Not much. I was hoping you could tell me a little about Mr. Mack."

"Varnell? Fair bass singer, better songwriter. Wrote 'Motor City Mama,' only song Sol didn't screw us out of, and he only missed that one 'cause he blew town in a hurry. That why Sol sent you around? Hell, I signed over my rights to that jam years ago."

"I'm not working for Sol Katz, Mr. DeWitt, I'm working for Varnell Mack."

"So you said." He nodded. "But if you workin' for him, why ask me about him?"

"Because I think he may be in some kind of trouble. Would you know a reason why anyone would be videotaping his movements? Police maybe?"

"Videotape?" the old man echoed, glancing up at me again, exasperated. "Sweet Jesus, what is this crap? The damn stroke messed up my arm some, but my brains ain't Alpo yet. At least the last dude Sol sent around askin' about Varnell came at me straight on. I don't know what kind of a scam you're tryna pull, but take your show on the road."

"I'm not pulling a scam, Mr. DeWitt."

"Hell you ain't," DeWitt snapped. "Look, I let you run your mouth to pass the time, but I'm tired of listenin' to jive 'bout friends of mine. Varnell Mack never hired you for a damn thing, sonny, so tell your story walkin' or I'm liable to get out' this chair and throw your jive ass outa here."

"Mr. DeWitt, why don't you think Varnell Mack hired me?"

"I don't think he didn't, boy, I *know*. Hell, he ain't even *been* Varnell for more'n twenty years. He went Muslim after the sixty-seven riots, changed his name to Raheem somethin' or other. Wouldn't hardly speak to a white man after that, say nothin' of hirin' one."

"Maybe he's mellowed."

"Musta mellowed one helluva lot. Musta mellowed hisself right outa the ground."

"What are you saying?"

"The man's dead, boy. Died back in eighty-three. Lung cancer. Wasn't but a dozen people at his funeral and most of them was Farrakhan Muslims. So you trot back an' tell Sol if he wants to use that jam, go ahead on. I won't give him no trouble, and Varnell sure as hell won't neither. You got what you came for, now get on away from me." He turned back to his game, shutting me out as effectively as if he'd slammed a door.

I rose slowly, trying to think of something to say. It wouldn't matter. He wasn't going to buy anything I was selling now. And maybe he was wrong, had Varnell and this Raheem whatever mixed up somehow. Maybe.

I stopped at the front desk on my way out and asked the Dresden milkmaid on duty if DeWitt had regular visitors.

"I wouldn't know offhand," she said, frowning. "We have so many patients. Why do you ask?"

"He seems to be a little confused. About who's alive, and who isn't."

"That happens quite a lot." She smiled, scanning the visitor's log. "Let's see, a Mr. Rothstein visited a few weeks ago. And a Mr. Jaquette. A Mr. and Mrs. Robinson. Does that help?"

"No one named Mack?"

"Apparently not, not recently anyway. I wouldn't be too concerned about it though," she added. "Residents often get confused about friends who've passed on. They even talk to them sometimes. It can give you shivers."

"Yeah," I said. "I know the feeling."

I found my steps quickening as I made my way out of the rest home, and when I hit the sidewalk I was sprinting for my car. I scrambled in and peeled out of the lot, pedal down, headed back to the heart of Motown.

And Rock 'n Soul Recollections. I barely made it. It was after five and the blinds were drawn, but I could still see movement inside. I hammered on the door. "Open up, Cal! It's an emergency."

"An emergency?" he said quizzically, letting me in. "At a record store?"

"You don't know the half of it," I said, stalking to the golden soul bin, riffling through the S's. The Sultans. Horace DeWitt grinned up at me from the jacket, young and strong. A rock. I scanned the faces of his backup singers. Their images were barely more than grey smears, blurred by the dance step they were doing. I just couldn't be sure.

"Have you got any other pictures of the Sultans?" I asked. "Posters? Anything?"

"The Sultans?" he echoed, eyeing me blankly, while he rapid-scanned the computer directory of his memory. "I have two playbills with the Sultans featured, but no pictures. . . ." He crossed to a file of publicity memorabilia, and expertly riffled through it. "Aha. A program for a Warfield Theater revue. Nineteen sixty-two. Sam Cooke, The Olympics, Millie Jump and the Jacks, and . . . the Sultans of Soul. Be careful now, it's a by God cherry original."

I checked the table of contents, then leafed through the program gingerly. And found the Sultans of Soul. A standard publicity shot of Horace DeWitt ringed by four dudes in gleaming lamé jackets. Except for Horace, I didn't recognize any of them. I checked the fine print beneath the photo. Varnell Mack was last on the left. He was tall, and had a Malcolm X goatee. But he definitely was not the man who hired me.

Damn.

"What's with you?" Cal said. "You look like you lost your best friend."

"Worse. I think I may be losing my touch. I'm being conned by a guy who can barely walk across a room."

"Conned out of what?"

"That's the hell of it. I don't know. Cal, why would anybody pretend to be a has-been soul singer? And a dead one at that?"

"Somebody's pretending to be one of the Sultans? But why? Even in their heyday they were strictly small change."

"It can't be for money," I said. "He's already paid me more than he's likely to get from any royalties. So what does he want?"

"You got any idea who this guy is?"

"All I know is that it has to be somebody from the old days who knew the Sultans. I'm guessing he found out Sol was looking for Varnell from Horace DeWitt, so his name could be Robinson, or maybe Jaquette."

"Jaquette?" Cal said, blinking. "First name?"

"I don't know. Why?"

"Because I know a few Jaquettes, but only one who would've known the Sultans," Cal said, taking the program from me and flipping through it. "Could this be your guy? The one in the middle?"

"Yes," I said slowly, "this is him. Or it was thirty years ago. But this pic isn't of the Sultans."

"Nope, it's the Jacks, Millie Jump's old group. Dexter Jaquette was their lead singer. And Millie's husband. She dumped him after he got busted."

"Busted for what?"

"A nickel-dime dope thing, couple of marijuana cigarettes. It'd be nothing now, but it was a hard fall back then. I think he did five years."

"All that was a lifetime ago. What could he possibly want now?"

"I don't know. Why don't you ask him?"

"Maybe I will," I said slowly, still staring at the smiling photo of Dexter Jaquette. "Can I take this with me?"

"Absolutely," Cal said. "That'll be twenty-four bucks plus tax, an extra ten for opening late, call it thirty-five even."

I raised an eyebrow, but paid without carping. He'd been a huge help and we both knew it.

I left the program open on the seat as I drove back to my apartment, and my eye kept straying to it. It was a jolting contrast, the faded photo of Dexter Jaquette the singer, and the broken man who'd hired me. My God, he was so young then. Younger than I am now. But there was more to it than that. Something about that picture that I was missing.

Pictures. The guy with the videocam. What was that all about? The only thing I was sure of was that Jaquette had gone to a lot of trouble to set this up. If I confronted him, he'd probably just back off and try again later. Assuming he lived long enough.

Should I warn Sol? A double conundrum. Sol wasn't my client, Dexter was. And if I warned Sol, he'd sic Roddy Rothstein on Jaquette. The fact that he was a cripple wouldn't bother Roddy. He'd rough him up, run him off, or worse, and I'd still never know what I'd bought into.

Unless I played it out. Seemed to me this show had been in rehearsal for thirty years. It would be a shame to close it before the last act.

* * *

The Cadillac rolled up in front of Papa Henry's a little after nine. I climbed out of my Buick and trotted over just as Mack's chauffeur opened the back door.

"There's been a change in plans," I said. "We'll take my car. Give your man the night off."

Mack/Jaquette eyed me a moment, then shrugged. "My car, your car, I guess it doesn't matter."

"Good. And Mr. Mack, I mean give him the night off. I don't want to see him in my rearview mirror, or the meet's canceled. Understood?"

"Yeah," he said, smiling faintly. "I think I understand." He spoke briefly to the chauffeur, who started to argue, then gave it up. He looked me over slowly, memorizing my features, then helped Jaquette out of the car, and drove off.

Jaquette made his way slowly to my car. He'd changed into a tux, with a gleaming ebony cane to match. The suit was an immaculate fit, and broken and bent as he was, he looked elegant. Dressed to kill.

After he'd eased into my car, I leaned in and snapped his seat belt, fussing over his suit to make sure the belt didn't muss it. And gave him a none-too-subtle frisk at the same time. I expected him to object, but he didn't. He seemed amused, energized. Wired up and ready.

Costa Del Sol is one of the hottest discotheques in Detroit. Tucked away on the fifteenth floor of the Renaissance Center, it's trendy, expensive, and *very* exclusive, with memberships available only to the very chic, and the very rich. I'd been there a few times as Desirée's bodyguard, but the bouncers working the front door still wouldn't admit us until Roddy Rothstein bopped out to okay it.

The Costa is on two levels, a huge, lighted dance floor below, a Plexiglas-shielded balcony above, with a deejay suspended in a pod between them, cranking out power jams loud enough to give the Statue of Liberty an earache. A state-of-the-art laser system plays on the dance floor, psychedelic starbursts competing with the camera flashes of the paparazzi shooting the celebrities at play from the press section of the balcony.

We followed Roddy up the escalator to the second floor, the dining, observing, deal-making area. Shielded from the blare of the sound-system, the music from below is reduced to a pulse up here, a thump you feel through your soles like a heartbeat.

Roddy threaded his way slowly through the tables, adjusting his pace to Jaquette's limp, leading us to the head table, where Sol and Millie were chatting up the entertainment editor of the *Detroit Free Press*. Sol had changed jackets, black, with a black shirt, to highlight a heavy gold Jerusalem cross. Millie was dazzling in a white sequined jumpsuit, a spray of diamonds in her hair. Desi was her usual fashionably frumpy self, street-person chic. In the bustle, nobody noticed us, until Jaquette spoke.

"Hello, Sol," he said quietly. "How's the leech business?"

Sol glanced up, annoyed, and the color bled from his face. "My God. Dexter." He glanced quickly around, but Roddy had already moved off into the crowd. "What do you want?"

"To settle up. To close out my account."

"There's nothing to close out," Millie said, glaring furiously at me. "It was all settled a long time ago."

"Maybe not," Jaquette said, glancing at Desi. "What do you think, girl? You know who I am?"

"You're nobody," Sol snapped. "History."

"Maybe it's history to you," Jaquette said. "It's not for me. You got any idea what it's like to see a girl's face on a billboard, have it nag at you? Knowin' there's somethin' familiar about her? Bugged me so much I went to a shop to buy her album, and as soon as I saw her picture up close I knew. I mean I *knew*. It was like bein' struck by lightning. She looks like you, Millie, even sounds like you. But she looks like me, too. And like my mama. The record jacket said she was only twenty-five, but I knew it was a damn lie. She's mine. You were pregnant when you quit me, hid it from me so you could cop yourself a honky meal ticket."

"That's enough," Sol snapped. "I don't know what you think you got comin', Dex, but if it's trouble, you're at the right place. Roddy!" Rothstein hurried toward us, bulling his way through the crowd, signaling to another security type standing near the balcony rail. Beyond him, I glimpsed a familiar silhouette, the man I'd seen on the rooftop that afternoon. He was in the press gallery now, with a camera, or a weapon, I couldn't be sure.

"Too late, Sol," Jaquette said, reaching under his coat. "You took everything, the music, my woman, even my child. It's time to pay up."

"Roddy!" Sol screamed, backing away, stumbling over his chair. Rothstein broke through the crowd and jerked his piece from under his coat, aiming at Dexter's belly, two-hand hold.

"No!" I yelled, stepping between them. "Don't. It's what he wants!"

"Kill him!" Katz shouted. "Do it! Axton, get out of the way!"

"For godsake Sol, he's unarmed! He didn't come here to kill you, he came here to die! To take you with him! He's got a guy in the balcony filming the whole thing!" Nobody was listening. Rothstein was circling to get a clear shot, and he was going to do it, I could read it in his eyes. Dammit!

I shoved Jaquette down out of the line of fire and threw myself at Roddy, tackling him chest high, the two of us crashing over a table. He hacked at me with his pistol, slamming me hard over the ear. I clutched desperately at his arm, but I was too dazed to hold it. He wrenched free, aiming his automatic past me at Dexter.

"Stop it!" Desi screamed, freezing us all for a split second, long enough for me to grab Rothstein's wrist and clamp onto it with my teeth. He roared, and dropped his weapon, hammering my face with his free hand. Sol scrambled after Roddy's piece, grabbed it, and swung it to cover Dexter.

"The balcony, Sol," I managed. "Look at the press box."

He risked a quick glance, spotted the guy with the camera. Then slowly got to his feet. He stood there, in a killing rage, his weapon centered on Jaquette's chest, and if I've ever seen one man ready to kill another, it was Sol at that moment. The moment passed.

"Get up and get him out of here, Axton," he said, lowering the pistol slightly. "But by God, if I see either of you again, I'll be the last thing you ever see."

I shook my head trying to clear it. Rothstein was still clutching his bloodied wrist. His eyes met mine for a moment, and I knew that it wasn't finished between us. It was personal now. I'd be seeing him again. Terrific.

I lurched to my feet, and hauled Jaquette to his. He was spent, ashen, barely able to stand. I got an arm around him, picked up his cane, and helped him walk out, one slow step at a time. He hesitated at the escalator and I let him. He'd paid the price of admission.

He turned to look back a moment; God only knows what he was thinking. Sol and Millie were trying to calm Desi, all of them shaken to the core. Jaquette swallowed, and I thought he was going to say something, but he didn't. Maybe he couldn't. I walked him out to the car.

We drove in silence for twenty minutes, the only sound the rumble of the Buick's big V-8 and the rasp of Jaquette's breathing. He rolled down the window, letting the rain sprinkle his face and trickle down his goatee and his collar. It seemed to help.

"I thought it'd be easier," he said softly, more to himself than to me.

"What would be?"

"Dying. I thought it through, thought I was ready. But at the last second there, I thought, maybe it's not worth it. *He's* not worth it. Not even after . . . everything. That, ahm, that was a bold thing you did back there. I'm sorry I dragged you into my trouble."

"Why did you?" I asked.

"I needed somebody to walk me through Sol's security. Went to the concert at the Palace to . . . to see the girl. Couldn't even get close. Spotted you. Asked around, found out who you were, what you do. Took me a month to figure this thing out, set it up. The guy with the camera's a film student from U of Detroit. Thinks he's makin' a documentary about an old-time singer tryin' to collect some back royalties from a rip-off record company. Would've worked too. I figured everything but you."

"How so?"

"Willis told me you were honest. He never said you were crazy. When it come down to it, I thought you'd stand aside, let it happen.

And the whole thing'd be on film. No way Sol could duck the rap for takin' me out."

"And that'd be worth dying for?"

"Hell, I'm dyin' anyway, boy, slow and hard. I was lucky to see Christmas. I won't see another. I figured if I could just take Sol down with me. . . . Maybe you shoulda let it happen. Hate's all I had left," he said, sagging back in his seat, closing his eyes. "Ain't even got that now. I'm tired. To my bones. I wish I could just . . . be gone."

"You can't though. It's not over."

"No? Why not?"

"You hired me to collect some money, Mr. Jaquette. I haven't done it yet. How would you like to meet your daughter? One on one? I think I can arrange it."

His eyes blinked open. "Meet her? Why? To say goodbye?"

"Or hello. You might have more to talk about than you think. Business, for instance."

"What business I got with her?"

"None. But the Sultans have business. With Sol."

"Man, that was all smoke. A way to get to him is all. He screwed 'em for true, but it was all legal."

"That doesn't make it right. And Desi might not think so either. She's got a good heart, and a hard nose. I think if you asked her right, you bein' a dyin' man and all, she'd talk Sol into doin' the right thing by the Sultans."

"It's too late for that. The Sultans are gone, all but Horace. And he ain't got long."

"Then do it for the others. The Sultans weren't the only group who got ripped off. Maybe you could establish a legal precedent other old-timers can use to get a fairer shake. It might not amount to much. But it's better than nothing."

"Maybe so, I don't know. I'm too tired to think now. Drop me off at the corner. I wanna walk awhile."

"It's raining."

"I know," he said. "Stop the car."

* * *

I watched him limp away, step, lean, step, lean. An old man in a tuxedo, in the rain. I wasn't worried about him. His Cadillac had been tailing us since we left the Costa Del Sol.

I think he's wrong about wanting to give up. A man who worked as hard as Jaquette to settle a score would find enough juice to talk to his daughter.

And he's wrong about the Sultans, too. They aren't gone. Not really. Nor are the hundreds of others who sang their souls out in warehouses and storefronts for pocket change. And altered the musical culture of the world. Shysters like Sol were so intent on cheating them out of every last nickel's worth of rights and royalties that they let one minor asset slip past.

Immortality.

When Sol and his ilk are gone, who will remember? But the Sultans? And Sam Cooke? Otis Redding? As long as anyone's left to listen, they'll sing. Forever young.

I slid the worn cassette into the Buick's player, felt the pulse of the kick drum in the pit of my stomach, then the thump of the bass. And Horace DeWitt sang to me. Not the stroke-shattered hulk in Riverine Heights, but the big-shouldered, brown-eyed, handsome man with conked hair, grinning up from the Warfield Theater program. And he was young again.

And so was I.

"I'm comin' home, Motown Mama, I just can't live without ya . . ."

The Cry of a Violin

by Seymour Shubin

Jealous? I was jealous? It was not true! Oh, maybe for just a few moments. But that was earlier, before I saw what I swear I saw and heard what I swear I heard. After all, what I have had out of life has been considerable, has it not? My life has been a full one, no? It has been enriched by music but not consumed by it, and no man could ask for more—the complete love and admiration of a wife, the joy of children and grandchildren, a house that has brought me so much pleasure (four of the Orchestra live on the same quaint little street, and we have a small chamber group too), the affection of my pupils (I would take only three), and prestige and recognition enough.

We of the Civic are not exactly looked down upon, you know. I mean, even the grocer—I say this only in passing—even he showed a certain, well, a certain respect. Or take the evening of the boy's concert, for instance. Abbie (she's the one who looks so like Margaret, though she has my temperament) Abbie said excitedly, "Papa, Mr. Hendrickson at school found out you were with the Civic! Oh, you should have heard him! I was so proud. And do you know what? He asked would you play the violin at assembly some time.

Would you, Papa? Would you?" She was so happy when I said yes, and I remember when I did it years ago for the married ones also. It is good to see that pride for you in your children's eyes.

Or take later that evening when Margaret drove me to the Town Hall (do you know she would not let me drive after we were married, and that once in a while she would still hold my hands so gently in hers, as though my hands were jewels?), we were walking toward the entrance through the crowd when there was a whisper, "The white-haired one—that's Franchetti," in such a tone of adulation that Margaret pressed my arm, though neither of us looked. This happened often and I just mention it to show you that I did not lack for certain things.

As for the boy, I assure you his name in large letters on placards did not arouse the slightest envy in me. It so happened that night the posters were for Anton Slubiak, "seven-year-old violin virtuoso" whose debut this was in America; but on another night they would tell of someone else. We in the Orchestra had seen child prodigies come and go and we took them quite calmly. And remember too that each of us had been a prodigy in our time.

Backstage that night there was the usual banter and humor and even horseplay, for you will find that with most of us in the Civic the human being is not lost in the artist, yet through it raced that pulse of excitement the years never take away. Then, once again, came the good feeling of stepping on the stage and walking to your chair and tuning your instrument or practising intricate little passages amid the cacophony that is so stirring to the blood.

And then, the applause for the conductor fading, there was that moment of waiting, which is so much like a held breath, for the thrust of the poised baton; and now the quick stern motion and a sudden glorious flooding of sound into what had been a vacuum, and over each of us the exalted sense of being a part of one of the world's most perfect instruments, where anything less than the sheerest artistry from the farthest chair can jar and distort the whole.

The boy did not come out until much later, when the orchestral part of the program was over and, at our conductor's gesture, we had risen to thunderous applause. He stepped from the wing, a small round-faced boy in short trousers, with large solemn eyes and sandy hair clipped evenly across his forehead. He walked to the center of the stage and stood there uncertainly, then looked back at the wing, at a tall balding man whose face was grave and whose forehead glistened. This was his father, who had brought the boy here from some mountain village in Europe and was, I recalled reading somewhere, his teacher.

The father nodded once, sternly, then again, urging him on, and now the boy put the violin awkwardly to his throat and I felt a hot flush of nervousness for him—but only until, with a suddenly graceful, delicate motion, he touched bow to string, and in that magic instant I found myself leaning forward, drawn by a force that was almost magnetic. For standing on that stage—oh, there is a difference, there is a difference—was not simply a superbly talented child with a violin tucked under his chin but one of those rare few, a handful in this world at most, who seem to open their own veins to an instrument, so that each becomes part of the other and fired by the same heartbeat.

I forced myself to sit up after a time, aware that for the past few hypnotic moments I had been fantasying myself out there, with that music flowing from my violin and all those eyes, all of them on me. And even now I had to catch myself from slipping off again, from calling back old dreams, things I had thought long dead in me, and I tried to keep telling myself that what I had now was the good life, it was better—and yet hadn't that music been in me once? Oh, I had it at one time, I had that fire, that certain genius, that— but where did it go? Where had I lost my way?

And now, though I struggled against it, my thoughts were going back, probing, searching—to that little immigrant boy at the settlement-house music school and his teacher taking him to play for a rich old woman and her kissing him afterward and touching her eyes and then more lessons and playing for the old woman's friends and then concerts and the scrapbook growing and then meeting Margaret, and at nineteen, to be tugged in two directions, for the old woman said no, go to Europe, but getting married instead and accepting an offer from the Civic, proud he was the youngest and certain some day he still would be a concert violinist, but then the first child came, and finding so much more to the world, so many new and marvelous things, and then the other children, and one day no longer caring that he was not the youngest any more . . .

Shouting and wild applause shook me then, as if from a dream, and Anton, awkward once more, was looking around in childish bewilderment during one of the most tumultuous ovations I have ever heard, and it took frantic gesticulations from his father before the boy bowed. I glanced at those nearest me, at Krakoff with his violin on his knees, and Heller with his cello between his legs, and their faces seemed tired and a little sad, though Krakoff's had a tremble of a smile; and now, even as we joined in and tapped our bows against the edges of our stands, I wondered were they thinking of old scrapbooks too.

Later, backstage, Anton and his father were surrounded by a loud and enthusiastic group of people who were joined presently by the mayor and his wife, led by the animated chairman of the Civic Orchestra Association. They were patting the boy's head and talking into his face, some of it in his language, but he never spoke a word; indeed, he seemed frightened, it was in his eyes and face, especially as he darted little glances at his father. And the father—it amazes me that no one else seemed to notice—had a look of restrained fury, even though he spoke with a touch of a smile, a forced smile, to the group, explaining in broken English how he himself "before the arthritis" had hoped to be a concert violinist and how Anton had first picked up the violin at two and had been playing less than a year after that.

"Nine, ten hour a day he practise," the father said. But all the while I could see the fury. I had seen it in the faces of other teachers in my time, before it would finally burst out; but usually it was over some obvious error, perhaps a strident note or too much dallying over decorative arpeggios or some overly stretched phrasing. But, in God's name, here? I had heard perfection. What more could he want?

I walked to the dressing room. Changing into street clothes, I thought of Margaret waiting for me near the car and how she would want to go to a restaurant as we usually did, to talk about the concert over coffee and cigarettes. I had always looked forward to it, but not that night. Not totally, that is. A part of me wanted to be with

Margaret and go to that restaurant and later, perhaps, watch television—do all the normal, joyous things of life. But another part of
me, though loathing that father, wondered what heights I might
have reached had I had someone to drive me even beyond my gifts.

The other men were leaving now. I did not know I was alone
until I heard the music.

From the corridor came a lament—a violin's lament—so thin and
tender and hauntingly sad it was as though the instrument itself were
whimpering gently and full of tears. I walked out, puzzled and
moved, and looking down the empty corridor saw that it was coming from the partly open door to Anton's dressing room. I wanted
to leave and yet was unable to tear away, for the quivering beauty
of what I heard, now like a pleading, now a cry, touched something
in me and held on, bringing a tightness to my throat.

I stood there, wondering so deeply stirred how any child could
know of such emotion and give it tongue, when suddenly I heard
his father's voice, cutting harshly through those strains. Astonished,
I took a few steps forward, trying to hear; and though I could not
understand the language, I could the tone, and it was as if he wanted
the boy to be quiet, for he repeated his name several times in a stern
and warning way. Yet, even though his voice ran angrily through
it, that music kept pouring out, as tremulous and plaintive as a sob;
and now, a shiver on my flesh, it drew me closer to the room.

Soon I was standing next to the door, a little beating in my temples, peering anxiously through the slight opening but seeing only
part of the father's arm. I pushed the door open a little wider. The
father, his back to me, stood facing Anton. He whirled. For moments
we stared at each other. Then I looked at Anton, and my whole
body went glazed.

I do not know what happened inside my head. But it was as
though every vein burst, and suddenly I was in the room, grabbing
hold of something—a lamp, a marble-based lamp, I learned—and
I was swinging it at the father's head, again and again. Then I turned
blindly on the child, unable to hold back in horror. I wanted the
father dead, but God forgive me for the child.

They said at my trial that jealousy drove me insane, that I wanted
to believe the father had so pressured and driven the child, had

worked him so long and so relentlessly, that he had turned him into something monstrous. They said it was my mind's way of clinging to the belief that I had taken the right route in life, had not made the violin my life. And sometimes, as I pace the locked confines of the ward, I wonder if they are right, if some dark part of me had imagined what I saw and heard. But no. I must believe it—or agree I am mad.

The boy was staring at his father, tears pouring down his cheeks and chest heaving. And he was crying the cry of a violin.

Death Between Dances
by Cornell Woolrich

Every Saturday night you'd see them together at the country-club dance. Together, and yet far apart. One sitting back against the wall, never moving from there, never once getting up to dance the whole evening long. The other swirling about the floor, passing from partner to partner, never still a moment.

The two daughters of Walter Brainard (widower, 52, stocks and bonds, shoots 72 at golf, charter member of the country club).

Nobody seeing them for the first time ever took them for sisters. It wasn't only the difference in their ages, though that was great enough and seemed even greater than it actually was. There was about 12 years' difference between them, and 50 in outlook.

Even their names were peculiarly appropriate. Jane, as plain as her name, sitting there against the wall, dark hair drawn severely back from her forehead, watching the festivities through heavy-rimmed glasses that gave her an expression of owlish inscrutability. And Sunny, dandelion-colored hair, blue eyes, a dancing sunbeam, glinting around the floor, no one boy ever able to hold her for very long (you can't make sunbeams stay in one place if they don't want to).

Although Tom Reed, until just recently, had had better luck at it than the rest. But the last couple of Saturday nights he seemed to be slipping or something; he'd become just one of the second-stringers again.

Sunny was usually in pink, one shade of it or another. She favored pink; it was her color. She reminded you of pink spun-sugar candy. Because it's so good, and so sweet, and so harmless. But it also melts so easily . . .

One of them had a history, one hadn't. Well, at 18 you can't be expected to have a history yet. You can make one for yourself if you set out to, but you haven't got it yet. And as for the history—Jane's—it wasn't strictly that, either, because history is hard-and-fast facts, and this was more of a formless thing, a whispered rumor, a half-forgotten legend. It had never lived, but it had never died either.

Some sort of blasting infatuation that had come along and changed her from what she'd been then, at 18—the darling of the dance floors, as her sister was now—into what she was now: a wallflower, an onlooker who didn't take part. She'd gone away for a while, around that time, and then she'd suddenly been back again.

From the time she'd come back, she'd been as she was now. That was all that was definitely known, the rest was pure surmise. Nobody had ever found out exactly who the man was. It was generally agreed that it wasn't anyone from around here. Some said there had been a quiet annulment. Some—more viperishly—said there hadn't been anything to annul.

One thing was certain. She was a wallflower by choice and not by compulsion. As far back as people could remember, anyone who had ever asked her to dance received only a shake of her head. They stopped asking, finally. She wanted to be left alone, so she was. Maybe, it was suggested, she had first met him, whoever he was, while dancing, and that was why she had no use for dancing any more. Then in that case, others wondered, why did she come so regularly to the country club? To this there were a variety of answers, none of them wholly satisfactory.

"Maybe," some shrugged, "it's because her father's a charter member of the club; she thinks it's her duty to be present."

"Maybe," others said, "she sees ghosts on the dance floor; sees someone there that the rest of us can't see."

"And maybe," still others suggested, but not very seriously, "she's waiting for him to come back to her: thinks he'll suddenly show up some time in the Saturday night crowd, and come over to her and claim her. That's why she won't dance with anyone else."

But the owlish glasses gave no hint of what was lurking behind them; whether hope or resignation, love or indifference or hate.

At exactly 9:45 this Saturday, this Washington's Birthday Saturday, tonight, the dance is on full-blast; the band is playing an oldie, *The Object of My Affections*, Number Twenty in the leader's book. And Jane is sitting back against the wall. Sunny is twinkling about on the floor, this time in the arms of Tom Reed, the boy who loved her all through high school, the man who still does, now, at this very moment—

She stopped short, right in the middle of the number, detached his arm from her waist, and stepped back from its half embrace.

"Wait here, Tom. I just remembered. I have to make a phone call."

"I no sooner get you than I lose you again."

But she'd already turned and was moving away from him, looking back over her shoulder now.

He tried to follow her. She laughed and held him back. A momentary flattening of her hands against his shirtfront was enough to do that. "No, you can't come with me. Oh, don't look so dubious. It's just to Martha, back at our house. Something I forgot to tell her when we left. You wouldn't be interested."

"But we'll lose this dance."

"I'll give you—I'll give you one later, to make up for it," she promised. "I'll foreclose on somebody else's." She gave him a smile, and even a little wink, and that held him. "Now, be a good boy and stay in here."

She made sure that he was standing still first. It was like leaving a lifesize toy propped up—you wait a second to make sure it won't fall over. Then she turned and went out into the foyer.

She looked back at him from there, once more. He was standing

obediently stock-still in the middle of the dance floor like an own-
erless pup, everyone else circling around him. She raised a caution-
ing index finger, shook it at him. Then she whisked from sight.

She went over to the checkroom cubbyhole.

"Will you let me have that now, Marie."

"Leaving already, Miss Brainard?" The girl raised a small overnight case from the floor—it hadn't been placed on the shelves,
where it might have been seen and recognized—and passed it to
her.

Sunny handed her something. "You haven't seen me go, though."

"I understand, Miss Brainard," the girl said.

She hurried out of the club with it.

She went over to where the cars were parked, found a small
coffee-colored roadster, and put the case on the front seat.

Then she got in after it and drove off.

The clubhouse lights receded in the indigo February darkness. The
music got fainter, and then you couldn't hear it any more. It stayed
on in her mind, though: still playing, like an echo.

"The object of my affections
Can change my complexion
From white to rosy-red—"

The car purred along the road. She looked very lovely, and a little
wild, her uncovered hair streaming backward in the wind. The stars
up above seemed to be winking at her, as though she and they
shared the same conspiracy.

After a while she took one hand from the wheel and fumbled in
the glittering little drawstring bag dangling from her wrist.

She took out a very crumbled note, its envelope gone. The note
looked as though it had been hastily crushed and thrust away, to
protect it from discovery, immediately after first being received.

She smoothed it out now as best she could and reread it carefully
by the dashboard light. A part of it, anyway.

"—there's a short cut that'll bring you to me even quicker, darling.
No one knows of it but me, and now I'm sharing it with you. It

will keep you from taking the long way around, on the main road, and risk being seen by anyone. Just before you come to that lighted filling station at the intersection, turn off, sharp left. Even though there doesn't seem to be anything there, keep going, don't be frightened. You'll pick up a back lane, and that'll bring you safely to me. I'll be counting the minutes—''

She pressed it to her lips, the crumpled paper, and kissed it fervently. Love is a master alchemist: it can turn base things to gold.

She put it back in her bag. The stars were still with her, winking. The music was still with her, playing for her alone.

> "—every time he holds my hand
> And tells me that he's mine."

Just before she came to that lighted filling station at the intersection, she swung the wheel and turned off sharp left into gritty nothingness that rocked and swayed the car.

Her headlights picked up a screen of trees and she went around to the back of them. She found a disused dirt lane there—as love had promised her she would—and clung to it over rises and hollows, and through shrubbery that hissed at her.

And then at last a little rustic lodge. A hidden secret place. Cheerful amber light streaming out to welcome her. Another car already there, offside in the darkness; his.

She braked in front of it. She took out her mirror, and by the dashboard light she smoothed her hair and touched a golden tube of lipstick lightly to her mouth. Very lightly, for there would be kisses that would take it away again soon.

She tapped the horn, just once.

Then she waited for him to come out to her.

The stars kept winking up above the pointed fir trees. Their humor was a little crueler now, as though someone were the butt of it. And in the lake that glistened like dark-blue patent leather, down the other way, their winking still went on, upside down in the water.

She tapped the horn again, more heavily this time, twice in quick succession.

He didn't come out. The yellow thread outlining the lodge-door remained as it was; it grew no wider.

An owl hooted somewhere in the trees, but she wasn't afraid. She'd only just learned what love was; how should she have had time to learn what fear was?

She opened the car door abruptly and got out. Her footfalls crunched on the sandy ground that sloped down from here all the way to the lake. Silly, fragile sandals meant for the dance floor, their spike heels pecking into the crusty frosty ground.

She went up onto the plank porch, and there they sounded hollow. She knocked on the door, and that sounded hollow too. Like when you knock on an empty shell of something.

The door moved at last, but it was her own knock that had done it: it was unfastened. The yellow thread widened.

She pushed it back, and warmth and brightness gushed out, the night was driven to a distance.

"Hoo-hoo," she called softly. "You have a caller. There's a young lady at your door, to see you."

A fire was blazing in the natural-stone fireplace, gilding the walls and coppering the ceiling with its restless tides of reflection. There was a table, all set and readied for two. The feast of love. Yellow candles were twinkling on it; their flames had flattened for a moment, now they straightened again as she came in and closed the door behind her.

Flowers were on it in profusion, and sparkling, spindly-stemmed glasses. And under it there was a gilt ice pail, with a pair of gold-capped bottles protruding from it at different angles.

And on the wooden peg projecting from the wall, his hat and coat were hanging. With that scarf she knew so well dangling carelessly from one of the pockets.

She laughed a little, mischievously.

As she passed the table, on her way deeper into the long room, she helped herself to a salted almond, crunched it between her teeth. She laughed again, like a little girl about to tease somebody. Then she picked up a handful of almonds and began throwing them one by one against the closed bedroom-door, the way you throw gravel against a windowpane to attract someone's attention behind it.

Each one went tick! and fell to the floor.

At last, when she'd used up all the almonds, she gave vent to a deep breath of exasperation, that was really only pretended exasperation, and stepped directly up to it and knocked briskly.

"Are you asleep in there, or what?" she demanded. "Is this any way to receive your intended? After I come all the way up here—"

Silence.

A. log in the fire cracked sharply. One of the gilt-topped bottles slumped lower in the pail, the ice supporting it crumbling.

"I'm coming in there, ready or not."

She flung the door open.

He was asleep. But in a distorted way, as she'd never yet seen anyone sleep. On the floor alongside the bed, with his face turned upward to the ceiling, and one arm flung over his eyes protectively.

Then she saw the blood. Stilled, no longer flowing. Not very old, but not new either.

She ran to him, for a second only, tried to raise him, tried to rouse him. And all she got was soddenness. Then after that, she couldn't touch him any more, couldn't go near him again. It wasn't he any more. He'd gone, and left this—this thing—behind him. This awful thing that didn't even talk to you, take you in its arms, hold you to it.

She didn't scream. Death was too new to her. She barely knew what it was. She hadn't lived long enough.

She began to cry. Not because he was dead, but because she'd been cheated, she had no one to take her in his arms now. First heartbreak. First love. Those tears that never come more than once.

She was still kneeling there, near him.

Then she saw the gun. Lying there. Dark, ugly, dangerous-looking. His, but too far across the room for him to have used it himself. Even she, dimly, realized that. How could it get all the way over there, with him all the way over here?

She began crawling toward it on hands and knees.

Her hand went out toward it, hesitated, finally closed on it, picked it up. She knelt there, holding it between both hands, staring at it in fascinated horror—

"Drop that! Put it down!"

The voice was like a whip across her face, stinging in its sudden-ness, its lashing sharpness. Then leaving her quivering all over, as an aftermath.

Tom Reed was standing there in the doorway, like a tuxedoed phantom. Bare-headed, coatless, just as he'd left the dance floor and run out after her into the cold of the February night.

"You fool," he breathed with soft, suppressed intensity. "You fool, oh you little fool!"

A single frightened whimper, like the mewing of a helpless kitten left out in the rain, sounded from her.

He went over to her, for she was crouched there, incapable of movement; he raised her in his arms, caught her swiftly to him, turned her away, with a gesture that was both rough and tender at the same time. The toe of his shoe edged deftly forward, and the gun slithered out of her sight somewhere along the floor.

"I didn't do it!" she protested, terrified. "I didn't! Oh, Tom, I swear—"

"I know you didn't," he said almost impatiently. "I was right behind you, coming up here. I would have heard the shot, and I didn't."

All she could say to that was, "Oh, Tom," with a shudder.

"Yes, 'Oh, Tom,' after the damage is done. Why wasn't it 'oh, Tom' before that?" His words were a rebuke, his gestures a con-solation that belied them. "I saw you leave and came right after you. Who did you think you were fooling, with your 'phone-call home'? You blind little thing. I was too tame for you. You had to have excitement. Well, now you've got it." And all the while his hand stroked the sobbing golden-haired head inert against his shoulder.

"You wanted to know life. You couldn't wait. Well, now you do. How do you like it?"

"Is this—?" she choked.

"This is what it can be like—if you don't watch out where you're going."

"I'll never—I'll never—oh, Tom, I'll never—"

"I know," he said. "They all say that. All the little, helpless purr-ing things. After it's too late."

Her head came up suddenly, in renewed terror. "Oh, Tom, is it too late?"

"Not if I can get you back to that dance unnoticed—you've only been away from the club about half an hour—" He drew his head back, still holding her in his arms and looked at her intently. "Who was he?"

"I met him last summer, when I was away. All of a sudden he showed up here. I never expected him to. He's only been here a few days. I lost my head, I guess—"

"How is it nobody ever saw him around here, even the few days you say he's been here? Why did he make himself so inconspicuous?"

"He wanted it that way, and I don't know—I guess to me it seemed more romantic."

He murmured something under his breath that sounded like, "Sure, at eighteen it would." Then aloud, and quite bitterly, he said, "What was he hiding from? Who was he hiding from?"

"He was going to—we were going to be married," she said.

"You wouldn't have been married." he told her with quiet scorn.

She looked at him aghast.

"Oh, there would have been a ceremony, I suppose. For how long? A week or two, a month. And then you'd come creeping back alone. The kind that does his courting under cover doesn't stick to you for long."

"How do you know?" she said, crushed.

"Ask your sister Jane sometime. They say she found that out once, long ago. And look at her now. Embittered for all the rest of her life. Eaten up with hate—"

He changed the subject abruptly. He tipped up her chin and looked searchingly at her. "Are you all right now? Will you do just as I tell you? Will you be able to—go through with this, carry it off?"

She nodded. Her lips formed the words, barely audible, "If you stay with me."

"I'm with you. I was never so with you before."

With an arm about her waist, he led her over toward the door. As they reached and passed it, her head stirred slightly on his shoul-

der. He guessed its intent, quickly forestalled it with a quieting touch
of his hand.

"Don't look at him. Don't look back. He isn't there. You were never
here either. Those are the two things you have to keep saying to yourself. We've all had bad dreams at times, and this was yours. Now
wait here outside the door a minute. I've got things to do. Don't
watch me."

He left her and went back into the room again.

After a moment or two she couldn't resist: the horrid fascination
was too strong, it was almost like a hypnotic compulsion. She crept
back to the threshold, peered around the edge of the door-frame
into the room beyond, and watched with bated breath what he was
doing.

He went after the gun first. Got it back from where he'd kicked
it. Picked it up and looked it over with painstaking care. He interrupted himself once to glance down at the form lying on the floor,
and by some strange telepathy she knew that something about the
gun had told him it belonged to the dead man, that it hadn't been
brought in from outside. Perhaps something about its type or size
that she would not have understood; she didn't know anything
about guns.

Then she saw him break it open and do something to it with deft
fingers, twist or spin something. A cartridge fell out into the palm
of his hand. He stood that aside for a minute, upright on the edge
of the dresser. Then he closed up the gun again. He took out his
own handkerchief and rubbed the gun thoroughly all over with it.

Each time she thought he was through, he'd blow his breath on
it and steam it up, and then rub it some more. He even pulled the
whole length of the handkerchief through the little guard where the
trigger was, and made that click emptily a couple of times.

He worked fast but he worked calmly, without undue excitement,
keeping his presence of mind.

Finally he wrapped the handkerchief in its entirety around the
butt, so that his own bare hand didn't touch it. Holding it in that
way, he knelt down by the man. He took the hand, took it by the
very ends, by the fingers, and closed them around the gun, first

subtracting the handkerchief. He pressed the fingers down on it, pressed them hard and repeatedly, the way you do when you want to take an impression of something.

Then he fitted them carefully around it in a grasping position; even pushed one, the index-finger, through that same trigger guard. He watched a minute to see if the gun would hold, that way, on its own, without his own supporting hand around the outside of the other. It did; it dipped a little, but it stayed fast. Then very carefully he eased it, and the hand now holding it, back to the floor, left them there together.

Then he got up and went back to the cartridge. He saw her mystified little face peering in at him around the edge of the door.

"Don't watch, I told you," he rebuked her.

But she kept right on, and he went ahead without paying any further attention to her.

He took out a pocketknife and prodded away at the cartridge with it, until he had it separated into two parts. Then he went back to the dead man and knelt down by him. What she saw him do next was sheer horror.

But she had only herself to blame; he'd warned her not to look.

He turned the head slightly, very carefully, until he'd revealed the small, dark, almost neat little hole, where the blood had originally come from.

He took one half of the dissected cartridge, tilted it right over it, and shook it gently back and forth. As though—as though he were salting the wound from a small shaker. Her hands flew to her mouth to stifle the gasp this tore from her.

He thrust the pieces of cartridge into his pocket, both of them. Then he struck a match. He held it for a moment to let the flame steady itself and shrink a little. Then he gave it a quick dab at the gunpowdered wound and then back again.

There was a tiny flash from the wound. For an instant it seemed to ignite. Then it went right out again. A slightly increased blackness remained around the wound now; he'd charred it. This time a sick moan escaped through her suppressing hands. She turned away at last.

When he came out he found her at the far end of the outside room, with her back to him. She was twitching slightly, as though she'd just recovered from a nervous chill.

She couldn't bring herself to ask the question, but he could read it in her eyes when she turned to stare at him.

"The gun was his own, or the user wouldn't have left it behind. I had to do that other thing. A gun suicide's always a contact wound. They press it hard against themselves. And with a contact wound there are always powder burns."

Then he said with strange certainty, "A woman did it."

"How do you—?"

"I found this in there with him. There must have been tears at first, and then later she dropped it when she picked up the gun."

He handed it to her. There wasn't anything distinctive about it— just a gauzy handkerchief. No monogram, no design. It could have been anyone's, anyone in a million. A faint fragrance reached her, invisible as a finespun wire but just as tenuous and for a moment she wondered at the scent.

Like lilacs in the rain.

"I couldn't leave it in there," he explained, "because it doesn't match the setup as I have it arranged now. It would have shown that somebody was in there, after all." He smiled grimly. "I'm doing somebody a big favor, a much bigger favor than she deserves. But I'm not doing it for her, I'm doing it for you, to keep even a whisper of your name from being brought into it."

Absently she thrust the wisp of stuff into her own evening bag, where she carried her own, drew the drawstring tight once more.

"Get rid of it," he advised. "You can do that easier than I can. But not anywhere around here, whatever you do."

He glanced back toward the inside room. "What else did you touch in there—besides the gun?"

She shook her head. "I just stepped in and—you found me."

"You touched the door?"

She nodded.

He whipped out his handkerchief again, crouched low on one knee, and like a strange sort of porter in a dinner jacket, scoured the doorknobs on both sides, in and out.

"What about these? Did you do that?" There were some almonds lying on the floor.

"I threw them at the door, like pebbles—to attract his attention."

"A man about to do what he did wouldn't munch almonds." He picked them up, all but one which already had been stepped on and crushed. "One won't matter. He could have done that himself," he told her. "Let me see your shoe." He bent down and peered at the tilted sole. "It's on there. Get rid of them altogether when you get home. Don't just scrape it; they have ways of bringing out things like that."

"What about the whole supper table itself? It's for two."

"That'll have to stay. Whoever he was expecting didn't come and in a fit of depression aging Romeo played his last role, alone. That'll be the story it tells. At least it'll show that no one did come. If we disturb a perfect setup like that, we may prove the opposite to what we're trying to."

He put his arm about her. "Are you ready now? Come on, here we go. And remember: *You were never here. None of this ever happened.*"

A sweep of his hand, behind his back, a swing of the door, and the light faded away; they were out in the starry blue night together.

"Whose car is that?"

"My own. The roadster Daddy gave me. I had Rufus run it down to the club for me and leave it outside, after we all left for the dance."

"Did he check it?"

"No, I told him not to."

He heaved a sigh of relief. "Good. We've got to get them both out of here. I'll get in mine. You'll have to get back into the one you brought, by yourself. I'll lead the way. Stick to my treads, so you don't leave too clear a print. It will probably snow again before they find him, and that'll save us."

He went on ahead to his own car, got in, and started the motor. Suddenly he left it warming up, jumped out again, and came back to her. "Here," he said abruptly, "hang onto this until I can get you back down there again." And he pressed his lips to hers with a sort of tender encouragement.

It was the strangest kiss she'd ever had. It was one of the most selfless, one of the nicest.

The two cars, trundled away, one behind the other. After a little while the echo of their going drifted back from the lonely lake. And then there was just silence.

The lights and the music, like a warm friendly tide, came swirling around her again. He stopped her for a moment, just outside the entrance, before they went in.

"Did anyone see you leave?"

"Only Marie, the check girl. The parking attendant didn't know about the car."

"Hand me your lipstick a minute," he ordered.

She got it out and gave it to him. He made a little smudge with it, on his own cheek, high up near the ear. Then another one farther down, closer to the mouth. Not too vivid, faint enough to be plausible, distinct enough to be seen.

He even thought of his tie, pulled it a little awry. He seemed to think of everything. Maybe that was because he was only thinking of one thing: of her.

He slung a proprietary arm about her waist. "Smile," he instructed her. "Laugh. Put your arm around my waist. Act as if you really cared for me. We're having a giddy time. We're just coming in from a session in a parked car outside."

The lights from the glittering dance floor went up over them like a slowly raised curtain. They strolled past the checkroom girl, arm over arm, faces turned to one another, prattling away like a pair of grammar-school kids, all taken up in one another. Sunny threw her head back and emitted a paean of frivolous laughter, at something he was supposed to have said just then.

The check girl's eyes followed them with a sort of wistful envy. It must be great, she thought, to be so carefree and have such a good time. Not a worry on your mind.

At the edge of the floor they stopped. He took her in his arms to lead her.

"Keep on smiling, you're doing great. We're going to dance. I'm going to take you once around the floor, until we get over to where your father and sister are. Wave to people, call out their names as we pass them. I want everyone to see you. Can you do it? Will you be all right?"

She took a deep, resolute breath. "If you want me to. Yes. I can do it."

They went gliding out into the middle of the floor.

The band was back to Number Twenty in the books—the same song they had been playing when she left. It must have been a repeat by popular demand, it couldn't have been going on the whole time, she'd been away too long. What a different meaning it had now.

> "—But instead I trust him implicitly
> I'll go where he wants to go,
> Do what he wants to do, I don't care—"

That sort of fitted Tom. That was for him; nobody else. Sturdy reliability. That was what you wanted, that was what you came back to, if you were foolish enough to stray from it in the first place. Sometimes you found that out too late; sometimes it took you a lifetime, it cost you your youth. Like what they said had happened to poor Jane, ten or twelve years ago when she herself, Sunny, had been still a child.

But Sunny was lucky, she had found it out in time. It had only taken her—well, the interval between a pair of dance selections, played the same night, at the same club. It had only cost her—well, somebody else had paid the debt for her.

And so, it was back where it had begun. And as it had begun.

At exactly 10:55 this Saturday, this Washington's Birthday Saturday, the dance is still on full-blast; the band is playing The Object of My Affections, Number Twenty in the leader's book. Jane is sitting back against the wall. And Sunny is twinkling about on the floor, once more in the arms of Tom Reed, the boy who loved her all through high school, the man who still does now at this very moment, the man who always will, through all the years ahead—

"Here are your people," he whispered warningly. "I'm going to turn you over to them now."

She glanced at them across his shoulder. They were sitting there,

Jane and her father, so safe, so secure. Nothing ever happened to them. Less than an hour ago she would have felt sorry for them. Now she envied them.

She and Tom came to a neat halt in front of them.

"Daddy," she said quietly. And she hadn't called him that since she was fifteen. "Daddy, I want to go home now. Take me with you."

He chuckled. "You mean before they even finish playing down to the very last half note? I thought you never got tired dancing."

"Sometimes I do," she admitted wistfully. "And I guess this is one of those times."

He turned to his other daughter. "How about you, Jane? Ready to go now?"

"I've been ready," she said, "ever since we first got here, almost."

The father's eyes had rested for a moment on the telltale red traces on Tom's cheek. They twinkled quizzically, but he tactfully refrained from saying anything.

Not Jane. "Really, Sunny," she said disapprovingly. And then, curtly, to Tom: "Fix your cheek."

He went about it very cleverly, pretending he couldn't find it with his handkerchief for a minute. "Where? Here?"

"Higher up," said Jane. And this time Mr. Brainard smothered an indulgent little smile.

Sunny and Tom trailed them out to the entrance, when they got up to go. "Give me your spare garage key," he said in an undertone. "I'll run the roadster home as soon as you leave, and put it away for you. I can get up there quicker with it than you will with the big car. I'll see that Rufus doesn't say anything; I'll tell him you and I were going to elope tonight and changed our minds, at the last minute."

"He's always on my side, anyway," she admitted.

He took a lingering leave of her by the hand.

"I have a question to ask you. But I'll keep it until next Saturday. The same place? The same time?"

"I have the answer to give you. But I'll keep that until next Saturday too. The same place. The same time."

She got in the back seat with her father and sister, and they drove off.

"It's beginning to snow," Jane complained.

Thanks, murmured Sunny, unheard, Thanks, as the first few flakes came sifting down.

Jane bunched her shoulders defensively. "It gets too hot in there, with all those people. And now it's chilly in the car." She stifled a sneeze, fumbled in her evening bag. "Now, what did I do with my handkerchief?"

"Here, I'll give you mine," offered Sunny, and heedlessly passed her something in the dark, out of her own bag.

A faint fragrance, invisible as a finespun wire but just as tenuous. Like lilacs in the rain.

Jane raised it toward her nose, held it there, suddenly arrested. "Why, this is mine! Don't you recognize my sachet? Where'd you find it?"

Sunny didn't answer. Something had suddenly clogged her throat. She recognized the scent now. Lilacs in the rain.

"Where did you find it?" Jane insisted.

"Hattie—Hattie turned it over to me in the ladies' lounge. You must have lost it in there—"

"Why, I wasn't—" Jane started to say. Then just as abruptly she didn't go ahead.

Sunny knew what she'd been about to say. "I wasn't in there once the whole evening." Jane disliked the atmosphere of gossip that she imagined permeated the lounge, the looks that she imagined would be exchanged behind her back. Sunny hadn't thought quickly enough. But it was too late now.

Jane was holding the handkerchief pressed tight to her mouth. Just holding it there.

Impulsively Sunny reached out, found Jane's hand in the dark, and clasped it warmly and tightly for a long moment.

It said so much, that warm clasp of hands, without a word being said. It said: I understand. We'll never speak of it, you and I. Not a word will ever pass my lips. And thank you, thank you for helping me as you have, though you may not know you did.

Presently, tremulously, a little answering pressure was returned by Jane's hand. There must have been unseen tears on her face, tears of gratitude, tears of release. She was dabbing at her eyes in the dark.

Their father, sitting comfortably and obliviously between them, spoke for the first time since the car had left the club.

"Well, another Saturday-night dance over and done with. They're all pretty much alike; once you've been to one, you've been to them all. Same old thing week in and week out. Music playing, people dancing. Nothing much ever happens. They get pretty monotonous. Sometimes I wonder why we bother going every week, the way we do."

Elvis Lives

by Lynne Barrett

"Vegas ahead—see that glow?" said Mr. Page. "That's the glow of money, babes."

Lee looked up. All the way from Phoenix he'd ignored the others in the car and watched the desert as it turned purple and disappeared, left them rolling through big nothingness. Now lights filled his eyes as they drove into town. Lights zipped and jiggled in the night. Ain't it just like humans, he thought, to set up all this neon, like waving fire in the dark to scare away the beasts, to get rid of your own fear. Lights ascended, filling in a tremendous pink flamingo. There was something silly about Las Vegas—he laughed out loud. "What's so funny, man?" the kid, Jango, asked with that flicker in the upper lip he'd been hired for, that perfect snarl.

Lee shrugged and leaned his cheek against the car window, studying the lights.

"He's just happy 'cause we're finally here," said Baxter. "Here where the big bucks grow and we can pick some, right?" Baxter was a good sort, always carrying Lee and the kid. A pro.

"Just you remember, babes, we're here to collect the bucks, not throw 'em down the slots." Mr. Page pulled into the parking lot of the Golden Pyramid Hotel and Casino. On a huge marquee, yellow on purple spelled out E L V I S, then the letters danced around till they said L I V E S. The lights switched to a display of Elvis's face. "They do that with a computer," said Mr. Page.

Lee, Baxter, and Jango were silent, staring up. The same look came over them, a look that spoke of steamy dreams and sadness women wanted to console. The face—they all three had it. Three Elvises.

It was surely a strange way to make a living, imitating another man. Sometimes Lee thought he was the only one of them who felt its full weirdness. As they moved their gear into the suite of the hotel provided for Talent, the others seemed to take it all for granted. Of course, Baxter had been doing Elvis for ten years. And the kid thought this was just a temporary gig that would bankroll a new band, a new album, where he'd be his punk-rock self, Jango. But Lee had never been in show business before. Maybe that was why it kept striking him as something horrifying, bringing the dead to life.

He threw his suitcase on a bed and went out to the living room where the bar was stocked for Talent. He poured himself a whiskey and carried it back to sip while he unpacked. Or maybe, Lee thought, he was just getting into the role, like Mr. Page said to, understanding Elvis Presley's own hollow feeling. He played the sad, sick Elvis, after all. Maybe his horror was something the man had had himself in his later years as he echoed his own fame.

Lee snapped open his old leather suitcase, the same valise his mamma had forty years ago when she was on her honeymoon and getting pregnant with him. "Why buy something new?" he'd said when Cherry pestered him before their trip to New York that started all the trouble. "This is leather, the real thing—you can't get that any more."

Cherry admired fresh vinyl, though. Her wish for new things was so strong it tore her up, he could see. Game shows made her cry. She entered sweepstakes, stayed up late at night thinking of new ways to say why she should win in twenty-five words or less. There was so little he could give her, he *had* to let her enter him in the contest the Bragg *Vindicator* ran. New York wanted, as part of its Statue of Liberty extravaganza, dozens of Elvis Presley imitators, and Bragg, Tennessee, was going to send one. Cherry had always fancied he resembled Elvis—she used to roll around with delight when he'd sing "hunka hunka burnin' love" to her in bed. She borrowed a cassette deck and sent a tape of him in, along with a Polaroid taken once at a Halloween party.

When he won, Lee said he didn't have the voice for it, that great voice, but they said no one would notice, there'd be so many others up there, he could mouth the words. He could too sing, Cherry said—oh, she still loved him then—he sang just beautifully in church. There was little enough Cherry was proud of him for any more. They still lived in the trailer on his mamma's land, and now that he'd put it on a cement foundation and built on a porch it seemed all the more permanently true that they were never going to have it any better. He was picking up what jobs he could as an electrician since the profit went out of farming and their part of the country got depressed. A free trip to the Big Apple was maybe what they needed.

And it was fun. Lee liked the pure-dee craziness of the celebration, a whole city in love with itself. Cherry bought one of those Lady Liberty crowns and wore it with a sexy white dress she'd made with just one shoulder to it. When they were riding on the ferry he heard a man say, looking at them, "Duplication is America's fondest dream," and the man's friend laughed and answered, "Such is identity in a manufacturing nation." Lee glared at them, I ain't a duplicate, and anyway, he noticed, they both had the same Fifties' sunglasses and wrinkled jackets as everyone in soda-pop commercials. But when he got to rehearsal with all the other Elvises, he knew that, yes, it was hard to see them as real men instead of poor copies.

Because he had some age and gut on him, they put him toward the back, which was just fine. He didn't even feel too embarrassed during the show. After, he and Cherry were partying away when a white-haired man, very sharp in his western-tailored suit, came up and said Lee was just what he needed. Lee laughed loudly and said, "Oh, go on," but Cherry put Mr. Page's card inside her one-strap bra.

And when they were back home and Cherry sighing worse than ever over the slimy thin blond people on *Knots Landing*, Mr. Page showed up, standing on their porch with a big smile. Cherry had called him, but Lee couldn't be mad—it meant she thought he was good for something.

Mr. Page's plan was a show like a biography of Elvis in songs. And he wanted three impersonators. For the kid Elvis, who drove truck and struggled and did those first Sun sessions and Ed Sullivan, he'd found Jango, a California boy with the right hips and snarl. He had Baxter, who had experience doing Elvis at his peak, the movie star, the Sixties Elvis. And he wanted Lee to be late Elvis, Elvis in gargantuan glittery costumes, Elvis on the road, Elvis taking drugs, Elvis strange, Elvis dying. "It's a great part, a tragic role," said Mr. Page. "The King—unable to trust anyone, losing Priscilla, trapped by his own fame—lonely, yes, tormented, yes, but always singing."

"Have you heard me sing?" Lee asked. He was leaning against the fridge in the trailer, drinking a beer.

Mr. Page beamed at his pose, at his belly. "Why, yes," he said. "I listened to the tape your lovely wife sent. You have a fine voice, big whatchacallit, baritone. So you break up a bit now and then or miss a note—that's great, babes, don't you see, it's his emotion, it's his ruin. You'll be beautiful."

And Cherry's eyes were shining and Mr. Page signed Lee up.

"Check, check, one two three," Baxter said into the mike. His dark Presley tones filled the Pharaoh's Lounge, where they'd spent the morning setting up.

"Man, what a system," Jango said to Lee. "If they'd let me do my stuff, my real stuff, on a system like this, I'd be starsville in a minute."

Lee looked over at the kid, who was leaning against an amp in the black-leather suit he'd had made after they played Indianapolis. Jango wasn't saving a penny, really—he kept buying star gear.

"Yeah, one of these nights," Jango said, "when I'm in the middle of a number—'All Shook Up,' I think—I'm just gonna switch right into my own material. You remember that song I played you, 'Love's a Tumor'?"

Lee grinned and finished his can of beer. Worst song he'd ever heard in his life.

"Yeah, they'd be shook up then, all right," said Jango.

Mr. Page came over to them. "Go hit some high notes on there, kid," he said, "let's check out the treble." While Jango went over to the mike, Mr. Page said to Lee, "How you doing?"

Lee squatted down by the styrofoam cooler they always stashed behind the drummer's platform, fished out a Coors, popped it open, stood drinking.

"You seem a little down, babes. Can I do something?"

"You can let me out of the contract so I can go on home," Lee said.

"Now, why should I do that? I could never find somebody else as good as you are. Why, you're the bleakest, saddest Elvis I've ever seen. Anyway, what home? But let me fix you up with a little something—some instant cheer, you know?" Mr. Page leaned over and put some capsules into the pocket of Lee's western shirt.

"What home" is right, Lee thought. He dug out one of the pills and washed it down with beer. Why not?

"Yeah, babes," said Mr. Page, "party. Here." He gave Lee a twenty. "After you get through here, go take a shot at the slot machines. But don't bet any more than that, right? We don't want you to lose anything serious."

"Oh, right," said Lee. He moved downstage to where Jango and Baxter were hacking around, singing "Check, Baby, Check" and dancing obscenely.

"My turn," said Lee and they went off so he could do his sound check.

He looked out into the theater filled with little tables set up in semicircles. Looks like a wedding reception, he thought, and laughed and then jumped back—he was always startled when he first heard his voice coming out through the speakers, it sounded so swollen and separate from him. It made him feel shy. He'd been so shy and frightened, he'd had to get drunk as hell the first time they did the show, and he'd been more or less drunk ever since. He started sweating as the men up on the catwalk aimed spots at him. They always had different lighting for him because he was bigger than the others. He squinted and went through his poses, singing lines for the sound check. The band took their places and swung in with him for a few bars of "Suspicious Minds," and then he was done and they started working on the band's levels.

He toured around the theater a bit, nodding to the technicians. Everywhere they went, Mr. Page hired local crews and Lee had found they were the only people he felt comfortable with. He'd always been good at electronics, ever since they trained him in the service, and hanging out with those crews the last few months he'd learned a lot. The Golden Pyramid had the most complicated system he'd seen. Up in the control booth, a fellow showed him the setup, talking about pre-sets and digital display. The show always had the backdrop with pictures suggesting what was happening in Elvis's life. Up until now they'd done this with slide projections, but here it would be computerized, same as the sign outside. Lee looked out at the stage and the fellow tapped into a keyboard and showed him Graceland all made of bits of light and then the blazing THE KING LIVES! that would come on with his finale.

He said thanks and made his way back down behind the set. Might be computers that were the brains of it, but there was a whole lot of juice powering the thing back here. Usually, he could stand behind the scrim backstage and follow what was going on, but now he faced a humming wall of wires. He knelt down by a metal box with power cables running out of it and held out his hands. Seemed like he could feel the electricity buzzing right through the air. Or Mr. Page's party pills, maybe.

Lee went through the backstage door and found his way into the casino. Bright? The place made his head whirl. He changed his twenty and the cashier gave him a chit. If he stayed in the casino an hour, he got a free three-minute call anywhere in the country.

He got a waitress to bring him a drink and started feeding quarters into a slot machine. He had a hard time focusing on the figures as they spun. He was buzzed, all right. He tried to go slow. If he made his money last an hour, who would he call?

* * *

When they began rehearsing in Nashville, he called Cherry every Saturday. Cherry would put on the egg timer so they'd keep track of the long distance. Mr. Page was giving a stipend, but he said the real bucks would have to wait till they were on the road. Lee, Baxter, and Jango shared a room, twin beds with a pull-out cot, in a motel. Mr. Page drilled them every minute, made them walk and dance and smile like Elvis. They practiced their numbers all day and studied Elvis footage at night. To Lee, it was a lot like the service, being apart from Cherry and having all his time accounted for. In '68, when Lee was drafted, Cherry was still in high school—too young, her daddy said, to be engaged. He remembered calling her from boot camp, yearning for the sound of her but terrified when they did talk because she seemed so quiet and far away. Just like she sounded now.

They'd barely started on the road, trying out in Arkansas and Missouri, when Cherry gave him the axe. She'd filed papers, she said when she called. She was charging him with desertion—gone four months now, she said.

"I'll come right back tonight," said Lee.

"I won't be here. You can send the support money through my lawyer." She said she'd hired Shep Stanwix, a fellow Lee knew in high school and never did like. He'd grown up to play golf and politics.

Cherry was still talking about money, how they wanted compensatory damages. "I gave up my career for you, Lee Whitney," she said.

She'd gotten her cosmetology license when they were first married, but she'd never gone past shampoo girl. She always said it was hopeless building up a clientele out there in the country, anyway—everybody already had their regular. Only hair she ever cut was his. She said she liked its darkness and the way it waved up in the front, like Elvis's.

"You can come along with us," Lee said, his voice breaking. "I'll get Mr. Page to hire you on as our hairdresser—he's spending money on that, anyway, dyeing us all blue-black and training our sideburns."

"There's no use talking. It's desertion and that's that."

"But, Cherry, this was all your idea."

"Oops, there's the timer," Cherry said. "Gotta go now."

"Wait—we can keep talking, can't we?"

"Save your money," Cherry said. "I need it." She hung up.

When he called back, he got no answer, then or all night. In the morning he called his mamma and she said Cherry'd been going into town till all hours since the day he left and now she'd taken everything out of the trailer that wasn't attached and moved into Bragg.

Lee went to Mr. Page—they were playing the Holiday House in Joplin, Missouri—and said he quit. That was when Mr. Page explained that Lee'd signed a personal-service contract for two years with options to renew and no way out. "Anyway," said Mr. Page, "what's one woman more or less? There's plenty of them interested in you—didn't you hear the sobbing over you last night? You were sad, babes, you were moving."

"Ain't the right woman," said Lee.

The women who came to the show only depressed him. Every night, die-hard Elvis Presley fans, women with their hair permed big and their clothes too girlish, were out there sighing, screeching, whimpering over Jango and Baxter and him. They'd come back after the show and flirt—hoping to get back their young dreams, it seemed to Lee, trying to revive what was in truth as lost as Elvis. Baxter took a pretty one to bed now and then—he considered it a right after so much time in the role. But then sometimes Lee wasn't sure Baxter fully realized he wasn't Elvis. Jango confided he found these women "too country." He waited for the big towns and went out in his punk clothes to find teenage girls who'd want him as himself. Lee slept alone, when he could get drunk enough to sleep.

When they were in Oklahoma, he got the forms from Shep Stanwix. He sent Cherry monthly checks. He had more money now than ever in his life and less to spend it on that mattered. Now and then he bought things he though were pretty—a lapis lazuli pin, a silver bracelet made by Indians—and sent them to Cherry, care of Shep. No message—no words he could think of would change her mind.

One night in Abilene Jango said he was going crazy so far from civilization and good radio and tried to quit. When he understood his contract, he went for Mr. Page in the hotel bar but Lee and Baxter pulled him off. Why? Lee wondered now. They dragged Jango up to his room and Baxter produced some marijuana and the three of them smoked it and discussed their situation.

"It's two years' steady work," Baxter said. "That's hard enough to find."

Lee nodded. He lay back across the bed. The dope made him feel like he was floating.

"Two years!" Jango stood looking at himself in the big mirror. "When two years are up I'll be twenty-three. Man, I'll be old."

Lee and Baxter had to laugh at him.

"Thing is," Lee said, "he tricked us."

"Not me," said Baxter. "I read the contract. Why didn't you?"

Lee remembered Cherry's hand on his shoulder as he signed. Remembered Mr. Page saying what a sweet Miss Liberty she made. And he felt Bax was right, a man's got to take responsibility for his mistakes.

Baxter passed the joint to Jango, who sucked on it and squinted at himself in the mirror.

"Mr. Page is building something up here," Baxter said. "What if we were quitting on him all the time and he had to keep training replacements? As it is—do you know he's hiring on a steady band? They'll travel in a van with the equipment while we go in the car. And he's upgrading the costumes. Not long, he says, till we'll be ready for Vegas. It's like what Colonel Parker did for Elvis."

Jango swiveled his hips slow motion in front of the mirror. " 'Colonel Tom Parker was a show-biz wizard,' " he quoted from his part of the show. He laughed. "Page wrote that. 'He guided me. And I—' " Jango's voice deepened into Memphis throb " '—I came to look upon him as a second father.' Shit. Isn't one enough?"

"My daddy died when I was a boy," said Lee dreamily.

"Mine's a money-grubbing creep," said Jango. "Just like Page."

" 'Course, Elvis should have broken with him in the Sixties," Baxter said. "That was his big mistake—he kept doing all those movies exactly alike because the Colonel was afraid to change the formula. No, at the right moment, you've got to make your break."

Jango snarled at the mirror. "I'm gonna save every dollar, and when I've got enough I'm going rent the best recording studio in L.A. and sing till I get Elvis out of my throat forever."

Lee circled quarters through the machine till they were gone. He hailed a waitress and while buying a drink asked her the time. Four o'clock here. It would be suppertime in Tennessee and darkness falling. Darkness never reached inside the casino, though—there were no windows, no natural light. Could you spend your life here and never feel it? He went and turned in his chit and they let him into a golden mummy case that was a phone booth.

He dialed his mamma. When she heard it was him, she went to turn down the pots on the stove and he was filled with longing for her kitchen. So far off. She exclaimed all right when he told her he was calling from a Las Vegas casino where he was to perform that night, but he could tell it didn't mean much to her, it was too strange.

The telephone glittered with gold spray paint.

"I only have a minute here, Mamma," he said, "so tell me straight—how's Cherry?"

"She was out here the other day. Kind of surprised me. Listen, Lee, you coming back soon?"

"I don't see how I can. Is something wrong?"

"It's Cherry. I know you're legally separate and all, but I don't think she's as hot on this divorce as she was. I was talking to my friend at the grocery, Maylene, she said to say hey to you—"

"Thirty seconds," said the casino operator.

"Mamma—" Lee's heart was pounding.

"Well, I mentioned Cherry stopping by for no good reason and Maylene said it's all over Bragg that Shep Stanwix dropped her to chase some country-club girl and—not that she deserves you, honey, after how she's acted—but maybe if you get back here right now, before she takes up with anyone else—"

Lee fell into a night with stars in it. When he came to, he was slumped in the golden mummy case and the line was dead. A lady from the casino leaned over him. "I'm fine," he said, "I just forgot my medicine." And he took a pill out of his pocket and washed it down with the last of his whiskey.

The lady was tall and half naked and concerned. "Is it heart trouble?"

"That's right, ma'am," said Lee. "My heart."

They ate dinner in their suite, at a table that rolled into the living room. The hotel sent up champagne in a bucket, for Talent on Opening Night. After they knocked it off, they ordered up some more to have while they got into costume in the mirrored dressing room off Jango's bedroom. Jango was ready first, in black jeans and a silky red shirt.

"Uhwelluh it's one fo the moneyuh," he sang into the mirror, warming up. "Uhwelluh it's one," he sipped champagne, "one fo the moneehah." He looked sulkier every day, Lee thought.

Baxter leaned into the mirror opposite, turning his head to check the length of his sideburns, which weren't quite even. He plucked out a single hair with tweezers. Beside him on the dressing table was a tabloid he'd picked up that had a cover story about how the ghost of Elvis got into a cab and had himself driven out past Graceland, then disappeared. Baxter read all this stuff for research.

"Uhwelluh it's two fo the show, damn it, fo the showowhuh," sang Jango.

Lee, who was drunk but not yet drunk enough to perform, confronted his costume. Hung up on wooden hangers, it looked like a man he didn't want to be—the vast bell-bottoms, the jacket with shoulders padded like a linebacker's, the belt five inches wide and jewel-encrusted. The whole deal heavy as sin. Lee sighed, took off his shirt and jeans, and stepped into the pants. The satin chilled his legs. He wrapped a dozen scarves around his neck to toss out during the show. He held out his arms and the others lifted the jacket onto him. The top of the sequined collar scratched his ears. He sucked in his stomach so they could fasten the belt on him, but just then Mr. Page breezed in, all snappy and excited.

"You know who we got in the audience tonight, babes? You know who?"

They all just looked at him.

"Alan Spahr!" he crowed. "I'm telling you, Alan *Spahr*. The Deal-maker!"

Baxter said, "What kind of deals?"

"Hollywood deals, babes. Hollywood. The Emerald City. We're talking moolah, we're talking fame, we're talking TV movie. What's this, champagne? Yeah, let's have a toast here." He filled their glasses. "Las Vegas to Hollywood—westward ho, babes, westward ho!"

"The Emerald City," said Lee.

The champagne was cool and sour. He poured some more and flexed his shoulders.

"Listen, man," Jango said. He still held Lee's belt in his hands. It flashed in all the mirrors. "I am not going to Hollywood. There's no way I'm going to play Elvis where anyone I know might see me."

"You won't be playing *in* Hollywood," said Mr. Page. "In fact, if we make this deal I'm going to see to it that the script is ex-panded—you know, do the whole life, filmed on location. Might even find a child, you know, to play Elvis at six, seven."

The poor kid, thought Lee.

"But a TV movie is on everywhere," said Jango.

"You betcha." Page drank champagne.

"I won't do it." Jango sneered. "Sue me—I don't have anything to lose."

Page leaned close to him. "Oh, no? A lawsuit lasts a long, long time, babes, and I would own all your future work if you quit me. Any albums, any concert tours, I would own your damn poster sales, babes, get it?"

"Mr. Page," Lee said, "you don't need me and Jango for a TV movie. Baxter is the real talent here. On film they can do everything with light and makeup—Baxter can go from twenty to forty, can't you, Bax?"

Baxter looked up from his tabloid and said, "I know I could do it. It'd be my big break, sir."

"Babes, I can see you wouldn't be anywhere without me," said

Mr. Page. "That there's three of you—" and he gestured at the mirrors where, small in his white suit, he was surrounded by ominous Elvises "—that's the whole gimmick. The three stages of the King. And with a TV movie behind us, babes, this show could run forever."

The show was on downstairs. Lee had finished the champagne and switched to whiskey. He had to find the right drunk place to be. The place without thought. Like in the Army. Which he never thought about. Stay stoned, don't think. He checked the clock—lots of time yet. He was in full costume, ready to go. Lee avoided the mirrors. He knew he looked bad. When he was young, he was dark and slim—like an Indian, Cherry used to say. Cherry had loved him. Cherry—better not think about Cherry. Where were his pills? In his shirt, on the floor of the dressing room. He tried to bend, but the belt cut into him, stopped him. He had to kneel, carefully, and then, as he threw back his head to wash down the pill, he saw. Who was that? Down on one knee, huge and glittery, his hair dark blue, his chest pale and puffy, his nose and eyes lost in the weight of his face. He looked like nothing human.

He had to get away. He took the service elevator down. It was smothering in there, but cold in the corridor, cold backstage. Sweat froze on his chest. Jango was on, near the end of his act. Off stage left, Lee saw Baxter talking to Mr. Page. He started toward them, then stopped.

Baxter had Mr. Page by his bolo tie. He pulled him close, shook him, then shoved him onto the floor. Baxter moved through the curtains, going on just as Jango came off with a leap, all hyped with performing and sparkling with sweat. Mr. Page was on his hands and knees, groggy. Jango did a swiveling dance step behind him and kicked out, sending him sprawling again. Then Jango saw Lee, shrugged, snarled, and flashed past.

Lee came forward and Mr. Page grabbed onto him and helped himself up. The old man was flushed—his red scalp glowed through his puffed white hair. He pulled at the big turquoise clasp of his tie and squawked. Baxter was singing "Love Me Tender." Lee shushed

Mr. Page and led him behind the back wall, where the music was muffled. Page kept shaking his head and squinting. He looked dizzy and mean.

"I got contracts," he said. "There's nothing they can do." He started brushing his suit—dust smeared the white cloth.

Lee held out his shaking hands. "Look—I can't go on."

"Oh, babes, you're a young man still," said Page. "You just gotta cut down on the booze some. Listen, I'll get you something that'll make you feel like a newborn child."

"When I get too old and sick to do this, will you let me free?"

"At that point Baxter'll be ready for your job. And Jango for Baxter's." Page patted his hair.

"And you'll find a new kid."

"That's the way this business goes, babes. You can always find a new kid."

Lee's heart was pounding, pounding. He had to look away from Mr. Page, at the wall of wires, lights, power.

"Yeah, kids are a dime a dozen. But I'll tell you what, babes," said Mr. Page, "you were my greatest find. A magnificent Elvis. So courtly and screwed-up. A dead ringer."

Lee looked away, listening to the noise of his punished heart.

"A dead ringer?" He remembered the first pills Mr. Page handed him, just after Cherry—don't think about Cherry—and Lee knew he would die, would die as Elvis had and never again see his wife, his mother, Tennessee.

"Magnificent," said Mr. Page, "we gotta get that look on film! It's gorgeous, it's ruinous—I tell you, babes, it's practically tragic."

And Lee struck him, with all his weight and rage. Mr. Page fell onto the metal box where the power cables met. Lee bent over him, working fast. Green sparks sizzled around them.

Onstage, Lee was doing the talk section of his last song, "Are You Lonesome Tonight?" He was supposed to get lost, say what he liked, then come back into the lyric with a roar. "Tell me, dear—" he murmured into the mike and remembered Cherry when she was just out of high school. "You were so lovely." Wrapping a towel around him with a hug before she cut his hair. "And I know, I know you cared—but the—" Oh, what went wrong? "What went wrong? You sent me away—"

He stood still and looked out at the people sitting at little tables like they were in a nightclub. Well, it is a nightclub, he remembered, a hot spot. And he laughed. "Watch out." He shook his head. "Gotta get straight," he muttered and, looking out, saw tears on faces. "Don't cry for me," he said, "she's waiting." And then the song came back to him as it always returned, the band caught it up, and behind him the wall of light blazed and then ripped open with a force that cast him out into the screaming audience.

Breakfast was cheap here. Even in the diners they had slot machines. Lee drank black coffee and scanned the newspaper. He read how Liberace's ex-chauffeur had plastic surgery to look more like Liberace and about the tragic accident backstage at the Golden Pyramid. The manager of the ELVIS LIVES show had been caught in the electrical fire caused by the new computer system. Now, days after the accident, the newspaper was running follow-up stories about past casino fires.

The first day or so, there had been investigators around, in and out of their suite, but they mostly left Lee alone. He'd been onstage during the fire, when the finale display overburdened the wires, causing a short and an explosion. And there'd been so much emphasis on how complex the system was, digital this and that, no one imagined a hick like Lee could understand it. Even to him, his own quick work seemed now beyond himself, like something done by someone else. Lee supposed the other two thought they'd contributed to Page's death—left him woozy so he passed out backstage and got caught in the fire. But they accepted the explosion as the dazzling act of some god of electricity looking out for them. The second night, when Baxter came in with their contracts, they ripped them up without a word.

A new three-Elvis act was opening soon—Mr. Page had owned them, but anyone could use his gimmick. Baxter was staying on in Vegas—he'd pitched himself to Alan Spahr and they were talking about cable. This morning Jango was heading west, Lee east. Wasn't everyone better off? Except Page—better not think about Page. Already he seemed far back in time, almost as far back as things Lee'd done in the Army. Anyway, Lee blamed the pills. He'd sweated himself straight in the hotel sauna and meant to stay that way.

Lee paid for breakfast, picked up his old leather valise, and went outside. This early, you could smell the desert. The sun showed up the smallness of the buildings, their ordinariness squatted beneath their flamboyant signs. Lee stuck out his thumb and began walking backward.

The trucker who picked him up was heading for Albuquerque. At the truck stop there, Lee drank some beers and hung around till he found a ride through to Memphis. He had resolved to cut back to beer only until he saw Cherry again, but in the middle of the night in Texas he felt so good, heading home, home, home, he wanted to stay up the whole way and bought some speed for himself and the guys who were driving him, and knocked it back with some whiskey the driver had. Home, home, home, they tore along Route 40, through the darkness, listening to the radio. When Elvis came on, they all sang along.

"Hey, Lee, you sound like Elvis. Look a little like him, too," the driver said. He nudged his buddy. "What do you think? Have we picked up Presley's ghost?"

"Naw," said Lee. "He's dead and I'm alive and going home." Sipping whiskey through the night, song after song, he felt so happy he just sang his heart out.

The Viotti Stradivarius

by Lillian De La Torre

(as narrated by James Boswell, April 1783)

The Viotti Stradivarius was detected by ear, a feat Dr. Sam: Johnson with his thickened and unmusical hearing could never have attained to; but so much does mind govern and even supply the deficiency of organs, that by mere ratiocination and knowledge of the world he was able to detect and restore, what the sharpest eye passed unseeing, the great Orloff diamond. The only loser by that night's strange work at Dr. Burney's was his daughter, Miss Fanny, whose little waxen figurine had to be destroyed beyond recall.

Eagerly I had accepted of that invitation to make one in a musical party of pleasure in St. Martin's Street. Men and manners are my study, and sure nowhere in London might one meet with such men, or such manners, as displayed themselves at the musical conversazioni of London's first musician and our very good friend, Dr. Charles Burney.

Behold me, then, James Boswell of Auchinleck, advocate and philosopher (if I may so stile an observer upon mankind) in my sky-blue sattin, attending, like a pinnace upon a man-o'-war, my stately friend Dr. Sam: Johnson. How well I remember the rugged countenance, the little brown wig, the massive figure, aye, the full-skirted snuff-coloured coat and the waistcoat with the brass buttons. How comfortably we were at home with handsome Dr. Burney.

We sat in his fine withdrawing room, once the study of Sir Isaac Newton. Every candle was alight, every sconce blazed, every prism shook with light. Seated by the fire, moulding a little waxen figurine with nervous fingers, mousy Miss Fanny was attired in violet brocade under tissue. I wondered much at such gaudy attire in the house of plain Dr. Burney.

The company that began to assemble was no great matter. First came the Bettses, father and son, violin-makers of St. Martin's Lane, small men, neat and cheerful, with quick brown eyes and respectful bows all round. Each carried an instrument, the father a violoncello, the boy a violin. The boy bore the flat cases with loving care into the little inner room adjoining.

Now came in Dr. Burney's favorite pupil, Miss Polly Tresilian, a Venus in miniature, a little perfection, with pouting red lips and her own yellow hair drest in the new round stile, set off with a baby's gown of clustering gauze, the colour maiden's blush. She was attended on the one side by her father, the portly rich jeweller of Cheapside, and on the other by his journeyman, young Chinnery, sandy and thin, and with eyes only for Miss Polly. 'Twas a trio known in every drawing-room and pleasure-garden of Mayfair.

But the trio had become a quartet. If Chinnery had eyes only for Polly, Polly had eyes only for the dark graceful young man who entered behind her. He wore his own raven curls clustering about a well-shaped head. His figure, though small, was well-proportioned and graceful, and set off by a quiet suit of gold brocade. His olive features were expressive, amiable, and radiant, and he bent his melting black eyes upon Miss Polly. He carried a violin in its flat case. Tresilian presented him with pride:

"Giovanni Battista Viotti, the wonder of the age! The sweetest fiddler that ever touched string! The favorite pupil of Pugnani, that has transcended the master! Honoured by Queen Marie Antoinette and the Empress Catherine! Yet now he comes to England as a simple fiddler, without fanfare; and had not my brother the lapidary of

Paris sent him to me for a banker, he had been lost to us in the crowd."

Upon this encomium, the famous Italian looked mighty abashed and put about; he bowed low, and looked for a corner to hide in. Dr. Burney made him most cordially welcome, and I would have escorted him to the seat of honour by the fire, had not Miss Fanny drawn him to her on the other side.

"Pray, pray," I cried, "Signor Viotti, let us not delay, but give us a touch of your string!"

Upon this an air of waiting settled upon Dr. Burney and Miss Fanny, and all was unaccountably delayed, so that I was constrained to whisper a question in Miss Fanny's ear.

"You think right," she whispered back, "there is indeed a guest to come, none other than the great Russian, Prince Orloff, lover to the Empress, whose terrible thumb strangled the Czar, as the whisper goes. He is music-mad, and resorts to us much. But perhaps this is he."

A mighty thundering upon the door promised no less. The door swung open, and an absolute giant of a man crowded through. He stood not an inch under seven feet high, a man handsome, well-fleshed, upright, and magnificent. He was superbly drest in the French stile, and adorned as for a court birthday. Besides the blue garter, he had a star of diamonds of prodigious brilliancy, and a shoulder knot of the same lustre and value. A picture of the Empress hung round his neck by a riband, set with diamonds of such brightness and magnitude that when near the light they were too dazzling for the eye, and made the lustres dim.

He made his greetings with an air and address shewy, striking, and assiduously courteous, with now and then a quick darting look that seemed to say, "I hope you observe that I come from a polished court?—I hope you take note that I am no Cossack?" Little Miss Polly positively took her eyes off young Viotti, and gasped, as the newcomer made her his bow, and favoured her with an ogling, half cynical, half amorous, cast of the eye.

She gasped again as she caught a first glimpse of the Prince's entourage: two great Cossacks who made up in the height of their fur hats what they lacked of Prince Orloff's stature. They flanked the door with folded arms and looked at nobody. Clearly they were to be regarded as furniture, most like the horses which waited with the Prince's carriage in the alley below.

Prince Orloff was mighty affable and complaisant. He and Dr. Johnson exchanged most respectful greetings. There was a brief flurry of bows as each ceded the other the place of honour, and then all subsided into silence and stared at the romantick Russian, while he stared back. This impasse was broken when little Miss Polly whispered a wish into Miss Fanny's ear, and she as ambassadress carried it to His Highness.

The little lady wished to see the miniature of the Empress a little nearer, the monstrous height of the wearer putting it quite out of her view.

The Prince laughed, rather sardonically; yet with ready good humour complied; telling Miss Fanny, *sans cérémonie*, to untie the riband round his neck, and give the picture into the possession of the Fair.

He was very gallant and debonnaire upon the occasion; yet through all the superb magnificence of his display of courtly manners, a little bit of the Cossack, methought, broke out, when he desired to know whether the Fair desired anything else? declaring, with a smiling bow, and rolling, languishing, yet half contemptuous eyes, that, if the Fair would issue her commands, he would be stript entirely! At this Miss Fanny flushed, and hastily passed the miniature into my hands.

There was hardly any looking at the picture of the Empress for the glare of the diamonds. They were crowded into a barbaric setting of pure gold, and pendant at the bottom from a loop of gold hung quite the largest diamond I have ever seen, cut *en pendeloque*, long and lustre-shaped, and something of the colour of a ripe pear. Dr. Sam: Johnson blinked nearsightedly at the thing over my shoulder.

"This is a prodigious gem," said I. "Pray, your highness, has it not a history?"

"A black one," said the Prince carelessly. " 'Twas stole from the forehead of a Hindoo idol by a rascally French sailor, and so passed by theft and violence from one scoundrel to another."

"Good lack!" cried little Miss Tresilian, "how if you should meet the three visiting Hindoo nabobs face to face!"

"But naturally I have met them," replied the Russian, showing all his teeth in a grin. "Mrs. Montague had the three Hindoos; Mrs. Vesey had the Russian Prince; naturally to maintain her supremacy, Mrs. Thrale was forced to have the three Hindoos *and* the Russian Prince."

"Oh, good lack," cried Miss Tresilian, pleased, "and what said they to the idol's ornament?"

"Never a word said they, but eyed it without blinking. 'Twas at their eye-level," added the Russian giant.

"You must keep a good look-out," said I, "against Lascars and darkavised men."

"Nay," roared the Russian giant, "let *them* look out for me. 'Tis mine, and so I will maintain, for I paid 200,000 rubles for it."

"So much?" breathed old Betts, and had the gems from my hand. He carried the thing under the mantelpiece lustres, and examined it with his glass to his eye, murmuring the while: "Nay, Arthur, I must get this by heart, I must fail of no detail, an account of this will be meat and drink to your uncle the Dutch merchant!"

Over his shoulder young Arthur regarded the precious thing with lacklustre eye. "Of what use is it?" he scoffed. "Can a man eat it? Will it cure the evil or the pthisick? No, Father, the famed Stradivarius of Signor Viotti is the treasure for my money."

"You say true," replied old Betts instanter, "and if I thought otherwise I had myself turned Dutch merchant and no fiddle-maker. Away, gross pelf!"

He yielded the blazing circlet carefully into the hand of Miss Tresilian.

"Welcome, gross pelf," murmured she with a rueful smile, and looked into Viotti's eyes, "for the tenth, aye the twentieth part of this gem would buy a life-time of happiness for two hearts."

The Italian pressed her hand, and together they gazed upon the famous Empress.

Chinnery bit his lip.

"Nay, then, let others see," he cried bitterly. He took the miniature. With professional attention he must needs examine the great stone through his lapidary glass, holding it in the glow of the mantelpiece sconces and turning it this way and that. Prince Orloff seized the occasion to murmur a word in Miss Tresilian's ear; clearly a Cossack compliment, for she mantled and shrank, and Viotti straightened his shoulders to glare at his highborn vis-à-vis.

Then Miss Fanny took the ornament again carefully in hand, and passed the riband over the bent head of the Russian giant. He settled the miniature in its frame of diamonds complacently against his massive chest.

"But come," I cried, "let us delay no longer to look upon the Prince of fiddles, the famed Stradivari of Viotti."

Viotti bowed, and fetched it from the inner room where our effects lay.

"You must know," said he, opening the clasps and revealing in the silk-lined flat case a violin-shape swathed in silk, "that Antonio Stradivari lived and worked at Cremona more than fifty years, and made many superb violins; but mine is the greatest of them all." He loosed it from its silk, and gave it into the eager hands of young Betts. All clustered about to view this second wonder.

" 'Tis a giant among fiddles!" cried young Betts—"even as [bowing] Viotti is a giant among fiddlers."

"What minuscule holes," said I, examining the graceful curved incisions, like an S, in the face of the instrument, "how does one get inside?"

"Minuscule!" cried young Betts, "they are quite the largest I have ever beheld."

"That is so," said Viotti, "it is to this grandeur of dimension that I attribute my instrument's grandeur of tone. Old Stradivari never quite repeated it; makers think that to make so large an incision, the grain must be right, or the face will break."

"I am of that mind," said old Betts; "and as to getting inside, one must take the instrument apart; failing which, he may use my new-invented instrument, which I use for adjusting the soundpost—" he displayed a specimen from his pocket—"you see it is curved so, and articulated so, and it goes inside with ease, so." With his neat little left hand, he manipulated the ingenious implement like a conjurer.

"Remarkable," cried Viotti, "I must have one."

"Pray," said Betts, "accept of this one."

"Sir," said Viotti, pocketing it, "I am your debtor."

"Then you shall repay me," said old Betts, "with a tune."

"At your service, sir. But I see tea approaching—" the fiddler began to case his instrument with loving care—"I shall fiddle for the company after our regale."

He bore the precious thing to the inner room as one carries a child to the nursery; and we all addressed ourselves to the tea-table.

Viotti drank his tea sitting at Miss Tresilian's feet. I thought the lady's eyes roved a bit as long as they were tête-à-tête; but when Mr. Chinnery came from the withdrawing closet and moved to her side, where he sat glowering and taking nothing, then who so gay, so mantling, so laughing and pert as pretty Miss Tresilian between her two swains? And who, when tea was over, pressed for a tune so irresistibly as she?

"I am all yours, ma'am," said the handsome fiddler, and fetched his violin.

Miss Tresilian settled her draperies at the harpsichord, Viotti brought down his bow, and I heard the storied Stradivari give forth a note as dismal and dull as ever blind crowder scraped out of his kit.

Viotti turned white, and set down the fiddle.

"This is not my violin," said he.

Dr. Johnson, to whom all musical notes, when not inaudible, are painful, picked up the instrument.

" 'Tis no other," he said positively.

"I know the voice of my violin as a mother knows the cry of her child," cried Viotti passionately, "and this is not my violin. 'Tis a clever copy, by eye alone you shall not tell them apart—but be assured, 'tis only a copy."

He put it angrily from him. I took the rejected instrument into my hands, I weighed it, I shook it against my ear. All seemed in order. I brought it to the light and peered into the f-hole.

"See, see," I cried, "the label! The Cremona label!"

Antonius Stradiuarius Cremonensis
Faciebat Anno 1709

"I see it," said Viotti bitterly. "He who can forge a violin can forge a label."

The Russian Prince, condescending to interest himself in the fate of the Viotti Stradivarius, bent down to peer in his turn. His miniature, dangling, caught in Viotti's raven curls, and as he straightened again the pendant stone parted from the soft gold loop with a jerk. 'Twas Viotti who first felt what had happened; he brought the stone from his locks with an exploring hand, and extended it to its owner, with a bow.

His Highness's answering bow was all civilized—but as his eye lit upon the stone his roar of anger was all Cossack. What he held was a prism of white glass. Dr. Burney turned pale; Dr. Johnson murmured in my ear: "Here is an artist at substitution!" and His Highness began to hiss through his teeth in Russian. Consternation struck the company; and futile though the gesture was, by common consent we turned to and scoured the rooms, inner and outer. The Orloff diamond was not to be found.

"This is a matter for Bow Street!" cried Dr. Johnson.

"This is a matter for me," replied His Highness, shewing his teeth and speaking too softly. "I am my own justice. I shall expose this thief, and my Cossacks will kill him for me."

Miss Tresilian rose in horror.

"Let no one move," said Prince Orloff, still between his teeth. "We will sit here, till my diamond is restored, and—" he bowed to Viotti—"we make common cause, Signor—till the Stradivarius is restored as well."

Never will I forget the next three hours. At first Mr. Tresilian tried to take the reasonable view, and was mighty prosy in respect to the hazard of jewel-thieves in his shop. But Prince Orloff grinned upon him without mirth until his voice dried to a trickle, and died away. Miss Fanny would have worked her beeswax figure, but 'twas not to be found, so she worked her fingers instead.

Upon this Dr. Johnson was seized with one of his strange rolling fits, and went about the room touching everything against the evil chance. Oscillating his head and ejaculating "Too, too, too," with tongue and teeth, he perambulated the rooms, both inner and outer. Often have I seen him thus in Fleet Street, touching the poles of the carriage in his absent fit. Tonight 'twas his humour to touch the under side of every thing, even the window-sills, in and out; and to tell the prisms of the lustres, every one. The self-imposed task was scrupulously performed before he returned to his seat by the fire, where he sat rolling and muttering in abstraction. Once Viotti opened the instrument-cases in the ante-room, but fruitlessly, for he returned to his place again in dejection. And again silence took us, and Prince Orloff's demoniack eye.

'Twas Miss Polly who finally broke the spell. She went off in hystericks.

"Pray, pray, your highness," said Miss Fanny in a small voice, "be pleased to take our parole, this is most unfitting for a young and tender female. Pray let the ladies depart."

"Why, ma'am," replied Prince Orloff courteously, "you may depart when you will—but"—the Cossack shewed his teeth—"you must leave your garments behind!"

Miss Tresilian wrung her hands, but Miss Fanny shewed better resolution.

"Be it so. My woman shall bring us others, and the ante-room shall serve for tiring-room."

So it was done. Though the discarded garments were stringently searched as to every seam, nothing of note was found except indeed that Miss Tresilian was revealed to be wearing the new female breeches richly laced, a practise which I shall recommend to my dear wife.

Miss Tresilian returned to us tripping in the hem of a gown of Miss Fanny's. Prince Orloff himself lunged his fingers into her soft hair, seemingly undecided whether as a caress or a punishment, and finding nothing there, not even a pad of wool, pronounced her ready to depart. Now a new question arose: how was an unprotected lady to make her way back to the City unattended?

"Let me be searched, and I will see her home," cried Chinnery.
" 'Tis my daughter," put in Tresilian. Orloff was sick of the sight

of them. He spoke in Russian to his entourage, and while one stood on guard the other laid hands upon Chinnery and bore him off to be searched. The ante-room was the scene of the proceedings, and Prince Orloff stood by to see that no seam, no curl of the wig was missed. Chinnery returned to Miss Tresilian very white, and fat old Tresilian took his place.

"At this rate I will go too," cried Viotti, and passed into the ante-room.

"Come," cried Chinnery, and without waiting for his rival swept his master and Miss Polly down the stair and away.

Viotti was seething upon his return to the withdrawing room, and when he saw the girl was gone his temper went higher. He rushed to the door. The Cossack without so much as by your leave wrenched the violin-case from his hand, had it open in a trice, and with one hand ripped out the silken lining while with the other he roughly shook aloft the substituted violin.

"Nay, keep it," shouted Viotti in a passion, and rushed without it down the stair. Fussy little Betts retrieved the lining from the floor, and restored the whole neatly to the case, shaking his head over the violin the while. Orloff eyed him malevolently.

"Let you begone," he shouted suddenly. "Search him, and away with him!—You, too," he added, scowling wolfishly upon the trembling boy.

They were searched and gone, and all the instruments with them, and still we sat about the dying fire, Dr. Johnson swaying and muttering, Miss Fanny working her fingers for want of her beeswax, Dr. Burney in gloomy reverie, Prince Orloff pacing the room in agitation, the Cossacks immovable with folded arms.

Suddenly Prince Orloff came and touched Dr. Johnson confidentially on the knee.

"For what do we wait?" he asked softly. "For a piece of dead stone? 'Twas mine, 'tis gone. It is the will of God. Let us go home."

"Now I see, Prince," said Dr. Johnson, "that you are a philosopher."

"It is the will of God," said the philosopher. "Let us go home."

* * *

Next morning betimes I waited upon Dr. Johnson; but early though I was, one was before me. 'Twas Dr. Burney's footman, his eyes starting from his face. He stood in the front room twisting his hands before him. Dr. Johnson signed me to listen.

"Which when I heerd this house-breaker a-prying and a-scratching at the entry-way, sir," said the footman earnestly, "I ons with my night-gown, and ups with my blunderbuss, and lets fly, Sir."

"What like was the miscreant?" enquired Dr. Johnson.

"Nay, Sir, 'twas that dark, I never looked at 'un, but let off my piece without waiting."

"Was he not a black man?" I asked eagerly.

The man shrugged.

"All cats is black in the dark, as they say, Sir."

"What wore he? A banjan? A turban, belike?"

"Nay, Sir, I cannot say, he was muffled to the brow in something, and when the blunderbuss went off he legged it mighty spry."

"Did you not hit him, then?"

"Never a whit, for I fired in the air."

" 'Tis a great pity," said Dr. Johnson thoughtfully, "for 'tis clear that the diamond is hid in that room, and the thief was forced to return for it in dead of night. Now had you scanned him, or marked him with a pellet, you might have known him again."

"Yes, Sir," said the man miserably, "I conceived it was my dooty, Sir."

"Very good, William," said Dr. Johnson kindly, "always do your duty, my man. Well, we must see what we can do. Pray, William, desire your master from me, to make the withdrawing room secure, and admit nobody, until I shall direct him further. Say to him, that as soon as Boswell and I have broken our fast, we shall be with him straight, and shall concert further measures."

Making a leg, the man withdrew, and soon the floating aroma of good India tea heralded Francis the manservant with our breakfast.

"Surely all is now clear," I cried in excitement, "I see it all. This olive-skinned, black-browed young man who calls himself Viotti has hypothecated Prince Orloff's diamond, and but for the vigilance of the good William he had already carried it in triumph to the hands of his masters the Hindoo princes."

Johnson swallowed a swig of tea.

"How do you make that good?" enquired he mildly.

"Why, thus, sir. Who is Viotti?"

"Why, Sir, Burney will tell you, Europe's rising young violinist, the favorite pupil of Pugnani, the fiddler who has played his way into every heart in Geneva, Dresden, Berlin, Warsaw, St. Petersburg, and Paris . . . and into one heart in London."

"Are you sure Viotti is in London?"

"My eyes tell me so."

"You judge over-hastily," I cried, triumphing to have so caught out my philosophical friend. "Who has seen Viotti? Have you? Has Burney? Who knows that this black-browed young man is in very truth Viotti, and not an impostor? Your eyes tell you, here is a young man. Mr. Tresilian tells you, this is the world's greatest violinist. Who tells him so? The man himself. But a man may lie. Letters from Paris. But letters may be forged."

"Yet what folly," suggested my learned friend mildly, mopping tea from the ridges of his waistcoat, "what folly to attempt the one personation a man cannot make good. 'Tis as if I were to strive to pass myself off as Johnson the equestrian. How long can I sustain the character? I must be detected the moment the company challenges me to mount and give an exhibition of my skill."

"Aye, sir," I exclaimed in excitement, "and so must he be the moment he puts bow to violin—unless he has the wit to extricate himself by pretending the sad lumpish wails he produces proceed from a violin bewitched, a changeling violin, a forgery. As indeed the instrument he carries must be a forgery, for how is a masquerader to come by a genuine Vremona? Nay, what need has he of a true Stradivari, who cannot play upon it like Viotti, be the instrument never so great? No, Sir, depend upon it, we have here to do with an impostor, come hither with no other object than to steal the great Orloff diamond from the Prince."

JOHNSON: "Surely 'tis a needless elaboration. A man may steal a diamond without giving himself out to be the world's greatest performer upon the violin, the haut-boy or the Jew's-harp."

BOSWELL: "How? How is one to take a diamond from a warrior seven feet high, unless by lulling him into security? For which, his easiness at the home of Dr. Burney is pitched upon. His partiality for music is known."

JOHNSON: "Well, Sir, say on. How did the pseudo-Viotti make off with the diamond after passing under the hands of the Cossacks?"

BOSWELL: "Nor did he so. He dared not attempt it. Hence his fit of passion in departing. He must depend upon his entrée at Burney's to carry it off subsequently from its hiding-place within the room."

"Why, Bozzy, you must consider," said my friend, peering into the empty tea-pot, "that our thief, whoever he be, was fain to gain entrée at dead of night, at risk of a blast from a blunderbuss. Is this your conception of the entrée at Dr. Burney's?"

"Perhaps passion warped his judgment. Or, it may be, the princely Hindoos his masters pressed him to the attempt."

"Pray, Bozzy," said my friend with asperity, setting down his cup with finality, "let us have no more of this romantick tale of the princely Hindoos, who in my belief know no more of the matter than the babe unborn. The diamond is to seek in Dr. Burney's with-drawing room, and the thief is to seek among those who were in it, so let's be up and doing, and leave the Hindoos to Mrs. Macau-lay."

So saying, he clapped his old cocked hat on his little brown scratch-wig and set forth. I followed suit, and we set out for St. Martin's Street.

Passing, as so often before, with admiration under Temple Bar, whom should we meet but the very man, him who called himself Viotti.

"Well-met, Dr. Johnson!" cried the volatile foreigner, "well-met indeed, for I am come forth to seek you. They give you a name, sir, for a detector of villainies, and I who have suffered one indeed, beg that you will put forth your endeavour to restore my priceless Stradivari and detect him who has made away with it."

I looked with amaze upon this impudence, but Dr. Johnson re-ceived the young man with unruffled complaisance.

"Pray, Sir, walk along with us, and let us take counsel together."

I fell back a pace, the better to have the suspected young man under my eye, the while my ear was alert to every word my astute friend might let drop.

"Well, Sir," began Dr. Johnson, "where, then, do you lodge?"

"At Joseph Hill's, Sir, at the sign of the Harp and Flute, in the Haymarket."

"Oho, the violin maker! Here's a man who knows a good fiddle when he sees it! Pray, sir, how know you that 'twas your own fiddle you brought away from thence last night?"

"I played upon it, sir, and it was never sweeter. I played for a space of ten minutes together, and then I wrapped it in silk, and laid it in the case, and so brought it away to Dr. Burney's. No, Sir, the exchange was made under my nose as it lay in the inner room, and priceless instrument somehow spirited away from thence."

"No such thing, Sir," replied Dr. Johnson. "Did one of those who were searched to the skin by the Prince's Cossacks succeed in smuggling thence so large a thing as your Stradivari? Disguised, perhaps, as a walking-stick?"

"I give you back your question," replied Viotti doggedly. "My Stradivari cannot still remain at Dr. Burney's. Those rooms were stringently searched for a stone no larger than a nutmeg. Did we pass unseeing so large a thing as a fiddle? Disguised, perhaps, as a hearth-brush?"

I jerked my head at this impudence, and muttered "Tschah" between my teeth. Dr. Johnson cast me a lowering look, and as we approached St. Martin's Lane he continued.

"Let us approach the matter by logic. Who will steal a violin? He who can play upon it. Who will substitute a forged fiddle? He who can make one. 'Tis plain: if the thief be not your landlord Hill—"

"Sir, sir," I ejaculated, "the most honoured violin-maker in London—"

"Then it can only be . . ."

"Hark!" cried Viotti, oblivious, and stood quite transfixed. "I lark!"

Dr. Johnson frowned, and seemed to strain his dull hearing. I heard it plainly—the tones of a violin, of particular sweetness, and played with a practised hand. Viotti's eyes seemed to start from his head.

" 'Tis no other," he cried in a strangled voice, "I cannot be mistaken,'tis my own Stradivari, and played by the hand of a master!"

I looked at the house whence the strains floated. The narrow door was ajar. Above it hung a gilded fiddle, and the brass plate bore the legend:

"JOHN BETTS, Violin-maker."

Viotti rushed through the door instanter, and we were constrained to follow. Like the lute of Orpheus, the mellifluous voice of the fiddle pulled us irresistably into the violin-maker's workroom.

'Twas Arthur Betts who played. He held the shining fiddle like a lover, and the silver notes cascaded under his bow. Seated at his worktable in a litter of pegs and patterns, his father beamed upon him and kept time with his famous articulated instrument. Our tumultuous entry but redoubled his smile. He met the rush of the choleric violinist with a rush as swift, and enveloped him in an embrace.

"Signor Viotti," exclaimed he, "I give you joy! Your Stradivari is restored to you good as new. You have been made the victim of an infamous trick, Sir, but by my skill I have made all right."

Arthur Betts, his fiddling broken off, extended the violin.

"Do you set bow to it, Sir," he exclaimed, "and your heart will be at rest. Oh, Sir,'tis the sweetest, the most responsive . . .''

Viotti, in an agony of impatience, yet forbore to snatch the precious instrument. Gently he accepted it from the boy's hand, gently he set bow to it and drew it across the strings, and it answered him like honey from the comb. He began to play. If Arthur Betts had drawn sweetness from the famous instrument, now it was brought alive. It wept, it danced, it laughed, it sang. Never have I heard such fiddling. Even Dr. Sam: Johnson uncreased his brow. He looked at my rapt countenance.

"Is this Viotti?" he murmured in my ear.

"None other," I replied; and even as the great violinist dropped his bow and caressed the violin in the cup of his hand, I realized that all my conjecture was vain, and the answer to both our riddles was still to seek.

"Pray, Sir," demanded Dr. Johnson of Betts, "how have you wrought this miracle?"

"You must know, Sir," replied the violin-maker, "that I was no more satisfied than yourself that a substitution had been effected. I desired to examine into the matter more closely, and to that end, as you know, Sir, I carried the instrument away with me. This morning I set it on my workbench and opened it—and lo, the thing was made clear. Some enemy—jealous, as it might be, or desiring to damage the master's reputation, had with great subtlety introduced against the sound-post—a quantity of beeswax!"

He handed the substance in question to Dr. Johnson, a hardening wad of the stuff of about the bigness of a nut of Brazil. I peered over Dr. Johnson's shoulder as he turned it in his big shapely fingers. One side bore the grain mark of the sound-post; on the other, clearly impressed, was the mark of a finger.

"Beeswax!" cried Viotti. "Small wonder the sound was deadened!"

"How so?" enquired I. A new realm was opening to me.

"I will shew you, Sir," said Betts. From his work-bench he took the two halves of another instrument. "The sound, d'ye see, Sir, is made by drawing the bow over the string. But the sound is thin, and of no account, till it be resounded within the belly of the instrument. Now much depends on this strip of wood which lies in the belly, being made fast there—'tis by name the bass bar; and much depends on this peg which joins top and bottom. This peg we call the soundpost, and 'tis most particularly not to be meddled with. 'Twas just here, that our Vandal had loaded the Viotti Stradivarius with this pad of wax. How determined an enemy is he who takes such pains. Pray, Signor Viotti, have you ever an enemy in England?"

"None that I know. Yet stay, an enemy I have, so much is certain, for last night in my homeward way I was followed, and I feared a knife in the ribs."

"More like a horse-pistol, with a 'Stand and deliver.' Yet you came off unscathed after all."

"I shewed him a clean pair of heels; I can run with the best. Yet how have I earned such hatred? Who can hate me so?"

"Who," said Dr. Johnson with a laugh, "but another violinist?"

"Or," said Arthur Betts quickly, "a rival defeated in love?"

Johnson was staring at the lozenge of wax through the violin-maker's glass.

"I think," he said in an absent voice, "I think we may soon find out."

"How, Sir?" demanded Viotti eagerly. "I would give much to know the scoundrel."

"There is a way," said Johnson, "or my observation is much at fault. Let us gather tonight once more, in the withdrawing room of Dr. Burney. I'll engage him to receive us. 'Tis there I'll expose Signor Viotti's enemy; aye, and perhaps restore the diamond of Prince Orloff."

The musical trio strove to learn more, but not another word would Dr. Johnson say. They perforce consented to the rendezvous. We left Viotti descanting upon the art of violin-playing, and Arthur Betts hanging entranced upon his every motion.

"Pray, Sir," I enquired as we made the best of our way to Dr. Burney's, "how do you propose to lay your hand upon him who tampered with yonder violin?"

JOHNSON: "Look upon this wax. See the print of a finger upon it. I will engage, with luck, to fit this print to the finger that made it."

BOSWELL: "Nay, how? Remember the thumb-print at Stratford, where you said that some other means than gross measurement must be found to fit a finger to its print."

JOHNSON: "I have found the means. I will put my finger—nay, his own finger—"

BOSWELL: "Or *her* finger."

JOHNSON: "Or *her* own finger—'tis indeed a slim one—on the miscreant."

BOSWELL: "I muse who it may be?"

"An avenging Hindoo," hazarded Dr. Johnson slily, "passing himself off as Viotti?"

"Why, no, sir, no avenging Hindoo could win such sweetness even from a Stradivarius," I owned. "Nor would any avenging Hindoo have an interest in harming even the first violinist of the age.

Sure such an one had attacked Prince Orloff direct . . . Prince Orloff!
Pray, Sir, how do we know that he is Prince Orloff? Or that yonder
yellow sparkler is indeed a diamond, or ever saw the land of the
Hindoos? Is not all perhaps a hoax?—the seven-foot hero and his
blaze of brilliants, and Viotti's fiddle choked with beeswax till it
croaks again—"

"Nay, Bozzy, spare me this while!" cried Dr. Johnson. "Be not
so finespun in conjecture. I cannot see that massive thumb that
choked the emperor brought to the finicking task of introducing a
lozenge of wax through an f-hole with a hump-backed darning-
needle, and there's an end on't."

"Yet Orloff works in my mind," continued I presently. "How if
he has hypothecated his own diamond? Perhaps he has insured it at
Lloyd's coffee-house, and will have its value again from the gentlemen there."

"Oh, the diamond," said Dr. Johnson. "Well, I have my eye on
the diamond, never fear."

"Or perhaps," I went on, "Prince Orloff fancies his diamond, and
would keep it. How long, think you, will it be his after the Empress's
greedy eye has lighted upon it? How better keep it, than to noise
after the story of its greatness the story of its loss?"

"At last!" Dr. Johnson breathed in relief. "St. Martin's Street!"

Dr. Burney readily assented to another gathering in his withdrawing
room. A card was sent to Mr. Tresilian, and another to Prince Orloff.
The Prince's reply was characteristick: "If it is the will of God His
Highness will come." Mr. Tresilian, entertaining no doubts of the
efficacy of his own will, as touching not only himself, but also Miss
Polly and young Chinnery, sent a curt assent in the name of all three.
All that remained was to make the withdrawing room fast and wait
the event.

Once more the company was gathered in Dr. Burney's withdrawing
room. Once more the candlelight sparkled on Sir Isaac Newton's
prisms, and the firelight warmed Miss Fanny's slender hands, busy
with fresh beeswax. Once more Viotti languished, and Miss Polly
mantled, and young Chinnery glowered, and old Tresilian watched

the three. Once more the Bettses, neat and respectful, wore smiles unchangingly cheerful. As to Prince Orloff, he was tranced in apathy, resigned in fatalistick Russian pessimism to the will of God.

"Pray, Boswell, be so good as to assist me."

I leaped to my feet with alacrity. Dr. Johnson handed me Miss Fanny's lump of softened beeswax, with the injunction still to keep it warm.

"Good friends," he addressed the quiet circle, "we are here for a double purpose, to detect the Vandal who tampered with Signor Viotti's Stradivarius, and to discover the whereabouts of His Highness's diamond."

"If it be the will of God," said His Highness.

"If it be the will of God," said Johnson solemnly. "The lesser puzzle first. Pray, Mr. Boswell, a lump of beeswax. Mr. Betts, oblige me by setting your fore-finger to the wax."

The violin-maker looked up at him with quick intelligence; he saw what we would be at. He pressed his right fore-finger to the wax. Arthur Betts followed, staring in wonder. Miss Fanny was next. Dr. Johnson scanned each imprint eagerly through a glass.

Now we approached the group about Miss Polly Tresilian. She graciously complied with my humble request.

"Signor Viotti?"

Quick colour rushed up his dusky cheeks.

"Have I tampered with my own most precious possession?" he began hotly.

Dr. Johnson shrugged.

"Mr. Chinnery?"

"I will not, unless Signor Viotti precedes me."

Angry glances crossed. Dr. Johnson turned suddenly upon old Betts.

"You, Sir, if memory serves you are left-handed?"

"Yes, Sir."

"Then touch your left fore-finger, and do not trifle with me."

The violin-maker shrugged, and touched. Johnson scanned the imprint, and shook his head. What did he seek? Or was this perhaps but a pretence, designed to force the guilty to betray himself?

"I am brought to a standstill, unless you, Sir—" to Viotti.

Viotti shrugged, and touched. Now Johnson turned to Chinnery. The thin young man felt every eye, and rose slowly.

"Pray, Sir, touch."

"I will not."

Quick as a snake striking Johnson had the slim wrist in his grip of iron, and pressed against the fore-finger the softened wax.

Chinnery was white as his ruffles as he nursed his wrist. "What signifies this hocus-pocus?" he demanded angrily.

Johnson produced the lump of beeswax he had brought from Betts's shop. At sight of it Chinnery went whiter yet.

"This," said my friend deliberately, "that when you tampered with Viotti's violin"—he held the young man's eyes with his in a gaze deep and full of meaning—"when you tampered with Signor Viotti's violin out of mere spite and jealousy, you left your finger-print on the wax plain as a foot-print, and a finger-print so singular that none in this room but you could have made it."

Viotti rose from the girl's side, dints of rage whitening his nose, fists clenching and unclenching; but Tresilian stopped him with a heavy hand on his arm.

"I deny it," said Chinnery in a strangled voice, "make that good."

" 'Tis easily made good," said Dr. Johnson, still engaging his eyes. "I have long observed the pad of the human fore-finger . . ."

"Holy Mother," remarked Orloff, his interest finally piqued, "what a man is this, that goes about peeping at fore-fingers! To what end, in God's name?"

"Why not?" said Johnson over his shoulder, "Nihil humanum a me alienum. Now the human fore-finger, in the inscrutable wisdom of God, bears a pattern, as it were an eddy or a spiral, that goes to one center where the pad is highest. Never have I seen a triple center, and only twice in my life a double one—once on the finger of the Rector of St. Olave's, and once on your fore-finger, Mr. Chinnery. Now the finger-print on the wax has a double center. Was it made, think you, by the Rector of St. Olave's?"

Chinnery stood irresolute.

"Come, Mr. Chinnery," said Johnson perswasively, "this is not a crime you stand charged with, unless loving a lady too well be a crime. I counsel you, give me best, and be off with you."

Chinnery seemed to make up his mind.

"You have the right of it," he confessed, " 'twas I tampered with the Italian's Stradivarius."

"Then satisfy us," cried Betts eagerly, "how you contrived to introduce a lump of beeswax through the f-hole and that without the use of my ingenious instrument."

" 'Twas done by depression," muttered Chinnery. Viotti ground his teeth. "I am indifferent deft, Sir, being a lapidary, and as to your instrument, I made shift to copy it, having in my pocket a sufficiency of silver wire which I designed braiding into a ring for Polly Tresilian." His voice broke. " 'Twas all for love of Polly, I could not bear he should make music with her,'twas his playing bewitched her."

"Good lack, Tom!" cried Polly, and ran to him.

Viotti uttered a round oath in Italian, but upon his threatening motion Tresilian pinioned him. Polly had her arms about Chinnery.

"Poor, poor Tom," she murmured, "I love you best, indeed I do."

"Then be satisfied, and be off with you," said Johnson sharply. Viotti muttered curses, and wrenched against the restraining arms of Tresilian. "Take my counsel, lad, with an Englishman 'tis a word and a blow, or he takes you to law, and so an end; but a foreigner will have it out of your hide. Be off, and look to your skin."

"I'll go with you, Tom!" cried Miss Tresilian.

"Not so, Miss, you'll bide. Now be off, young Sir, and repent in time."

Quickly young Chinnery touched his lips to Polly's hand, and was gone. Polly burst into tears.

"Unhand me, Sir," said Viotti quietly to Tresilian. "You have my parole."

"A pretty comedy, Dr. Johnson," said Prince Orloff languidly. "Now for the after-piece. Where is my diamond?"

"Sir," replied Dr. Johnson, " 'tis in this room. Yet I do not choose to sniff about like a dog after truffles. I shall look in my head, and find your diamond. Pray, Dr. Burney, have you ever a bowl of *poonch*? Your downright English *poonch* is a great quickener of the intellects."

"Now, Sir," said I with resolution, "you shall not take me twice in the same springe. Trust me, gentlemen, in these exact words did my learned friend engage with Bonnie Prince Charlie that he would find his missing ruby in the bottom of Miss Flora MacDonald's punch-bowl; and drown me therein if he did not know where the thing was all along!"

Dr. Johnson flashed me a look so imperious and full of meaning that my voice died in my throat.

"Nay, Dr. Burney, I do but jest," I added in a small voice, "pray let the punch-bowl be brought."

"With all my heart," cried Dr. Burney. As the punch was brewed I reflected anxiously what my venerable friend could mean with his carousing. Could he intend the thief of the diamond should become befuddled, and so betray himself? My eye lit upon Orloff, and I saw it all plainly. As the glass went round I set myself assiduously to drink with Orloff, designing he should become liquored as my friend desired. As to myself, I had no care if I could be of service to his scheams.

The chimes of St. Martin's told the hour round, an hour of toasts and pledges. I looked upon my princely charge. His countenance seemed to waver like a face under water. The moment is at hand! said I to myself.

I sought my learned friend where he stood by the punch-bowl with his back to the company, intending to impart this news to him. He held a fruit-knife in his hand, and seemed to be peeling a prune.

"The moment is unmanned," said I.

"How?" said he, dropping the prune-pit into his cup.

"Unmanned," said I.

"Alack, Bozzy, so are you," said he.

He approached Prince Orloff where he sat wabbling by the fire. The next to the last thing I remember is the triumph in his voice as he cried:

"My inebrious friend Boswell was a true prophet, your Highness. I have found your diamond—in the bottom of the punch-bowl!"

The last thing I remember is the rough feel of the carpet under my cheek.

* * *

I opened my eyes with difficulty in the morning light. Dr. Johnson seemed to be sitting at my bedside.

"How now, Bozzy," cried he with unwonted geniality, "still un-manned?"

"Yes, Sir," I replied sheepishly. "And how do all friends in St. Martin's Street—" memory began to return—"is Signor Viotti rec-onciled to lose his Miss and gain his Stradivarius? And has Prince Orloff indeed his Hindoo stone again?"

"He has, then," replied Dr. Johnson, "and the thief is much be-holden to you for an hour's clear start."

I rose to an elbow in excitement.

"Pray tell me the story, Dr. Johnson, how came it out of the punchbowl so pat?"

JOHNSON: "Because I put it in there."

BOSWELL: "Where did you find it?"

JOHNSON:"Where the thief had hidden it to be carried away, in a lump of beeswax affixed to the sound-post of Viotti's violin. This is an old trick of the professional jewel-thief. He'll come into a shop, and snatch up a ring or a gem while the 'prentice's back is turned, and quickly with a lump of softened beeswax he has brought with him he'll affix it to the under side of the counter. The shopman may search him all day long, he'll never find the ring: and tomorrow comes in his doxy, she knows where the beeswax is, and will quietly pick it off and carry it away."

BOSWELL: "Yet which of Dr. Burney's guests was a professional jewel-thief?"

JOHNSON: "Not one of them; but two were professional jewellers, to whom the trick is known. Neither do I think it a plot, whether against the diamond or the Stradivarius. But put yourself in the place of the young lapidary. He desires the girl, yet cannot have her with-out money. He sees her turning from him to a dangerous and charming new rival. He is deft and bold, and seems to himself to have lost all that makes life dear. Into his hands is passed a diamond of 50-odd carats, slightly held to a frame by a loop of soft gold. He examines it under a sconce set with prisms much the same size and

shape. Now the theft of such an object, to any other man foolhardy
and without profit, is to him exactly a source of pelf. He is himself
a lapidary. He can cut the stone himself, thus destroying its identity,
and providing himself with valuable gems that can be gradually in
the course of his master's business turned to profit. It is the work
of a reckless moment to substitute a prism, and make the diamond
his own. Fortune favoured him, in that Miss Burney and not Orloff
restored it to its place about the neck of the Prince. Now the diamond is upon his person. He cannot keep it there; the risk is enormous.

He must hide it. He remembers the jewel-thief's trick, abstracts
Miss Burney's softened beeswax, and looks about for a place that
cannot be searched, preferably one that he can later come at with
ease. The violins! Can he affix the diamond to the inside of one of
them, where short of taking it apart it cannot be come at? He is deft
and desperate; he will try. He chooses Viotti's. From this alone we
might have concluded the Bettses were innocent; they would have
pitched upon their own instrument. But Chinnery would choose
Viotti's, not only to throw the risk upon his rival, but also because
Viotti frequents his master's house; it will be easiest to come at. I
do not think he would have blenched at shattering the precious thing
to bits to come at the diamond again."

I shuddered.

JOHNSON: "Leaving first, he could not know how his plans had gone
awry when Viotti angrily repudiated the changed violin, and left it
for Betts to carry away and open. And when he lay in wait for Viotti
and saw him sans violin, what could he conclude but that the instrument was to seek at Burney's?"

BOSWELL: "I make sure 'twas Betts who tampered with the violin that
he might make it his own; and fobbed us off with a taradiddle when
we found it in his possession."

JOHNSON: "I thought otherwise when I saw 'twas beeswax had done
the damage. The jewel-thief's trick flashed into my mind, and I
made sure that I had recovered the Orloff diamond."

BOSWELL: "Yet how were you sure that Betts was not the thief?"

JOHNSON: "Because he yielded me the beeswax cheerfully and without a struggle, which he had not done had he hid therein a diamond

worth a Mogul's ransom. Yet I had not to guess, for the finger-mark with the double eddy promised to betray the thief with certainty."

BOSWELL: "Having discovered the thief, why did you let him go?"

JOHNSON: "Because I never doubted but that Prince Orloff spoke no more than the truth when he said the thief should die—and I could not turn the boy over to death, once I had discovered the diamond. He took the warning and fled for it; though 'twas most obliging in Viotti to be in such a mighty passion with him, and so cover my meaning."

BOSWELL: "You presumed on fortune, in letting him go before you had assured yourself that you had recovered the diamond indeed."

JOHNSON: "Am I so foolish? I stripped back from the under side only enough beeswax to assure myself that it contained the Orloff diamond indeed, before ever I left the sign of the Golden Violin."

BOSWELL: "Pray, Sir, tell me one more thing: how did you account to Prince Orloff, for having found his diamond at the bottom of a bowl of punch?"

Johnson fairly laughed aloud.

"Easily. I told him 'twas the will of God."

An Ear for Murder

by L. A. Taylor

"*S*ì, okay." Madame Spezzacristolo's plump, ring-encrusted fingers doodled a little musical figure on the piano keys. "You want to run through the 'Bell Song' now, before H. J. comes?" She took the music from the student and spread it out on the music rack. "All that wa-wa at the beginning, too, *cara*, or shall we just start at *où va la jeune?*"

Despite—or perhaps because of—the brilliant October morning, the lessons were running late today, so Madame was not particularly put out that the next student, her last until after dinner, didn't show up on time. But the soprano ran far over, twice through the *Lakmé* aria and once through a thing from *Tales of Hoffman*—she did like French!—and the big blond bass had still not arrived. Her *ciao* to the soprano was as cheerful as ever, but with her huge pouf of hennaed hair deep in the open refrigerator, Madame Spezzacristolo admitted to a twinge of worry.

Her hand detoured from the container of celery sticks intended to invite her interest and picked up a sinfully large wedge of brie: the big blond *basso* was a cop.

"What d'you s'pose happened to him, 'Rico?" she asked the little dog curled up on a scrap of carpeting at the end of the counter. Madame thought of the things that sometimes happen to police officers and absentmindedly bit into the brie.

That Harrison Jacob Anderson was her student was due to an accidental intersection of their professions (vocal instructor and homicide detective) a year and a half before. Madame often found it amusing to think that she was teaching a cop to sing, though not in the sense of singing with which cops were ordinarily associated. He had a nice voice, could be very good—not great, thank heaven, or she'd have bewailed the waste—but he was having trouble learning to focus the tone . . .

Surprised to find that the brie was no longer in her hand, Madame Spezzacristolo licked her teeth and rinsed the tips of her fingers at the sink. As she dried them, the telephone rang. Dropping the towel onto the counter, she hurried into her large living room where the telephone stood on a small table conveniently near the grand piano. " 'Allo?" she said eagerly.

"Lena, it's H. J.," said the hoped-for voice. "Sorry not to call you sooner, but I've been tied up with a case."

"*Non importa, caro,*" she assured him. "I'm just glad to hear that you're—that everything's all right. *Non ci pensi.*"

There was a pause. "Don't even think about it," she translated.

"Oh. Lena—" Anderson insisted on using her real name, now that he knew it "—I know the local music community is kind of, uh, ingrown. You wouldn't happen to have known a Craig Clayton, would you?"

"Craig Clayton?" Madame's eyes widened. She pressed a hand to the furrow in the mound of age-freckled flesh that strained through the rather low neckline of her dress. "But of course I know Craig, *caro.* We did a *Messiah* together, oh, ten, twelve years ago. Or was it—Well, anyway, I know him."

"You do." Another pause.

"Harrison Anderson, are you telling me Craig's been murdered?" Madame demanded. Every scrap of Italian vanished as New York City reclaimed her accent. "Is that the case that tied you up?"

"Yes, and yes," the cop replied in a washed-out version of his voice Madame had not heard for at least a year.

"Tell!" she ordered.

"Uh—it's a long story. Maybe it would be better if I came over on my way home. I was just going to catch a nap before I go back on duty."

"Be quick," Madame said crisply. "*Ciao.*"

By the time the doorbell chimed its diminished third and Enrico, who would never learn anything about harmony, dashed to the door to yap at it in a different key, Madame Spezzacristolo had finished the celery and started on lunch. She levered her bulk from the kitchen chair and swept, glorious in her violent green paisley tent, to the front door to greet the cop with a flutter of fake eyelashes. Damn, she thought. One's come loose again.

Anderson was far too much of a gentleman to comment on such things, so she just pressed the eyelash back into place as she let him in and wiped smudged purple eyeshadow off the tip of her finger onto a matching swirl in the paisley. "Now, what's this?" she demanded, dragging him into the living room by one wrist. "Craig Clayton murdered? That naive little wimp?" Schlemiel, more like it, she thought. Or schlimazel.

The detective's eyebrows twitched. "That's how you'd describe him?"

"*Bel ragazzo*, but he never grew up," Madame pronounced. "What is he, forty-five? I remember him squeaking out his little soprano in the boys' choir at St. Gremlin's. Germain's. Hasn't changed a bit, except his voice fell an octave and filled out better than anyone could have expected."

"What else do you know about him?" Anderson asked, dropping onto the couch as if he could barely hold himself upright.

"He teaches at the university," Madame said. "Voice, of course. He may not be a tenor to match Domingo or Pavarotti himself, but some of his students have turned out very well. There's a contralto in the chorus at the Met right now, and—"

"More personal than that," Anderson interrupted.

"Nothing really, *caro*," she said. "Rumors all over the place, but that's true of everyone, and nine out of ten of the rumors have nothing to them. The lovers I'm supposed to have taken, and at my age—'' She rolled her eyes. "Not Craig, though," she added hastily.

That evoked a quick smile and a sniff from the detective. "If one of the rumors is that his marriage is in trouble, that seems to be right on," he commented. "Clayton moved in with a colleague from the music department at the U a few weeks ago. Breathing space while he and his wife figured out how to get along with each other."

Madame Spezzacristolo felt her eyes narrow. She knew Craig Clayton's wife—about as well as she knew Craig—and doubted anyone would ever figure out how to get along with her, money or no money. No children, that was a blessing. She bit her tongue.

"They were separating?" she asked.

"Not precisely. According to the colleague, Clayton was a devout Catholic, and there was no question of a divorce. Besides that, the wife had all the money in the family."

"And he stood up to her? *Davvero!* I'm surprised he had it in him."

Anderson's eyes drifted to the spot by the piano where the students stood for each lesson, and to the lilac hedge beyond the french doors where someone had hidden a year and a half ago to shoot that poor girl. Madame could almost see the wheels turning in the detective's mind.

"Any suspects?" she asked.

"None."

"Who'd he move in with?"

"Willis Jespersen, a cellist."

She didn't know instrumentalists nearly as well as she did singers, but something clicked, far away in the back of her mind. Too far away to tell what it was.

"Lena," the detective said, "here's desperation. Would you be willing to come over to Jesperson's place with me, after my nap, and see if you see anything odd about it for a professional musician?"

She shrugged. "I could."

"Four o'clock? Are you free?"

"What is this, Thursday? Yes, I could do it. There's no, mm, gore, is there, *Caro?*"

"Cleaned up by now," Anderson replied. "Vinyl kitchen floor."

"Better than carpet, sì," Madame agreed, glancing at the spot Anderson's eyes had lingered on a moment before. "Four o'clock, then. I'll be ready."

"I'll have to set it up with Jesperson." The detective yawned. " 'Scuse me. You'll be here, so I can let you know if there's any change of plans?"

"Certo, H. J."

"I guess that means yes," he sighed and got to his feet.

Willis Jesperson lived in one of a neat row of townhouses on the university side of the city. Madame Spezzacristolo examined them from her comfortable seat as Anderson parked and turned off the car engine. Old buildings but painted a pleasant grey with white trim and looking very well cared-for, every bush in the yards sheared into an approximation of a globe. The detective opened her door. Madame heaved herself out of the front seat with his arm to lean on and teetered on her spike heels for a moment, looking at the flight of steps to the front porch.

"You won't have any trouble climbing the steps in those shoes, will you?" Anderson asked.

"I?" Madame chuckled. "I've been wearing heels like this for the past fifty-five years, carissimo. I couldn't climb the steps without them."

The townhouse shared its wide roofed porch with two others, one on each side. Two absurd little railings divided the floor area into precise thirds, preserving the fiction that each of the houses was separate first put forth by the three front walks and the three sets of steps. To the left, at the far end, a young woman in a wicker rocking chair had her feet against the front railing. A tow-haired two-year-old of indeterminate sex played nearby. The woman gave Anderson a friendly wave.

"Oh, let me introduce you," the detective said. "Mrs. Rokeach?" With a broad smile, the woman got up and came to the divider, a hand out to welcome Anderson.

The introductions were performed: at least H. J. remembered to call her Maria Spezzacristolo, and not Lena Goldfarb. The child proved to be a boy, Madame thought. At least, its name was Tommy.

Tommy stared at her open-mouthed, leading her to wonder if the eyelash had sprung loose again.

"I guess I was about the last person to hear that poor man sing," the young woman sighed. "Isn't that sad?"

"*Peccato*," Madame agreed. "How terrible for you!"

"And to think how annoyed I was," the girl went on. "It doesn't seem right, somehow."

Madame murmured something soothing sounding.

"Mrs. Rokeach heard Craig Clayton practicing yesterday afternoon," Anderson explained.

"Oh, every day since we moved in," the woman agreed eagerly, jouncing the child on her hip. "Last weekend, that was. Every day since Monday, I mean. And always exactly the same thing. How can he stand it? I know I can't—oh." She made a woeful face. Madame contained a spurt of inappropriate laughter.

"He was working something up," Anderson explained earnestly. "So he'd have to practice it over and over."

"Yeah, I guess," Mrs. Rokeach agreed, bouncing the child. "Still. And always when Tommy and I were trying to nap. I was going to speak to him about it." She sighed. "I guess I won't have to, now."

Madame Spezzacristolo turned another snort of nervous laughter into a clearing of her throat. "The other gentleman, the cellist, his practice didn't disturb you, hmm?" she asked.

"Cellist?" The younger woman frowned. "You mean Bill plays the cello? I don't think I ever heard him."

"Perhaps he practiced when you weren't at home," Madame conjectured.

"I'm *always* home," Mrs. Rokeach groaned. "At least, until I get a job. We moved here because Tom was transferred, but I haven't found anything yet."

Tommy abruptly made up his (or, still possibly, her) mind about this large-faced stranger and started to cry. Madame and the detective beat a polite retreat while the child's mother carried him back to the end of the porch and sat down in the rocker.

"You know, that's funny," Anderson commented as he opened the door to Jespersen's townhouse. "How come he didn't practice? Jespersen, I mean."

"He teaches at the university, isn't that what you told me, *carissimo?*" Madame pointed out. "So he has a studio he can practice in. Perhaps that's more convenient."

A closet projecting into the large room immediately inside the door divided off a small foyer paved with dark blue ceramic tile. The closet door was mirrored, giving the singer a start as she glimpsed herself in it: she really should not have eaten *all* of that brie! Anderson followed her in and shut the door.

Willis Jespersen has expensive tastes, Madame Spezzacristolo thought, poised at the archway into the living room. The carpet was lush, a deep grey-blue; velvety drapes in a slightly lighter shade covered the two wide windows, front and back; and the walls were covered in an elegant flocked stripe. The furniture, too, was plumply upholstered in fabrics that made one want to stroke them. Not a seat in the place that a fat old lady could get out of without help, except the one at the mahogany desk under the window. An end table next to the couch was covered to the floor with a cloth: Madame had an urge to look under the cloth to find out whether the table might be nothing more than a cardboard box. She'd feel reassured if it were: her experience of professional musicians would not have led her to believe in the availability of this much money to any but the most widely-known, which Jespersen was not. Maybe he'd inherited.

She moved into the room, absently humming. *Every valley shall be exalted,* ticked the words through her brain. Yes, it must have been the *Messiah* she and Craig Clayton had worked on together.

"You should work up 'The Trumpet Shall Sound,' " she said to Anderson. "For your voice, *perfetto.* Nice and smooth."

The area behind the projecting closet had been designated for music, apparently. A cello—or, more precisely, a hard case for a cello—leaned against the corner formed by the closet, a light film of dust on its shoulders and belly. Next to it, against the wall the house shared with the one belonging to the Rokeach family, stood a spinet piano. "Kind of a dinky instrument for a professional musician," Madame commented, then recalled that Jespersen as a cellist probably had no particular use for even a baby grand. Or might think the one the university provided sufficient. She walked over to the piano and played a couple of arpeggios. In tune, though the top was also somewhat dusty.

Ranged along the wall beside the piano were elegant built-in shelves containing something she might more readily have expected of a musician: speakers, tape deck, compact disc player and turntable, all hooked together with some other apparatus in that complex way that had always eluded her. Tapes and compact discs sat on their own small shelves, a large collection of records on one wider one along the bottom of the wall.

Madame perched on the piano bench. "So tell me," she said. "What exactly happened? *Da capo*, if you please."

Anderson rather uneasily sank into one of the overstuffed chairs. "Apparently Clayton moved in with Jespersen about three weeks ago. From what Jespersen says, Clayton and his wife had a real blowup, which ended with her demanding a divorce and him storming out of the house and phoning the first person he could think of for a place to stay while he and his wife sorted things out. Jespersen's single, he's got all this space, they've known each other a few years—I guess he was a natural choice. Jespersen says he thought a night, two or three—" the detective made a rocking motion with one hand "—but three nights turned into four, four into five, and Clayton was still here yesterday."

Madame nodded, sucking in her well-rouged cheeks. She'd done her share of sponging and being sponged upon.

"Yesterday morning Clayton went over to the university at his usual time, around nine o'clock. He had a couple of students and a music theory class to teach. Usually he was back here around two, then warmed up and practiced for an hour or so. Jespersen doesn't teach on Wednesdays, so he was here all morning, but he had a bunch of things to do and left before Clayton got back."

"What things to do? When?"

"I don't remember the exact schedule. A lunch date with two friends thinking of forming a string trio—that dragged on until well past three. Then the three of them walked over to the university, where Jespersen copied some music in the library. After that he stopped at an Arby's for dinner, then went back to the university to pick up his cello and to attend a rehearsal for an opera the music department's putting on."

"Verdi's *Otello*. You should go."

"Yeah, I've got tickets. All I need is not to get stuck with some job," Anderson said. "Jespersen's in the orchestra."

Madame nodded, her eyes straying to the cello case.

"I asked about that," the detective said. "It's an instrument he doesn't use very often. Apparently he has three, and he keeps the other two at the U. The rehearsal broke up around ten thirty. Jespersen went out to a bar with some of the other players. Left when they closed up, at one, came home, and found Clayton on the kitchen floor with a knife in him. Dead for hours."

"And you have no doubt he did all this?"

"None. The friends he ate lunch with agree that he met them around twelve thirty. The waiter remembers them because he thought they'd never give up their table. He was right about that— they got shoved out when the kitchen closed for the afternoon. The librarian remembers him because he needed help finding the part he wanted to copy and stood around awhile, talking. He had the Arby's register tape shoved into his pocket—date, time and location printed right on it. And he's got a whole thirty-piece orchestra with a leader, a chorus of twenty, and eight principal singers to say he was at the rehearsal. So he's covered from just after noon until better than twelve hours later."

"I see."

"And Clayton was alive between two and three. We know that because Tracy Rokeach heard him singing while she tried to take a nap."

"So what are you thinking?"

"Back door had been jimmied. Most likely he surprised somebody in the kitchen who shouldn't have been there—there've been a few daytime break-ins in the neighborhood—and got himself knifed. The knife belonged here."

"But you have doubts."

Anderson frowned at her. "Not really."

She spread her hands. "Here I am, no? Why, if you have no doubts?"

"I just wanted to be sure I hadn't missed anything."

"You have doubts." Madame got up and began wandering around the room. She stopped at the piano again, looking at it. Clearly someone had played it regularly since the last time the keys had been dusted. "He has a housekeeper, Jespersen?"

"Comes on Thursdays. We sent her away this morning. Weren't done with the place when she came."

"Mm." She studied the dust: no key below the C below middle C had been touched. What she might expect, if Clayton—a tenor— had just fingered out his part to learn it. But if he'd played the accompaniment, as surely he would, to see how the voice lay with it? That would have lower notes. Yet some keys were dustless well above a tenor range.

She remembered something about Jespersen. He was a not especially well regarded composer as well as a player. Maybe he'd been working out something for cello, without bothering to take the instrument in the corner out of its case and tune it? But something else teased at her.

"There's a tape in the player," Anderson commented. "Clayton must have been taping his practice, like I do."

Madame shot him a glance. "Oh, yes?" She moved to the sound system and studied it. "How do you work this thing?"

Work, she thought. They worked together, Jespersen and Clayton. Or, at least, in the same music department. And had been friendly enough that Craig would come here when he needed a place to stay. What was it about Jespersen? Something she'd heard? Women?

Anderson punched a couple of buttons. The tape began to play: a few notes of some warm-up vocalizing came from the speakers, not very loud. Funny enough for a professional to record at all, Madame thought. But to record warm-ups? She hummed a few notes along with Clayton's tenor.

Something seemed odd. She squinted at one of the speakers, trying to place it. "How do you turn this up?" she asked. "I need it louder."

"Why? Isn't that Clayton singing?"

"Certo. Yes, that's him." The voice, made louder, sounded even more like the one she remembered standing next to her on stage, chugging away at the Handel. "But wait a minute . . . turn it down."

Anderson did whatever was required. Madame turned toward the room and thought a moment, inhaling slowly.

"*Ritorna vincitor!*" she sang, as if she had to fill the whole of a large auditorium with the drama of those six notes.

"My god," Anderson commented.

Sì. She smiled, satisfied. "Like singing in one of those rooms, what do they call them, anechoic."

"An—what?"

"Made not to reverberate. This room sounds like that. Nothing comes back. *È morte*, don't you hear?"

Anderson, who for some reason had pressed a hand to the nearest ear, shook his head.

"Completely dead. But that tape was recorded in a room with nice, lively acoustics. Let's listen again, please?"

The detective rewound the tape. "Louder," Madame said, as he started it playing. "Now listen. You hear what I mean?"

The tape sped on. The voice of Craig Clayton moved from a simple exercise to a more difficult one, the tone light and clear. Anderson frowned. "I—yes, I guess . . ."

"No guess about it," Madame said decisively. "That was recorded in a room with a whole lot of life in it. This room—wait, what was that? Stop the tape and turn it back a little."

Anderson rewound the tape a few feet. They listened again. Clear in the background of Clayton's vocalizing was another voice, a lower voice, also singing, one phrase, very, very faint under the storm of tenor triplets. Madame grinned. "Aha. You hear that? That's Iago!" She snapped her fingers, too excited to even pretend to think in a foreign language. "Where he's bitching about God, second act, remember? And the opera the U music department is putting on next month is *Otello*, yes?" She inspected the controls of the tape deck and twisted the one marked Volume counterclockwise. "So that's how our friend Mr. Jespersen did it."

"You lost me on the last turn, Lena," Anderson complained.

She perched again on the piano bench. "Jespersen made this tape over at the university when poor Craig was singing in his studio. Have you ever been over there? No? All kinds of electronic equipment just there for the using. Simple to record what went on in a studio without anyone's ever knowing—I think they're even connected to a recording room of some kind. So Jespersen made this tape—"

Anderson turned the tape deck off. "Why?"

"Because he must have known the people next door were moving out, doesn't one always? And that, and when, new ones were moving in. People who had no idea what was usual for this house." It seemed so simple. Why couldn't this lunk see it? But his stare was still blank.

"Craig was here, and Bill Jespersen wanted him out of the way. Why, I don't know, that's for you to find out. So the plan was this. When the new people moved in, he played the tape at the same time every day—a time he told you that Craig was here, but I bet if you check far enough you'll find out he wasn't—and yesterday he killed him, put the tape deck on a timer, and went out. Miss Silly next door thinks she's been hearing a singer practicing every day, but it's this tape she's been hearing. Remember, she said it was the same every day?"

Anderson squatted down and examined the tops of the records on the bottom shelf without touching them.

"He goes about his business—lunch, the library where he makes a point of talking to the librarian, a fast-food place that gives him a slip with the date and the time, a rehearsal where the absence of a cello will quickly be seen. Then he comes back and removes the timer." Madame Spezzacristolo jumped up and trotted across the room to the desk. "After which, he calls you. Then or before, he damages the back door. You police are so good at telling us when crimes are repeated, surely he knows about the daytime break-ins?" She slammed the first drawer she'd pulled out and snatched open another one. "See? Here it is!"

"Don't touch," Anderson cautioned, almost running across the room.

Madame pointed at the timer shoved into the back of the desk drawer with all the drama a lifetime of conveying emotion on stage had taught her. "That, *caro*, is a part of your plot," she exclaimed in triumph, her chins held so high there were only two of them.

Anderson shut the drawer, less noisily than she had the one above it. "We'll come back with a warrant," he said, steering her by the elbow toward the front door. "I think you've got it, Lena. There's no dust on those records. Any of them. Why do that, unless to hide where you'd pulled some out to get at the power cords?"

Tracy Rokeach was standing at the dividing rail of the porch. "What are you doing?" she asked. "I heard that man singing, and— was that you, Mrs. Spitsacrystal?"

Madame graciously inclined her head, giving the young woman a first curtain call smile.

"It was a tape?" the girl asked. "All this week, that was a tape? Because it sounded just like—"

"Do me a favor," Anderson said. "Don't mention this to Jespersen."

"But he's such a *sweetheart*," Tracy Rokeach exclaimed. "You don't think he had anything to do—I mean, he's got a girlfriend comes over now and then, and—You're not saying that other guy was messing with Bill's girl?"

"I'm not saying anything," Anderson said. "Just keep your lip buttoned, understand?"

In the car, he engaged in an exchange over the radio, only the last part of which Madame understood: he was taking her home before he showed up at the precinct station.

The soprano ah'ed her way through the long unaccompanied opening of the "Bell Song," ending up only half a step flat. Madame Spezzacristolo gave her a second-balcony smile and exclaimed, "*Brava!* You'll get it yet."

"I don't know . . ." the girl began. The doorbell rang. Enrico Caruso erupted from the kitchen to bark at the door, almost losing the bow that kept his bangs out of his eyes in his enthusiasm. He jumped wildly at the big blond *basso* as Madame let him in.

" 'Rico," she ordered. "Go lie on your rug, that's a good boy."

Time to wind the soprano's lesson up, anyway: she'd had an extra half hour the week before.

"Well," she said the moment the door closed behind the girl. She perched on the edge of a chair. "What happened? I saw about the arrest on television, but they didn't explain anything."

Anderson nodded. "Your friend Mr. Clayton wasn't the luckiest of men," he said. "When he had an argument with his wife, who did he pick to put himself up with but his wife's boyfriend."

"I thought so," said Madame, who over the past week had had time to remember a few more rumors about Willis Jespersen's behavior with women—and his appetite for money.

The detective sighed. "You know, I really believed that tape was something Clayton made for himself. Jespersen never said a word about it—I suppose he thought we'd overlook it."

Not likely, Madame thought. Probably he meant to call attention to it when he got a natural chance, and say it was Craig's own tape— proof that he'd been practicing in that room, though not as to time, of course. But why bother, when the cop interviewing you starts talking about the opera? And no doubt mentions taking singing lessons?

"You'd think he'd have taken the chance when we got to talking about that *Otello* production," Anderson said, fingering the music he'd brought.

Uh-huh, Madame thought.

"Well. You were right. We've got people who saw Clayton earlier last week, at the time he was supposedly at home practicing, and Tracy Rokeach identified a picture of Dora Clayton as Jespersen's girlfriend. Still a lot of legwork to do, but we're on the way, thanks to you."

"*Prego*," Madame said, shrugging. "Any time. Now. We sing." She went to the piano and lowered her bulk onto the bench. "A little warm-up," she said. "Ee-ee-ee-ee-oh, yes?"

She watched indulgently as the big blond cop moved her telephone aside to set his portable tape recorder on the table near the piano, soberly checked the tape, and pressed the button to record. Ah, sweet amateur! Not too sure how to feel his tone production yet, so glad of this little crutch a professional would use far more sparingly.

A little learning may not always be a dangerous thing, she thought, but it can so often be misleading.

Mom Sings an Aria

by James Yaffe

*I*t was one of the greatest disappointments of my mother's life
that I never turned out to be a musical genius. For a couple of
years, when I was a kid, Mom made me take violin lessons. At
the end of the first year I played a piece called *Rustling Leaves*. At the
end of the second year I was still playing *Rustling Leaves*. Poor Mom
had to admit I wasn't another Jascha Heifetz, and that was the end
of my musical career.

Mom has always been crazy about music herself. She did a little
singing when she was a girl, and might have done something with
her voice—instead she got married, moved up to the Bronx, and
devoted herself to raising a future Lieutenant in the New York City
Homicide Squad. But she still listens regularly to the Saturday afternoon broadcasts of the Metropolitan Opera, and she can still hum
along with all the familiar arias. That was why—when my wife
Shirley and I went up to the Bronx the other night for our regular
Friday dinner—I knew Mom would be interested in my latest case.

"You're a music lover, Mom," I said. "Maybe you can understand
how a man could love music so much that he'd commit murder for
it."

"This is hard to understand?" Mom said, looking up from her roast chicken. "Why else did I stop your violin lessons? Once, while you were playing one of your pieces, I happened to take a look at your teacher, Mrs. Steinberg—and on her face was murder, if I ever saw it!"

"You don't mean that literally, do you, Mother?" Shirley said. "A woman wouldn't *really* feel like murdering a little boy because he played the violin badly."

"People can have plenty feelings that were never in your psychology books at college," Mom said. "Believe me, in my own family—my Aunt Goldie who thought the pigeon outside her window was actually her late husband Jake—"

Mom went into detail, and her story was fascinating. Then she passed the chicken a second time, and I was able to get back to my murder.

"Have you ever seen the standing-room line at the Metropolitan Opera House?" I said. "Half an hour before every performance the box office sells standing-room tickets at two-fifty each, on a first-come first-served basis. The opera lovers start lining up outside the house hours ahead of time. They stand on their feet for three hours *before* the opera just so they can stand on their feet for three hours *during* the opera! Talk about crazy human motives!"

"People with no ears in their heads," Mom said, "shouldn't be so quick to call other people crazy." And she gave me one of those glares which has been making me feel like a naughty little five-year-old ever since I *was* a naughty little five-year-old.

I turned my eyes away and pushed on. "Well, there are certain people who show up on the opera standing-room line night after night, for practically every performance throughout the season. These 'regulars' are almost always at the head of the line—they come earlier than anyone else, wait longer, and take the best center places once they get inside the house. And since most of them have been doing this for years, they know each other by name, and they pass the time gossiping about the opera singers and discussing the performances. You could almost say they've got an exclusive little social club all their own—only their meeting place isn't a clubhouse, it's the sidewalk in front of the Met. Anyway, you couldn't imagine a more harmless collection of old fogeys—the last group on earth where you'd expect to find a murderer!"

"Even an opera lover has to have a private life," Mom said. "He enjoys himself with the beautiful music—but he's still got business troubles or love troubles or family troubles waiting for him at home."

"That's just it, Mom. If one of these standing-room regulars had gone home and killed his wife or his mother-in-law or his business partner, this would just be a routine case. But what happened was, he killed one of the other people in the standing-room line."

Mom was looking at me with her eyes narrowed—a sure sign that I had her interested. "The two oldest regulars in the standing-room line," I said, "the charter members of the club, are Sam Cohen and Giuseppe D'Angelo. Cohen used to be a pharmacist, with his own drug store on West Eighty-third Street. He retired fifteen years ago, after his wife died, and turned the management of the store over to his nephew, though he went on living in the apartment above it. As soon as he retired, he started going to the opera almost every night of the season.

"D'Angelo was in the exterminating business out in Queens—insects, rodents, and so on—but he retired fifteen years ago too. His wife is alive, but she doesn't care for music, so he's been in the habit of going to the opera by himself—almost every night of the season, just like Cohen.

"The two old men met on the standing-room line fifteen years ago, and have seen each other three or four nights a week ever since—but only at the opera, never anywhere else. As far as we know, they've never met for a drink or a lunch, they've never been to each other's homes, and they've never seen each other at all in the summer, when the opera is closed.

"Opera is the biggest thing in both their lives. Cohen's mother was a vocal coach back in Germany, and he cut his teeth on operatic arias—D'Angelo was born and brought up in the city of Parma, which they tell me is the most operatic city in Italy—"

"I've read about Parma," Mom said. "If a tenor hits a bad note there, they run him out of town."

"How horrible!" Shirley said. "It's positively uncivilized!"

Mom shrugged. "A little less civilization here in New York, and maybe we wouldn't hear so many bad notes."

I could see the cloud of indignation forming on Shirley's face—she never *has* caught on to Mom's peculiar sense of humor. I hurried on, "Well, the two old men both loved opera, but their opinions about it have always been diametrically opposed. So for fifteen years they've been carrying on a running argument. If Cohen likes a certain soprano, D'Angelo can't stand her. If D'Angelo mentions having heard Caruso sing *Aida* in 1920. Cohen says that Caruso never sang *Aida* till 1923.

"And the old men haven't conducted these arguments in nice soft gentlemenly voices either. They yell at each other, wave their arms, call each other all sorts of names. 'Liar' and 'moron' are about the tamest I can think of. In spite of their bitterness, of course, these fights have never lasted long—before the night is over, or at least by the time of the next performance, the old men always make it up between them—"

"Until now?" Mom said.

"I'll get to that in a minute, Mom. Just a little more background first. According to the other regulars on the standing-room line, the fights between Cohen and D'Angelo have become even more bitter than usual in recent years. They've been aggravated by a controversy which has been raging among opera lovers all over the world. Who's the greatest soprano alive today—Maria Callas or Renata Tebaldi?"

Mom dropped her fork and clasped her hands to her chest, and on her face came that ecstatic, almost girlish look which she reserves exclusively for musical matters. "Callas! Tebaldi! Voices like angels, both of them! That Callas—such fire, such passion! That Tebaldi—such beauty, such sadness! To choose which one is the greatest—it's as foolish as trying to choose between noodle soup and borscht!"

"Cohen and D'Angelo made their choices, though," I said. "D'Angelo announced one day that Tebaldi was glorious and Callas had a voice like a rooster—so right away Cohen told him that Callas was divine and Tebaldi sang like a cracked phonograph record. And the argument has been getting more and more furious through the years.

"A week ago a climax was reached. Callas was singing *Traviata*, and the standing-room line started to form even earlier than usual. Cohen and D'Angelo, of course, were right there among the first. Cohen had a bad cold—he was sneezing all the time he stood in line—but he said he wouldn't miss Callas's *Traviata* if he was down with double pneumonia. And D'Angelo said that personally he could live happily for the rest of his life without hearing Callas butcher *Traviata*—he was here tonight, he said, only because of the tenor, Richard Tucker."

"That Richard Tucker!" Mom gave her biggest, most motherly smile. "Such a wonderful boy—just as much at home in the shul as he is in the opera. What a proud mother he must have !" And Mom gave me a look which made it clear that she still hadn't quite forgiven me for *Rustling Leaves*.

"With such a long wait on the standing-room line," I said, "Cohen and D'Angelo had time to whip up a first-class battle. According to Frau Hochschwender—she's a German lady who used to be a concert pianist and now gives piano lessons, and she's also one of the standing-room regulars—Cohen and D'Angelo had never insulted each other so violently in all the years she'd known them. If the box office had opened an hour later, she says they would have come to blows.

"As it turned out, the performance itself didn't even put an end to their fight. Ordinarily, once the opera began, both men became too wrapped up in the music to remember they were mad at each other—but this time, when the first act ended, Cohen grabbed D'Angelo by the arm and accused him of deliberately groaning after Callas's big aria. 'You did it to ruin the evening for me!' Cohen said. He wouldn't pay attention to D'Angelo's denials. 'I'll get even with you,' he said. 'Wait till the next time Tebaldi is singing!' "

"And the next time Tebaldi was singing," Mom said, "was the night of the murder?"

"Exactly. Three nights ago Tebaldi sang *Tosca*—"

"*Tosca!*" Mom's face lighted up. "Such a beautiful opera! Such a sad story! She's in love with this handsome young artist, and this villain makes advances and tries to force her to give in to him, so she stabs him with a knife. Come to think of it, the villain in that opera is a police officer."

I looked hard, but I couldn't see any trace of sarcasm on Mom's face.

"Those opera plots are really ridiculous, aren't they?" Shirley said. "So exaggerated and unrealistic."

"Unrealistic!" Mom turned to her sharply. "You should know some of the things that go on—right here in this building. Didn't Polichek the janitor have his eye on his wife's baby-sitter?"

Another fascinating story came out of Mom, and then I went on. "Anyway, for the whole weekend before *Tosca*, D'Angelo worried that Cohen would do something to spoil the performance for him. He worried so much that the night before, he called Cohen up and pleaded with him not to make trouble."

"And Cohen answered?"

"His nephew was in the room with him when the call came. He was going over some account books and didn't really pay attention to what his uncle was saying—but at one point he heard Cohen raise his voice angrily and shout out, 'You can't talk me out of it! When Tebaldi hits her high C in the big aria, I'm going to start booing!' "

Mom shook her head. "Terrible—a terrible threat for a civilized man to make! So does D'Angelo admit that Cohen made it?"

"Well, yes and no. In the early part of the phone conversation, D'Angelo says he and Cohen were yelling at each other so angrily that neither of them listened to what the other one was saying. But later on in the conversation—or so D'Angelo claims—Cohen calmed down and promised to let Tebaldi sing her aria in peace."

"Cohen's nephew says he didn't?"

"Not exactly. He left the room while Cohen was still on the phone—he had to check some receipts in the cash register—so he never heard the end of the conversation. For all he knows Cohen *might* have calmed down and made that promise."

"And what about D'Angelo's end of the phone conversation? Was anybody in the room with *him*?"

"His wife was. And she swears that he *did* get such a promise out of Cohen. But of course she's his wife, so she's anxious to protect him. And besides she's very deaf, and she won't wear a hearing aid—she's kind of a vain old lady. So what it boils down to, we've got nobody's word except D'Angelo's that Cohen didn't intend to carry out his threat.''

"Which brings us," Mom said, "to the night Tebaldi sang *Tosca?*"

"Cohen and D'Angelo both showed up early on the standing-room line that night. Frau Hochschwender says they greeted each other politely, but all the time they were waiting they hardly exchanged a word. No arguments, no differences of opinion—nothing. And her testimony is confirmed by another one of the regulars who was there—Miss Phoebe Van Voorhees. She's an old lady in her seventies, always dresses in black.

"Miss Van Voorhees came from a wealthy New York family, and when she was a young woman she used to have a regular box at the opera—but the money ran out ten or twelve years ago, and now she lives alone in a cheap hotel in the East Twenties, and she waits on the standing-room line two nights a week. She's so frail-looking you wouldn't think she could stay on her feet for five minutes, much less five hours—but she loves opera, so she does it."

"For love," Mom said, "people can perform miracles."

"Well, Miss Van Voorhees and Frau Hochschwender both say that Cohen and D'Angelo were unusually restrained with each other. Which seems to prove that they were still mad at each other and hadn't made up the quarrel over the phone, as D'Angelo claims—"

"Or maybe it proves the opposite," Mom said. "They did make up the quarrel, and they were so scared of starting another quarrel that they shut up and wouldn't express any opinions."

"Whatever it proves, Mom, here's what happened. On cold nights it's the custom among the standing-room regulars for one of them to go to the cafeteria a block away and get hot coffee for the others—meanwhile they hold his place in the line. The night of Tebaldi's *Tosca* was very cold, and it was D'Angelo's turn to bring the coffee.

"He went for it about forty-five minutes before the box office opened, and got back with it in fifteen or twenty minutes. He was carrying four cardboard containers. Three of them contained coffee with cream and sugar—for Frau Hochschwender, Miss Van Voorhees, and D'Angelo himself. In the fourth container was black coffee without sugar—the way Cohen always took it.

"Well, they all gulped down their coffee, shielding it from the wind with their bodies—and about half an hour later the doors opened. They bought their tickets, went into the opera house, and stood together in their usual place in the back, at the center.

"At eight sharp the opera began. Tebaldi was in great voice, and the audience was enthusiastic. At the end of the first act all of the standing-room regulars praised her—except Cohen. He just grunted and said nothing. Frau Hochschwender and Miss Van Voorhees both say that he looked pale and a little ill.

" 'Wait till she sings her big aria in the second act,' D'Angelo said. 'I hope she sings it good,' Cohen said—and Frau Hochschwender says there was a definite threat in his voice. But Miss Van Voorhees says she didn't notice anything significant in his voice—to her it just sounded like an offhand remark. Then the second act began, and it was almost time for Tebaldi's big aria—"

"Such a beautiful aria!" Mom said. "*Vissy darty*. It's Italian. She's telling that police officer villain that all her life she's cared only for love and for art, and she never wanted to hurt a soul. She tells him this, and a little later she stabs him." And in a low voice, a little quavery but really kind of pretty, Mom began to half sing and half hum—"*Vissy darty, vissy damory*—" Then she broke off, and did something I had seldom seen her do. She blushed.

There was a moment of silence, while Shirley and I carefully refrained from looking at each other. Then I said, "So a few minutes before Tebaldi's big aria, Cohen suddenly gave a groan, then he grabbed hold of Frau Hochschwender's arm and said, 'I'm sick—' And then he started making strangling noises, and dropped like a lead weight to the floor.

"Somebody went for a doctor, and D'Angelo got down on his knees by Cohen and said, 'Cohen, Cohen, what's the matter?' And Cohen, with his eyes straight on D'Angelo's face, said, 'You no-good! You deserve to die for what you did!' Those were his exact words, Mom—half a dozen people heard them.

"Then a doctor came, with a couple of ushers, and they took Cohen out to the lobby—and D'Angelo, Frau Hochschwender, and Miss Van Voorhees followed. A little later an ambulance came, but Cohen was dead before he got to the hospital.

"At first the doctors thought it was a heart attack, but they did a routine autopsy—and found enough poison in his stomach to kill a man half his age and twice his strength. The dose he swallowed must've taken two to three hours to produce a reaction—which means he swallowed it while he was on the standing-room line. Well, nobody saw him swallow *anything* on the standing-room line except that container of hot black coffee."

"And when the doctors looked at the contents of his stomach?"

"They found the traces of his lunch, which *couldn't* have contained the poison or he would've died long before he got to the opera house—and they found that coffee—and that was all they found. So the coffee had to be what killed him."

"And since that old man D'Angelo was the one who gave him the coffee, you naturally think he's the murderer."

"What else can we think, Mom? For five minutes or so—from the time he picked up the coffee at the cafeteria to the time he gave it to Cohen at the opera house—D'Angelo was alone with it. Nobody was watching him—he could easily have slipped something into it. And nobody *else* had such an opportunity. Cohen took the coffee from D'Angelo, turned away to shield the container from the cold wind, and drank it all down then and there. Only D'Angelo *could* have put the poison into it."

"What about the man at the cafeteria who made the coffee?"

"That doesn't make sense, Mom. The man at the cafeteria would have no way of knowing who the coffee was meant for. He'd have to be a complete psycho who didn't care *who* he poisoned. Just the same, though, we checked him out. He poured the coffee into the container directly from a big urn—twenty other people had been drinking coffee from that same urn. Then in front of a dozen witnesses he handed the container to D'Angelo without putting a thing in it—not even sugar, because Cohen never took his coffee with sugar. So we're right back to D'Angelo—he *has* to be the murderer."

"And where did he get it, this deadly poison? Correct me if I'm wrong, but such an item isn't something you can pick up at your local supermarket."

"Sure, it's against the law to sell poison to the general public. But you'd be surprised how easy it is to get hold of the stuff anyway. The kind that killed Cohen is a common commercial compound—it's used to mix paints, for metallurgy, in certain medicines, in insecticides. Ordinary little pellets of rat poison are made of it sometimes, and you can buy them at your local hardware store—a couple of dozen kids swallow them by accident in this city every year. And don't forget, D'Angelo used to be in the exterminating business—he knows all the sources, it would be easier for him to get his hands on poison than for most other people."

"So you've arrested him for the murder?" Mom said.

I gave a sigh. "No, we haven't."

"How come? What's holding you up?"

"It's the motive, Mom. D'Angelo and Cohen had absolutely no connection with each other outside of the standing-room line. Cohen didn't leave D'Angelo any money, he wasn't having an affair with D'Angelo's wife, he didn't know a deep dark secret out of D'Angelo's past. There's only one reason why D'Angelo could have killed him—to stop him from booing at the end of Renata Tebaldi's big aria. That's why he committed the murder. I'm morally certain of it, and so is everyone else in the Department. And so is the D.A.'s office—but they won't let us make the arrest."

"And why not?"

"Because nobody believes for one moment that we can get a jury to believe such a motive. Juries are made up of ordinary everyday people. They don't go to the opera. They think it's all a lot of nonsense—fat women screaming at fat men, in a foreign language. I can sympathize with them—I think so myself. Can you imagine the D.A. standing up in front of a jury and saying, 'The defendant was so crazy about an opera singer's voice that he killed a man for disagreeing with him!' The jury would laugh in the D.A.'s face."

I sighed harder than before. "We've got an airtight case. The perfect opportunity. No other possible suspects. The dying man's accusation—'You no-good! You deserve to die for what you did!' But we don't dare bring the killer to trial."

Mom didn't say anything for a few seconds. Her eyes were almost shut, the corners of her mouth were turned down. I know this expression well—her "thinking" expression. Something always comes out of it.

Finally she looked up and gave a nod. "Thank God for juries!"

"What do you mean, Mom?"

"I mean, if it wasn't for ordinary everyday people with common sense, God knows *who* you experts would be sending to jail!"

"Mom, are you saying that D'Angelo *didn't*—"

"I'm saying nothing. Not yet. First I'm asking. Four questions."

No doubt about it, whenever Mom starts asking her questions, that means she's on the scent, she's getting ready to hand me a solution to another one of my cases.

My feelings, as always, were mixed. On the one hand, nobody admires Mom more than I do—her deep knowledge of human nature acquired among her friends and neighbors in the Bronx; her uncanny sharpness in applying that knowledge to the crimes I tell her about from time to time.

On the other hand—well, how ecstatic is a man supposed to get at the idea that his mother can do his own job better than *he* can? That's why I've never been able to talk about Mom's talent to anybody else in the Department—except, of course, to Inspector Milner, my immediate superior, and only because he's a widower, and Shirley and I are trying to get something going between Mom and him.

So I guess my voice wasn't as enthusiastic as it should have been, when I said to Mom, "Okay, what are your four questions?"

"First I bring in the peach pie," Mom said.

We waited while the dishes were cleared, and new dishes were brought. Then the heavenly aroma of Mom's peach pie filled the room. One taste of it, and my enthusiasm began to revive. "What *are* your questions, Mom?"

She lifted her finger. "Number one: You mentioned that Cohen had a cold a week ago, the night Maria Callas was singing *Traviata*. Did he still have the same cold three nights ago, when Tebaldi was singing *Tosca*?"

By this time I ought to be used to Mom's questions. I ought to take it on faith that they're probably not as irrelevant as they sound. But I still can't quite keep the bewilderment out of my voice.

"As a matter of fact," I said, "Cohen did have a cold the night of the murder. Frau Hochschwender and Miss Van Voorhees both mentioned it—he was sneezing while he waited in line, and even a few times during the performance, though he tried hard to control himself."

Mom's face gave no indication whether this was or wasn't what she had wanted to hear. She lifted another finger. "Number two: After the opera every night, was it the custom for those standing-room regulars to separate right away—or did they maybe stay together for a little while before they finally said good night?"

"They usually went to the cafeteria a block away—the same place where D'Angelo bought the coffee that Cohen drank—and sat at a table for an hour or so and discussed the performance they'd just heard. Over coffee and doughnuts—or Danish pastry."

Mom gave a nod, and lifted another finger. "Number three: At the hospital you naturally examined what was in Cohen's pockets? Did you find something like an envelope—a small envelope with absolutely nothing in it?"

This question really made me jump. "We did find an envelope, Mom! Ordinary stationery size—it was unsealed, and there was no address or stamp on it. But how in the world did you—"

Mom's fourth finger was in the air. "Number four: How many more times this season is Renata Tebaldi supposed to sing *Tosca*?"

"It was Tebaldi's first, last, and only performance of *Tosca* this season," I said. "The posters in front of the opera house said so. But I don't see what that has to do with—"

"You don't see," Mom said. "Naturally. You're like all the younger generation these days. So scientific. Facts you see. D'Angelo was the only one who was ever alone with Cohen's coffee—so D'Angelo must have put the poison in. A fact, so you see it. But what about the *people* already? Who is D'Angelo—who was Cohen—what type human beings? This you wouldn't ask yourself. Probably you wouldn't even understand about my Uncle Julius and the World Series."

"I'm sorry, Mom. I never knew you *had* an Uncle Julius—"

"I don't have him no more. That's the point of the story. All his life he was a fan from the New York Yankees. He rooted for them, he bet money on them, and when they played the World Series he was always there to watch them. Until a couple of years ago when he had his heart attack, and he was in the hospital at World Series time.

" 'I'll watch the New York Yankees on television,' he said. 'The excitement is too much for you,' the doctor said, 'it'll kill you.' But Uncle Julius had his way, and he watched the World Series. Every day he watched, and every night the doctor said, 'You'll be dead before morning.' And Uncle Julius said, 'I won't die till I know how the World Series comes out!' So finally the New York Yankees won the World Series—and an hour later Uncle Julius went to sleep and died."

Mom stopped talking, and looked around at Shirley and me. Then she shook her head and said, "You don't follow yet? A man with a love for something that's outside himself, that isn't even his family—with a love for the New York Yankees or for Renata Tebaldi—in such a man this feeling is stronger than his personal worries or his personal ambitions. He wouldn't let anything interrupt his World Series in the middle, not even dying. He wouldn't let anything interrupt his opera in the middle—not even murdering."

I began to see a glimmer of Mom's meaning. "You're talking about D'Angelo, Mom?"

"Who else? Renata Tebaldi was singing her one and only *Tosca* for the year, and for D'Angelo, Renata Tebaldi is the greatest singer alive. Never—in a million years, never—would he do anything to spoil this performance for himself, to make him walk out of it before the end. Let's say he *did* want to murder Cohen. The last time in the world he'd pick for this murder would be in the middle of Tebaldi's *Tosca*—her one and only Tosca! Especially since he could wait just as easy till after the opera, when the standing-room regulars would be having cake and coffee at the cafeteria—he could just as easy poison Cohen *then*."

"But Mom, isn't that kind of far-fetched, psychologically? If the average man was worked up enough to commit a murder, he wouldn't care about hearing the end of an opera first!''

"Excuse me, Davie—the average man's psychology we're not talking about. The opera lover's psychology we are talking about. This is why you and the Homicide Squad and the District Attorney couldn't make heads and tails from this case. Because you don't understand from opera lovers. In this world they don't live—they've got a world of their own. Inside their heads things are going on which other people's heads never even dreamed about. To solve this case you have to think like an opera lover.''

"To solve this case, Mom, you have to answer the basic question: if D'Angelo didn't poison that coffee, who could have?''

"Who says the coffee was poisoned?''

"But I told you about the autopsy. The poison took two to three hours to work, and the contents of Cohen's stomach—''

"The contents of his stomach! You should show a little more interest in the contents of Cohen's pockets!''

"There was nothing unusual in his pockets—''

"Why should a man carry in his pocket an empty unsealed envelope, without any writing on it, without even a stamp on it? Only because it wasn't empty when he put it there. Something was in it—something which he expected to need later on in the evening—something which he finally took out of the envelope—''

"What are you talking about, Mom?''

"I'm talking about Cohen's cold. An ordinary man, he don't think twice about going to the opera with a cold. What's the difference if he sneezes a little? It's only music. But to an opera lover, sneezing during a performance, disturbing people, competing with the singers—this is worse that a major crime. A real opera lover like Cohen, he'd do everything he could to keep his cold under control.

"Which explains what he put in that envelope before he left his home to go to the opera house. A pill, what else? One of these new prescription cold pills that dries up your nose and keeps you from sneezing for five, six hours. And why was the envelope empty when you found it in his pocket? Because half an hour before the box office opened, he slipped out his pill and swallowed it down with his hot black coffee.''

"Nobody *saw* him taking that pill, Mom."

"Why should anybody see him? Like you explained yourself, to drink his coffee he had to turn his body away and shield the container from the wind."

I was beginning to be shaken, no doubt about it. But Shirley spoke up now, in her sweet voice, the voice she always uses when she thinks she's one up on Mom. "The facts don't seem to bear you out, Mother. All the witnesses say that Mr. Cohen went on sneezing *after* the opera had begun. Well, if he really did take a cold pill, as you believe, why didn't it have any effect on his symptoms?"

A gleam came to Mom's eyes, and I could see she was about to pounce. The fact is that Shirley never learns.

So to spare my wife's feelings I broke in quickly, before Mom could open her mouth. "I'm afraid that confirms Mom's theory, honey. The reason why the cold pill didn't work was that it wasn't a cold pill. It looked like one on the outside maybe, but it actually contained poison."

"I always knew I didn't produce a dope!" Mom said, with a big satisfied smile. "So now the answer is simple, no? If Cohen was carrying around a poison pill in his pocket, where did he get it? Who gave it to him? Why should he think it was a cold pill? Because somebody told him it was. Somebody he thought he could trust— not only personally but professionally. Somebody he went to and said, 'Give me some of that new stuff, that new wonder drug, that'll keep me from sneezing during the opera—"

"His nephew!" I interrupted. "My God, Mom, I think you're right. Cohen's nephew *is* a pharmacist—he manages the drug store that Cohen owned. He has access to all kinds of poison and he could make up a pill that would look like a real cold pill. And what's more, he's the only relative Cohen has in the world. He inherits Cohen's store and Cohen's savings."

Mom spread her hands. "So there you are. You couldn't ask for a more ordinary, old-fashioned motive for murder. Any jury will be able to understand it. It isn't one bit operatic."

"But Mom, you must've suspected Cohen's nephew from the start. Otherwise you wouldn't have asked your question about the empty envelope."

"Naturally I suspected him. It was the lie he told."

"What lie?"

"The night before the opera D'Angelo called up Cohen and tried to make up their quarrel. Now according to the nephew, Cohen made a threat to D'Angelo over the phone. 'When Tebaldi hits her high C in the big aria, I'm going to start booing!' A terrible threat—but Cohen never could have made it."

"I don't see why not—"

"Because Cohen was an opera lover, that's why. A high C—this is a tenor's note. It's the top of his range—when he hits one, everybody is thrilled and says how wonderful he is. But for a soprano a high C is nothing special. She can go a lot higher than that. A high E—sometimes even an E sharp—this is the big note for a soprano. In the *Vissy darty* from *Tosca*, any soprano who couldn't do better than a high C would be strictly an amateur. People who are ignoramuses about opera—people like Cohen's nephew—they never *heard* of anything except the high C. But an opera lover like Cohen—he positively couldn't make such a mistake. Now excuse me, I'll bring in the coffee."

Mom got to her feet, and then Shirley called out, "Wait a second, Mother. If his nephew committed the murder, why did Cohen accuse D'Angelo of doing it?"

"When did Cohen accuse D'Angelo?"

"His dying words. He looked into D'Angelo's face and said, 'You no-good! You deserve to die for what you did!' "

"He looked into D'Angelo's face—but how do you know it was D'Angelo he was seeing? He was in delirium from the weakness and the pain, and before his eyes he wasn't seeing any D'Angelo, he wasn't seeing this world that the rest of us are living in. He was seeing the world he'd been looking at before he got sick, the world that meant the most to him—he was seeing the world of the opera, what else? And what was happening up there on that stage just before the poison hit him? The no-good villain was making advances to the beautiful heroine, and she was struggling to defend herself, and pretty soon she was going to kill him—and Cohen, seeing that villain in front of his eyes, shouted out at him, 'You no-good! You deserve to die for what you did!' "

Mom was silent for a moment, and then she went on in a lower voice, "An opera lover will go on being an opera lover—right up to the end."

She went out to the kitchen for the coffee, and I went to the phone in the hall to call the Homicide Squad.

When I got back to the table, Mom was seated and the coffee was served. She took a few sips, and then gave a little sigh. "Poor old Cohen—such a terrible way to go!"

"Death by poisoning *is* pretty painful," I said.

"Poisoning?" Mom blinked up at me. "Yes, this is terrible too. But the worst part of all—the poor man died fifteen minutes too soon. He never heard Tebaldi sing the *Vissy darty*."

And Mom began to hum softly.

Cut from the Same Cloth
by George Baxt

I was kneeling on the floor with my head in the oven when the phone rang. Anyone with a stronger character than mine would have ignored the interruption and continued with this sorry business of self-destruction, especially as from the moment I had come to the decision to commit suicide, it had taken three days to select the method, muster the courage, and finally spur myself to this ultimate action. I did my best to prove to myself I was made of sterner stuff, as I had proved to myself (much to my delight and surprise) on at least three previous occasions.

So while the telephone continued nagging like some ubiquitous shrew, I inhaled deeply, which brought on a coughing fit. I had heard of fits like these causing heart attacks or fatal hemorrhages, which of course frightened the hell out of me, so I staggered to the sink for a glass of water.

Relief came almost instantly, but not from the telephone. It was still agonizing away, which was a clue to the probable identity of the dauntless party at the other end. My money was on Maud Magruder. Maud was one of that peculiar breed of rich (she said) middle-aged Middle Western widow who chose to settle in New York for the sole purpose, it seemed to me, of preying on unattached middle-aged men like myself.

I made my automatic move of reaching for cigarettes and lighter when I realized with horror and a cold shudder that in this gas-filled room I might blow myself up. I turned off the five jets, flung open the window, and was attacked by a hurricane of freezing wind. I drew my cardigan tightly around me for fear of pneumonia and hurried to the living room.

"Hello?" I said weakly into the mouthpiece.

"Oh, darling! You *are* at home! Did I get you out of the bath?" It was Maud Magruder.

"No, Maud, I was just lying down."

"You're not ill or anything, are you?"

Her concern was as automatic and impersonal as the mechanism responsible for this connection.

"I'm not ill. I just don't feel very well."

"You sound perfectly awful. How long have you been back?"

"Three days," I said without thinking, chalking up another reason for suicide.

"Three *whole* days! And you didn't *call*?" I could see that look of indignation, the one she had mastered and perfected to fill one (especially me) with guilt. Medusa's look turned men into stone, Maud's turned me into jelly. ("Oh, darling you didn't go see that movie without *me*! You *know* I was dying to see that movie." "You wretch! You had an invitation to that opening and took someone *else*?" "Blackguard! You know I've been aching to meet the Galtons and you took Bernice *Grimshaw* to their party?")

I tempted the Fates and lied. "I called you the day I got back but you weren't at home."

"What day was this? Wednesday?"

"Yes."

"What time did you call?"

"Oh, for God's sake, Maud, I don't remember what time I called."

"I was home all day Wednesday."

I stretched out on the couch and longed for a cold towel to soothe my aching forehead. "I'm positive I called," I continued, lying brazenly, devil may care, unconcerned by the consequences, knowing full well that soon I'd be back in the kitchen with my head in the oven, this time with the phone off the hook, and breathing deeply of Chanel Number Death.

"There's no need to sound so testy."

I thought I had sounded bored. "Let's not have an argument, Maud, I'm just not in the mood for an argument."

"Then you really must be ill. Is that why you cut the trip short?"

"More or less."

"Oh?" I could almost hear her cosying up to the phone. "Is Kurt there with you?"

"No."

"You didn't return *alone*, did you? Where did you leave *Kurt?*"

"Somewhere in Maine."

"Well, I'll be damned." Wishing won't make it so. "How'd you get *back?*"

"I walked."

"You *are* testy."

"I took a train."

"Why didn't you fly?"

"The weather was bad."

"I just knew you two would have a fight somewhere along the way. You *did* have a fight, didn't you?"

I was positive I heard her licking her lips. Maud thrived on other people's misfortunes. Tell Maud a mutual friend has a terminal disease and she'll insist on throwing a farewell party. Tell Maud old friends are divorcing and she'll announce plans for dinner at Lutece. A really splendid day for Maud is when The *Times's* obituaries list a minimum of three of her contemporaries.

I must have reclined silent for close to thirty seconds staring at the ceiling. Maud of course interpreted the silence as a tacit corroboration of her deduction. "What did you fight about?"

"Everything."

"Oh, come now!"

"He got on my nerves."

"Well, of course he did," she gurgled. "You two are *so* alike."

You've got to meet Kurt Ackerman. You'll adore him. He's so much like you.

"You remember I didn't like him the moment you brought him

around." Maud's voice was unpleasantly shrill. "Why does Bernice Grimshaw insist on thrusting so many unpleasant people on you?"

I couldn't resist it. "She introduced *you* to me." I heard her intake of breath followed by a brief pause and then an outburst of laughter. I can never win.

"Have you heard from Kurt?"

"No."

"It's just as well."

"I agree with you."

"You must have had one lulu of a fight."

"I prefer not to discuss it."

"As you wish." Her voice was stiff. "I don't suppose by any chance you're free tonight?"

I wanted to say, "With any luck I'll soon be free forever." Instead I said, "I told you I wasn't feeling very well."

"It's just that I'm having a divine group in tonight for drinks and dinner. The Escuderos are bring Tony Gompers."

"So?"

"Tony *Gompers*. The *cellist*."

"Never heard of him."

"You must be going out of your mind! You took me to his recital last spring! How could you forget? You thought he was immensely gifted. You couldn't have forgotten. I remember saying at the time, coming from a brilliant musician like yourself that it was *indeed* a compliment. I mean *you* who said Artur Rubinstein was an arthritic hack." Another pause. "You've been pulling my leg."

Fat chance. "I'm sorry, Maud, I'm a bit vague today. Yes, I remember Tony Gompers, and he was good."

"Well, his wife's just left him for a flautist, and the Escuderos are helping him get over her. Oh, do come! He's so terribly lonesome and the Escuderos say he needs a friend to talk to."

"That's what Bernice said about Kurt when *he* left *his* wife."

"Oh, to hell with Kurt."

I silently agreed with her.

"Are you still there?"

"Where's to go?" I made no attempt to disguise my irritation.

"Darling, you're not in one of your . . . *moods* again, are you?"

My moods are celebrated, famous, perhaps more correctly, infamous. All great artists are prey to them. My moods are matched only by my monstrous temper. Perhaps you remember the headlines when I threw the piano stool at that deplorable conductor at my last public concert two years ago. I haven't performed in public since then. There was five months in that so-called rest home during which my lawyers effected an out-of-court settlement with that deplorable conductor's widow. Thanks to my so-called breakdown, I escaped prosecution. During the past year and a half of my self-imposed retirement I have attempted suicide on seven different occasions. The scars on my wrists are the results of four of those attempts. It was Maud who unkindly suggested I have my wrists fitted with zippers.

I have nothing to live for. I have suffered three disastrous marriages. I have suffered the notorious court case when I sued my despicable parents for an accounting of my earnings as a child prodigy. (I had mastered every Chopin prelude by the age of four, and at five stunned the musical world by playing "The Minute Waltz" in 33 seconds. I filled the time remaining with "The Happy Farmer.") That trial left an ugly scar on my psyche. I received very bad press when I refused to attend their joint funeral following the tragic car accident when I was driving them to the Catskills during an attempted reconciliation. I had been miraculously thrown from the car before it went over the cliff.

So I am very much alone in the world, without friends (Maud Magruder is hardly an incentive to go on living), unloved (my wives didn't marry me, they married my reputation) and my gift completely dissipated (the piano in my soundproofed studio hasn't been tuned in over eighteen months).

"Zoltan!"

"What? What?" I stared at the phone and realized it was Maud who had shouted my name. "Oh, Maud, I am sorry. I think I dozed off."

"Well, thank you very much for that!"

"Don't be angry. You just don't understand."

"Zoltan"—her voice was unusually soft and compassionate—"you're crying."

"No, I'm not," I said through a sniffle. "I think I'm catching a cold. The window's open in the kitchen and I'm lying in a draft."

"What shall we do with you?" I heard her tongue clucking. "Now, darling, pull yourself together and come to dinner."

"I really don't—"

"I will not take no for an answer. Tony Gompers is just what you need. He's gifted and witty and terribly attractive. Really, darling, he's so much like you."

"Flatterer." *So much like you.*

"I'll expect you at seven. Meantime, soak in a hot tub."

She hung up before I could remonstrate. I slammed my phone down violently. I stomped into the kitchen like a petulant child and tested the air with a huge sniff. All trace of gas had disappeared. I banged the window shut and erupted with a fit of sneezing. I tramped with a house-shaking stride to my soundproofed studio at the rear of the apartment. There was the piano in the middle of the room. Untouched. Unloved. Unwanted. Like myself.

I stifled a sob as my eyes moved around the room. The six lithographs I kept delaying hanging on the walls were stacked in a corner, and on the floor were the box of nails and the hammer. The studio had been constructed by order of my lawyers during my stay in the rest home. The suggestion had been put to them by my psychiatrist. He had meant well. It would be there awaiting what he called "my new beginning." I didn't want a new beginning, which I dismissed along with the psychiatrist. I know my gift has also been my curse. Rejecting the piano was my way of exorcism.

Of course I attended Maud's dinner party. She's made of sterner stuff than I. (I assure you, I'll be back at that oven again, but not to prepare a meal.) Frankly, my curiosity overcame my morbid desire for death. I wanted to meet Tony Gompers. It fascinates and piques my interest when someone says, "You must meet so and so, he's so much like you." It's what drew me to Bernice Grimshaw's that night six weeks ago when she tempted me with Kurt Ackerman.

They say that one should profit by one's mistakes, but I'm a different sort of speculator. I'm not particularly religious, but I felt that Maud's phone call had in some way been preordained. I was not yet meant to die. It was destined for me to meet Tony Gompers.

If you're as myopic as I am, then you can honestly say Maud Magruder was a vision in her silver lamé pants suit, silver-rimmed harlequin glasses large enough to cover two faces instead of just hers, and glittering sandals to slightly minimize her height, which was one inch short of six feet. Her face as always looked as though the cosmetics had been applied by a mortician, and very thoughtfully (some might say thoughtlessly) one of my recordings, a Brahms Piano Concerto, was permeating the room from four cleverly concealed speakers.

Her left cheek brushed my right cheek as though I might carry an infection. "How good of you to come, darling," she said in her party voice which was terribly British except for the flat a's which were a dead giveaway of her Midwestern origin. I greeted Alphonse and Lolita Escudero (who were really Al and Lily Eichman), once celebrated professional ballroom dancers. They now owned dancing schools throughout the country and were immensely wealthy. Their hobby was collecting celebrities and sometimes trading their celebrities with a friend who had acquired a better celebrity. I had been traded at least four times. There were other guests, but they weren't important.

Maud took my sweaty hand and guided me to Tony Gompers, who was leaning disconsolately against the grand piano. I expected him at any moment to break into "Stout Hearted Men." My ego swelled a bit when Maud introduced us and Tony brightened on hearing my name. Maud beamed like a good deed in a naughty world.

"I just know you two have a great deal to talk about," Maud insisted. She left us to greet some late arrivals.

"Maud was afraid you might not come," said Tony.

"Maud is never afraid," I replied somewhat archly. It was meant to sound good-natured but somehow I didn't quite manage to catch the effect.

"Well, now," he said.

"Yes, indeed," I replied.

He lowered his head conspiratorially and whispered, "I didn't want to come." So at least we had this in common. "How's the music coming?"

"I don't play any more."

"That's what Maud said, but I didn't believe her. She said you're so much like me, but I said that's not possible because I couldn't live without my cello."

"But I used to play the piano." We both laughed.

"Don't say 'used to.' You'll play the piano again."

"I really don't miss it. After all, I've had forty years of it. Remember, I was a child prodigy."

"So was I. Didn't you know?"

I didn't. I felt like asking him if he had ever sued his parents for an accounting of his earnings.

"Of course there was that awful mess with my parents," he said. "Much like yours, I suppose." I wondered if the change in my face was noticeable. I could feel the blood draining from it.

I managed to stammer out, "I didn't know about that."

"Well, why should you?" he asked with a pleasant smile. "I didn't really begin to make it on the concert stage until long after the lawsuit. I was strictly local stuff. The South." There was no trace of an accent. "I did pretty damned well for some fifteen years." His face darkened. "Then I met my wife. She took over from my parents. She was a successful manager." He mentioned her name and I recognized it.

"I didn't know you were married to her."

"Oh, yes, indeed I was. Twenty very long years. I suppose Maud's told you she's left me."

"For a flautist."

"He's fifteen years younger than she is."

"Then his wind's still good." We broke up into laughter together over that one and he slapped me on the back in one of those hail-fellow-well-met gestures that had my back stinging for quite a while. We bantered back and forth amiably and jovially for at least half an hour until Maud announced dinner. The meal was a delicious and delightful affair and impeccably served. Maud held court at the head of the table, and every so often I would catch her glowing with motherly pride at Tony and myself, who kept up a steady stream of chatter and jokes, batting dialogue back and forth across the table like tennis champions.

I could tell that Maud considered the dinner party a huge success—the instant camaraderie between Tony and myself could only be exceeded for her by one of the Escuderos slumping over the dessert from a heart attack, which of course did not happen.

When I arrived home alone shortly after midnight, I was in amazingly good spirits. I even poured myself a brandy, which is something I rarely do as brandy stimulates my adrenaline and causes a sleepless night. As a matter of fact, for the first time in over a year I played one of my own recordings and sat back in an easy chair, sipping brandy and listening to the ghost of my earlier genius. And then the phone rang.

"Good evening," I said somewhat mockingly into the mouthpiece, assuming the caller would be Maud to rehash the evening.

"Zoltan!" It was Bernice Grimshaw. "Maud told me you were back." Maud would. "What the hell happened?"

I swished the brandy lazily and said, "Kurt was a very disappointing traveling companion."

"Really!" You'd have thought I had slapped her in the face.

"He didn't like any of the accommodations. He complained about the food. He made snide remarks about the people we met, and he drove like a maniac."

"Well, you're the same way, for God's sake!" Bernice should know. We once took a trip together to Canada which was another mistake.

"I suppose so," I said somewhat airily. "Maybe that's why I couldn't stand it. So I defected."

"Poor old Kurt," whimpered Bernice, "having to drive all the way back from Maine by his lonesome."

"He enjoys talking to himself."

"Don't be so cruel," she snapped. "You're both cut from the same cloth. I should have known better than to bring you two together."

"Don't blame yourself, dear," I said rather wearily, "I really didn't want to make that trip, if you recall."

"Well, I should have thought you two would have gotten along famously, larking your way across New England." Bernice was fishing for information. She was desperately in love with Kurt, who, of course, was not encouraging her. He was at the blue-jeaned tight-behind, teenage stage, an affliction that attacks many men in their forties. I had passed through that stage myself rather swiftly.

"There wasn't very much of that, Bernice."

"Hmmm. Well, have you any idea when he's getting back?"

"None whatsoever."

"You men. You're absolute babies, all of you." And Bernice wished she could diaper each and every one of us. "Are you free for lunch tomorrow?"

"I'm sorry, but I'm not." I wasn't lying. I was having lunch with Tony Gompers.

"I gather you and Tony Gompers got along famously tonight." I groaned inwardly. I knew whatever she had gathered was from a crop seeded by Maud Magruder.

"I found him quite affable." In the middle of this statement I stifled a yawn. There was no stifling Bernice.

"I'm quite friendly with his wife." Somehow I had the feeling she was delivering a subtle warning rather than imparting an innocuous bit of information.

"Have you met her flute player?" I asked.

"I certainly have, and he's a vast improvement on Tony."

"How can you tell? They play different instruments."

"Don't be so snide. That's one of the reasons she decided to leave Tony."

"Because I'm so snide?"

"That's almost funny. Tony's snide, possessive, has a vicious temper, is given to childish tantrums, he's mean to her friends—"

"And on the seventh day he rested."

"Have I touched an exposed nerve? It must all sound so familiar. He's so much like you."

You're mean. You're vicious. You're vindictive. How dare you drag us through the slime like that. You're driving much too fast. Are you trying to get us killed? Are you listening? Oh, you are impossible! You're just like your father! You're so much like him!

"Bernice, it's terribly late, and I'm terribly tired."

"What's the music I hear?"

"Liszt."

"Seems to me I have that recording." There was a dramatic pause followed by, "Why, it's *your* recording!"

"I only listen to the best."

Her voice dropped an octave. "Are you entertaining someone?"

"Myself." I took a sip of brandy. "We missed you at dinner tonight."

"Oh, go to hell."

"If you'll lead the way."

She slammed the phone down and almost gave me an earache.

As you may have gathered by now, Bernice and Maud are sisters under the skin. The catalogue of Tony's (and by inference, my) deficiencies could well apply to themselves. But I forgive them their sins as they do not forgive others. To be perfectly honest, I had planned to cancel the luncheon engagement with Tony Gompers. I know now that I don't really get along with men. I loathe sports, drinking in bars, and comparing notes on romantic triumphs.

I suppose you're thinking that Tony and I do have music in common, but I happen to find the cello a rather unpleasant instrument. It is frequently too guttural for my taste, which is lyrical. I should have studied the harp. It could have served two purposes—the second, of course, in my afterlife.

After turning off the stereo and finishing the brandy, I went to bed and suffered a series of incredible nightmares. Twice I awakened in a cold sweat and briefly considered retenanting the oven right then and there. My knees felt stiff and my nose was clogged, usually the symptoms of an oncoming cold. You wonder why I don't jump off a tall building? I have a fear of heights.

In the morning over toast and coffee and the *Times* crossword puzzle, Tony Gompers phoned. I tried to use my cold to beg off lunch, but he's as stubborn as I am about rejection. He was having none of my canceling and it finally ended up with me offering to cook lunch for the two of us. One way or another there's no avoiding that stove. Even the mean offering of eggs and sausage would not put Tony off. He insisted he wasn't much of a lunch eater and neither am I. Oh, what the hell, I decided, the hour or two will pass quickly.

Tony arrived promptly at one. To my very obvious chagrin he was toting his cello.

"I hope you don't mind," he said with a big smile as he followed me into the living room. "There's a piece I'd like you to hear and advise me on. I composed it myself." I could feel my spine freezing. "If you think it's any good, I'll play it at my next recital."

"I'm not a very good judge of modern music," I said weakly.

"I'm sure you have a fine ear." I glanced at my ear as we passed a mirror and agreed with him. "It's a lyrical piece." I almost stumbled on the way to the kitchen. "They don't compose enough of them for the cello, don't you think?"

"I sure do."

The sausages were sizzling in a pan. "Oh," he said in an almost petulant voice, "you fry your sausages, you don't broil them." Little did he know how close he came to suffering a shower of sausages.

"I *always* fry sausages," I said with a rasp as I took the eggs from the refrigerator. There was something very déjà vu about the scene. I consider myself a superior cook and have frequently been guilty of dismaying a host or hostess who hadn't prepared a dish in a manner I prefer.

Tony said, through a laugh, "I suppose you've said something similar in somebody else's kitchen at one time or another."

Is the clown a mind reader? Can there really be such a thing as thought transference? "Would you like a drink?"

"No, thanks, I never drink in the afternoon."

"Neither do I." I almost dropped an egg.

Somehow we managed to get through lunch. We had coffee in the living room and chatted—rather, Tony chatted and I listened. He monopolized the conversation much in the way I do when I find a fresh audience. It was most discomforting. I was very much on edge and not successfully camouflaging my feelings. I kept referring to my wristwatch and stifling yawns and picking nonexistent lint from my trousers and growing bored with all the uh-huhs and I *sees* and of *courses* I was interjecting into his conversation by way of letting him know I was still alive.

Then there was still the cello concerto to endure. In the past, I wondered, was this the effect I had on people when I asked them to listen to a new piece I was attempting to master? Of course it was, and it frightened me. He's so much like me, and I could feel a trickle of perspiration down my side.

Just when I was about to suggest we go to my soundproofed studio, the phone rang.

I reached for it hungrily.

"Zoltan . . . oh, my God, Zoltan." It was Maud, the voice of doom.

"What's wrong, Maud? What is it?"

"Bernice just phoned, weeping bitterly. It was on the one o'clock news."

I must have grown pale because Tony leaned forward anxiously and I averted my eyes from his. "What was?"

"Kurt's been found dead."

"What—how—what are you talking about?"

"What is it?" whispered Tony but I waved him to be quiet.

Maud told me Kurt's body had been found in the car in an isolated patch of woods near Portland, Maine. He had apparently gone off the road during a heavy fog and crashed into a tree. His skull had been crushed. "How awful," I said hoarsely.

"They say he's been dead for several days," continued Maud at her most tragic. "It must have happened shortly after you left him."

"How awful," I said again, because there was nothing else for me to say.

"But Zoltan," Maud continued, "the police suspect foul play."

"How can they?" It was a stupid thing to ask, but it was the first thing that came to my mind, and I am frequently guilty of speaking the first thing that comes to my mind.

"The monkey wrench in the trunk of the car had traces of blood on it."

"I didn't notice when we changed the tire. We—we'd had a blowout going at seventy. We were almost killed. That's what caused the argument. Oh, God. What a mess."

"Zoltan."

"What?"

"Bernice has phoned the police. She's told them you'd been traveling with Kurt."

I fought hard to keep from exploding. Tony's curiosity was now more than piqued. His hands were making semaphores trying to get me to give him some hint of what Maud was telling me. Obviously he had gathered Kurt was dead and under suspicious circumstances—at least, I assumed he had if he was so much like me. "She didn't have to do that. I would have gotten in touch with them."

"Oh, darling, of all times to put you under such stress."

"It's all right." I was amazed at how calmly I spoke. "It will be all right. Tony's here. We've just had lunch. He's brought his cello. He's going to play his new piece for me."

Tony was flexing his fingers.

"You're taking it beautifully," said Maud. I might have just refused the handkerchief before the firing squad. "Please call me later. I'm terribly concerned for you." I promised I would and hung up. I told Tony about Kurt. All he did was shrug.

"He was a bore," said Tony.

He shouldn't have said that. He really shouldn't have said that. Of course Kurt was a bore. And Tony Gompers is a crashing bore. So much like me, of course. I stood up abruptly and Tony followed me to the studio carrying his cello. I flung open the door and stood aside for Tony. Then I slammed the door shut and the sound that reverberated through the studio was hollow and empty. Tony crossed to the piano and ran his fingers across the keys.

"My God, this is out of tune. How could you do it to this lovely instrument?"

The veins in my temples were throbbing and I pressed my fingers against them. Then I rubbed my sweaty palms together as Tony unpacked his cello. "Look, Tony," I stammered nervously, "I don't think I could be much of a judge of anything right now. Do you mind terribly?"

He looked up at me sharply and said in a tone of voice I found offensive, "It's a very short piece. This might be the only chance I'll get to play it for you."

I remember wondering then why he had said something like that. It sounded in a way sadistic and I know I have sounded that way on similar occasions. I spat an epithet and moved past him to where the lithographs were tacked. I couldn't resist a deliciously nasty impulse to hang one of them while Tony attempted to tune up the cello. I lifted the hammer, selected a nail, and began pounding it into the wall.

"Well, this is a fine time to do that!" Tony shouted angrily. "Are you afraid to hear this piece because it might be too good?"

There must have been a hideous look on my face when I rounded on him, clutching the hammer. He leaped from the seat so abruptly that he stumbled over the cello, lost his balance, and sprawled backward onto the floor.

I pounced on him like some wild animal, my left hand clutching his neck, my right hand holding the hammer poised to strike. Tony screamed and tried to scratch my face, just the way Kurt had tried.

"Don't!" he shouted hysterically, "Don't! Don't!"

I rained blow after blow on his skull. I could hear the bone crack as rivers of blood erupted.

"Why—why—" he gasped.

"You're so much like me!" I screamed in a voice I did not recognize. "You're so much like me . . . and I hate myself!"

Death at the Opera
by Michael Underwood

*W*henever I have occasion to dip into *Who's Who*, I usually look first to see what the contributor has listed under "Recreations." This can often tell one more about the person than all the lines taken up with his accomplishments. It invariably paid me dividends when I was still an estate agent and dealing with important clients. It always helped if I was able to talk to the person concerned about gardening or theater or sailing or whatever the subject might be. The fact that my own knowledge of it might be minimal mattered far less than that I showed an interest.

Of course, sometimes the failure to mention a particular hobby could prove even more revealing. I recall selling a property for a High Court judge on one occasion. He was a stiff, unbending man without any noticeable sense of humor. "Walking" and "Reading" were listed as his unexceptionable recreations. It was only when I visited his house I learned quite by chance that he would pass his winter evenings doing embroidery. His obvious desire to keep this fact secret lowered him still further in my estimation.

But all this is really by the way. What I had been going to say was that, had I ever been invited to contribute an entry to that prestigious volume, I would have headed my list of recreations with "Opera, especially Wagner."

I have a passion for Wagner that has taken me to performances in places as far apart as Moscow and San Francisco, Vienna and Buenos Aires. In fact, since I retired five years ago, most of my traveling has been devoted to his cause, with an annual statutory visit to Bayreuth, the shrine for all Wagnerians.

I ought perhaps to say that my passion is unshared by most of my friends who regard it as an aberration in an otherwise reasonably normal person.

But however strong the lure of Wagner, attendance at his operas can bring hazards of their own. For example, you can find yourself sitting next to someone who fidgets or coughs, or be faced in the foyer by a notice regretting the indisposition of one of the leading singers. These things can, of course, happen at performances of other operas, but with less disastrous effect. And even if you manage to escape these particular hazards, others still lurk, for no composer loaded his singers and musicians, not to mention his producers and stagehands, with such superhuman difficulties. Even when the singing and orchestral playing are sublime, disaster can still strike. The dragon in Siegfried can get inextricably caught up in a piece of scenery, the hero's sword can break in two just after it has been invincibly forged, and majestic Valhalla can develop an incurable wobble like a jelly on a vibrating surface. The list is almost inexhaustible.

And recently I was involved in a nightmarish drama that not even a practised Wagnerian has ever envisaged. Death on the stage is one thing, but sudden death in the auditorium is something different altogether, particularly when, to use the police colloquialism, foul play is suspected.

When a few years ago the well-known philanthropist, Sir Julius Meiler, announced that he was proposing to build an opera house in the park of his Oxfordshire home and devote it primarily to an annual festival of Wagner operas, there was great enthusiasm among us devotees. Sir Julius went quietly ahead with his plans. Since he could no longer travel to Wagner, he would realize an ambition and bring the composer's work to his own doorstep. He employed top men at heaven knows what expense and from his drawing-room window he was able to sit and watch the edifice slowly rise up a quarter of a mile across the parkland.

Even if he never entertained any doubts about the ultimate success of the project, there were many, like myself, who saw it all ending with the old boy's death or in hideous bankruptcy. But neither of these events occurred and six months before the first performances were due to be given, the box office opened.

Needless to say, Sir Julius had himself decided which operas were to be performed and long before the final bricks were laid, conductors, singers, and producers had been engaged for the first season. There were to be two cycles of The Ring and three performances each of Parsifal and Tristan and Isolde.

Though, as I say, I had been skeptical about the outcome of the project, I had made up my mind that, if it did come off, I would be there, come hell or high water. Fortunately I had a contact in the box-office manager who was a friend of a friend.

I can still remember my excitement the day my tickets arrived. They were for the second cycle of The Ring and for performances of the other two operas. Not even the horror of subsequent events has dimmed my recollection of that sunny June morning when our cheerful postman delivered the self-addressed envelope that had accompanied my application.

There were still three months to go before that fateful performance of Die Walküre on Tuesday, the 22nd of September.

For the non-Wagnerian, I ought to explain that The Ring (full title: Der Ring des Nibelungen) consists of four operas amounting to about twenty hours of music, if you include the intervals. Wagner believed in giving his fans their money's worth and some of his "acts" are as long as whole operas by other composers. So far as The Ring is concerned, Das Rheingold, which is the first, is the shortest. It lasts just under two and a half hours and is performed without an interval. From this you will gather that stamina is almost as important as love of the music. If you're given to fidgets, you'd better stay at home and listen to recordings.

I had been over to Bargewick Park, Sir Julius Meiler's place, a couple of times before the festival opened. Once to a large and noisy party to which I was invited by my friend, the box-office manager, and once for a privately conducted tour of the opera house itself which I had found much more interesting. It wasn't an elegant building to look at, but the acoustics were said to rival those at Bayreuth. Sir Julius had insisted that everything should be subordinated to the acoustics, hence the somewhat functional interior. The seats might be on the hard side, but they were guaranteed not to absorb any of the sound.

I greeted Monday, the 21st of September with a sense of great exhilaration. It was almost beyond the dream of any Wagnerian that the operas were about to be performed with internationally famous singers in a brand-new theater almost on his own doorstep. Bargewick Park was, in fact, twelve miles from where I lived. The Gods could not have been more beneficent.

Das Rheingold was scheduled to start at half past seven and I arrived a good hour before that. The car park was already quite full and I made my way to the long bar which ran the length of one side of the building and bought myself a glass of champagne. What else on such an occasion! Almost everyone was in evening dress and the air of expectation was enormous. Wagnerians had flocked from all points of the compass to attend the opening performance.

After a second glass of champagne to put the seal on my mood, I decided to go and claim my seat. I had studied the plan in advance and knew exactly where it was—one from the end of the twelfth row of the stalls.

An elderly man and his arrogant-looking younger companion were already occupying the two seats to the right of mine. They tucked their legs in with a poorly concealed lack of grace to let me pass, for which I murmured my thanks. Seeing that there were still fifteen minutes to go before the curtain rose, their attitude seemed rather churlish. Wagner may bring us together, but, as I've discovered before, he doesn't necessarily make us love each other.

The seat on my left, which was against the wall, was still empty and I wondered who was to be my neighbor on that side.

A sudden outburst of applause greeted the arrival of Sir Julius

Meiler, who was wheeled in his chair into a specially prepared space in the center of the circle.

The house lights were dimming when I became aware of upheaval at the end of our row as a middle-aged woman pushed her way along to the empty seat on my left.

She was obviously hot and bothered and almost fell headlong over the feet of the two men next to me. I stood up to let her pass more easily and then held her seat down for her. She murmured profuse thanks and sank back with an audible sigh of relief as those incredible opening chords rose from the orchestra pit, signifying our immediate transportation to the bottom of the Rhine.

It was not long, however, before I became aware of suppressed coughing on my left and I shot her a quick glance to indicate my awareness. Then at the very moment when Alberich the dwarf seized the Rhinemaiden's gold, she began rummaging in her handbag. Recognizing the symptoms all too well, I realized that in her rush to arrive on time she had left her cough lozenges at home.

She held a tissue to her mouth and tried to clear her throat in silence, which, as everyone knows, is quite impossible. Hastily I reached into my pocket for the throat pastilles I always carry on visits to the opera. I seldom require them myself and am motivated entirely by self-protection. I passed her the whole tin and she communicated her gratitude by patting my hand.

They obviously did the trick for there were no further disturbances and the performance reached its majestic end with the Gods making their entry into a satisfyingly solid-looking Valhalla.

"Wonderful, wonderful," she murmured to me several times in the course of the curtain calls, which continued for fifteen minutes.

Eventually the house lights came up and we both sat back in our seats temporarily exhausted while the two men on my other side thrust their way out as if they had a last train to catch.

"You enjoyed the performance?" I said to her after the curtain had come down for the last time.

"Enormously. Surely you did, too?"

"Very much. Though wasn't it Ernest Newman who said one'll have to wait till one reaches heaven for the perfect performance of Wagner?"

"If the rest of the cycle is as good as that, it'll be an unnecessary wait as far as I'm concerned," she said.

I laughed. "I'll reserve judgment until we've heard more."

She reached down for her program which had fallen to the floor and gave a hitch to her shawl which had slipped from one shoulder. "I do hope I didn't disturb you with my chokes. You saved my life with your cough sweets. I was sure I had some in my bag, but I must have forgotten them in the rush of leaving home. I kept on being held up and thought I was never going to get here. I think I'd have lain down and died if they hadn't let me in."

"You certainly ran it rather close," I remarked. "Don't forget that tomorrow's performance starts at six."

"My husband'll be at home to see I set off in good time. He was out at a meeting this evening or I'd never have been late. He's one of those punctual people who has never missed a train in his life. I shan't dare tell him I forgot to bring my cough lozenges." With a laugh she added, "He regards them as a minimum requirement for sitting through Wagner. But then he's hopelessly unmusical. We have a pact. He lets me come to the opera and I let him go off catching butterflies."

"He's an entomologist?"

"He's written a book on the subject," she said with a touch of pride.

As we walked together toward the car park, she told me a bit more about herself. She lived in North Oxford and her husband, who had been a supply officer in the navy, now worked in the bursar's office of one of the colleges.

I estimated her age as being around sixty. She had a pleasant round face and, I suspected, a perennial weight problem.

We reached the car park and were about to part company when she let out an exclamation.

"I've never given you back your cough sweets." She fumbled with her handbag and promptly dropped it.

"Keep them," I said, retrieving her bag. "You may need them tomorrow. And, anyway, I've got more at home."

With that I bade her good night and went in search of my car.

The next evening I arrived at Bargewick Park soon after five o'clock and once more fortified myself with two glasses of excellent champagne before going to my seat.

I was both surprised and gratified to find Mrs. Sharpe already in her place—she had told me her name was Helen Sharpe before we parted company the previous evening.

"See!" she said with a note of triumph. "I'm not the scatty female you obviously thought I was."

"No problems getting here this evening then?" I said with a smile.

"My husband pushed me out of the house far sooner than was necessary and I've even brought my own cough sweets this time." She gave me a rueful look. "But I've just discovered that I've left yours at home. I'm terribly sorry. They were in my other handbag."

"Don't worry. I've brought a further supply."

"What a couple of philanthropists you and Sir Julius are! One provides the music, the other the cough sweets," she said with a merry laugh.

Shortly afterward the two men on my right took their seats without so much as a nod or glance in my direction and a few minutes later the cellos were whipping up the storm music that forms the prelude of the opera.

Act I of Die Walküre is one of my favorite parts of the whole Ring. It lasts over an hour, but, for me, there is never one flagging second. And when the roles of Siegmund and Sieglinde are sung as gloriously as they were that evening, I quickly become immersed in the music and oblivious of everything else around me. Mrs. Sharpe could have been coughing her head off and I don't believe I'd have noticed.

I turned to her as soon as the curtain came down and was surprised to see her leaning against the wall on her other side in apparent sleep.

It was only when the lights came up and people began to leave the auditorium that I turned back to her.

With horror I realized it wasn't sleep that had overcome her, but death.

I must say that the authorities at Bargewick Park were as efficient at removing bodies from the auditorium as they were at putting on an opera. In no time at all Mrs. Sharpe's remains were carried out with the minimum of fuss.

I went off to the bar and had a large brandy to help me recover from the shock of my discovery. When we returned for Act II, I realized I was more distracted by the empty seat on my left than I had been by the poor woman's coughing the previous evening. My discomfort was compounded by the man on my right who seemed deliberately to turn his shoulder on me. For the first time I glanced round at the occupants of the two seats immediately behind. They were a middle-aged couple and the woman gave me a nervous smile before quickly looking elsewhere.

I have seldom enjoyed anything less than I did those two remaining acts. When the performance was finally over, I decided I ought to go back and make myself known to someone in authority. It had only occurred to me toward the end that they might still be trying to identify Mrs. Sharpe. I could at least help with that.

Accordingly, I hung back until the theater was almost empty. Even so, I received a number of curious stares and it suddenly dawned on me that people had taken her to be my wife or, at least, my companion for the evening, and were now regarding me as some sort of callous monster.

I had just reached the foyer when a man stepped forward.

"Excuse me, sir, but may I have a word with you for a moment?"

"Of course. Is it about Mrs. Sharpe?"

He didn't reply, but led the way to a door marked "Private." It was a small office and there was a man inside whom I recognized as the house manager. His photograph appeared in the souvenir program.

"I believe you're Mr. Mason, sir?" the first man said.

"Yes. Charles Mason." For a second I couldn't think how he knew my name, but then I realized he had obviously found out by checking my seat number against my application form.

"I'm Detective Chief Inspector Jackley," he said. "I gather you knew Mrs. Sharpe?"

"No, I'm afraid not."

He frowned. "But you mentioned her name when I first spoke to you, sir."

"We'd exchanged names when we left together after last night's performance."

"You'd not met her previously?"

"I'd never seen her before in my life."

"I see," he said, in a tone which clearly implied that he was reserving judgment on every word I uttered.

"If you look at my written application for tickets," I said slyly, "you'll see that I'm on my own. I imagine Mrs. Sharpe's will show the same. She told me that her husband wasn't at all musical and never accompanied her on these occasions."

"I see," Jackley said again in the same faintly disconcerting tone. "Well, I think that's all for the moment, Mr. Mason. Can we reach you, if necessary, at the address given on your ticket application form?"

"Yes, that's my home."

"Good, then I needn't detain you further."

I got to the door and paused. "Did she have a sudden heart attack or something?" I asked.

"We shan't know the cause of death until after the autopsy," Jackley said, giving me a funny look.

It was only when I was driving home that it occurred to me to wonder what on earth a Detective Chief Inspector would be doing investigating a case of heart attack.

I spent the next day pottering about the garden trying to take my mind off what had happened, entirely without success. Normally I would have been eagerly looking forward to *Siegfried* the following night and to the final opera of the cycle, when the whole monumental undertaking reaches its musical and dramatic climax. It was no use telling myself that there couldn't be a better way of dying, because I kept on remembering Detective Chief Inspector Jackley's intrusion on the scene.

About half past five I went indoors and had a wash. I had just settled down to watch the early evening news on television when a car drew up outside and two men got out. One of them I recognized immediately as Jackley. For a few seconds they stared up at the roof as if searching for some structural fault. Then they advanced up the path. I waited until they had rung the bell before going to open the door.

"Good evening, Mr. Mason," Jackley said. "I wonder if my colleague and I might come in and have a word with you? Incidentally, this is Detective Sergeant Denham."

I led the way into the living room.

"Nice home you have," Jackley remarked, glancing about him. "But then it would be surprising if a retired estate agent couldn't pick himself a plum." He gave me a small smile.

My ex-profession had certainly not appeared on my application form for opera tickets, so it was obvious that the police had been doing some homework on me. Moreover, they were ready to let me know the fact. I decided to hold my tongue and oblige them to state their business, which Jackley wasn't long in doing.

"I understand you supplied Mrs. Sharpe with some cough lozenges," he said with a mildly quizzical expression.

"Not last night. It was during the performance the previous evening."

"That agrees with what Mr. Fox and Mr. Driver have told us."

"And who might they be?"

"They occupied the two seats on your right. They saw you pass Mrs. Sharpe your tin of cough lozenges."

"Oh, did they!" I exclaimed in a nettled tone.

"You sound put out," Jackley said equably. "I thought you Wagner worshippers were all chums together."

"There was nothing chummy about those two as far as I was concerned."

"But you're not denying you handed Mrs. Sharpe your lozenges?"

"Of course not. Why should I deny it? And, anyway, so what?"

"Ah, so what, you ask. Well, the answer to that, Mr. Mason, is it appears Mrs. Sharpe didn't die a natural death, but was poisoned. Murdered by a dose of potassium cyanide. Now, that's a poison that acts very rapidly and so the irresistible inference is that she must have ingested it during the actual course of the performance. That's where your cough lozenges become relevant."

"Oh, my God, that's terrible!" I said, feeling as if the Chief Inspector had given my room a sudden violent spin. "But it certainly couldn't have been anything to do with the ones I gave her. She left them at home yesterday and brought her own."

"What makes you say that, Mr. Mason?"

"She told me so. Apologized for not returning mine. Said she'd left them in her other bag, the one she'd been carrying the previous evening."

For a moment Jackley looked nonplused. "She told you that?"

"Yes."

"When?"

"When we met at our seats yesterday evening."

"I can't understand why she should have said that," he remarked in a tone of clear disbelief, "because it wasn't true." He reached into his pocket and pulled out a tin which was enclosed in a cellophane envelope. "Is this the tin you gave her?"

"Yes, that's the sort I buy. Buckland's."

"We found this tin in her handbag when we were called to Barge-wick Park last night. There was also a packet of Coff-Stop lozenges in the bag. Can you explain why she should have lied to you, Mr. Mason?"

"I can only repeat what she said to me."

"Doesn't it strike you as very odd?"

"I don't know enough about the lady to answer that," I said warily.

"And you still say that you had never met her before?"

"Never."

"You don't live far apart."

"Nor do I from a hundred and twenty thousand other people in this area, but I assure you I don't know them all."

"That's the best you can say?"

"It's all I can say."

"Do you have a further supply of Buckland's lozenges?"

"Yes."

"Any objection to handing them over?"

"None."

"If you tell Sergeant Denham where they are, he can fetch them."

"I'll fetch them myself," I replied frostily.

"You don't trust the police?" Jackley said with an air of faint amusement.

"It doesn't seem that they trust me."

"I assure you I'm doing no more than duty requires, Mr. Mason. At this stage of an inquiry it's questions, questions all the way."

"And I've given you truthful answers."

"Every answer has to be tested. You say that yours are truthful, but I have to be sure."

"You can be."

"But can I?" He fixed me with an intent look. "It doesn't exactly tally with what Mrs. Sharpe told her husband when she arrived home the night before last." The room seemed to take another violent spin as Jackley went on. "According to Mr. Sharpe, you had considerably upset his wife. You behaved so strangely that she began to wonder if you mightn't be a mental patient. And she became even more apprehensive when you forced your cough lozenges on her."

"What absolute rubbish! I don't believe for one moment that she ever said anything of the sort. I've never been a mental patient in my life and there was nothing remotely strange about my behavior. You can ask the couple who were sitting behind us."

"The fact still remains, Mr. Mason, that she did have your tin of Buckland's lozenges in her handbag last night. Are you quite sure she told you she'd left them at home?"

"Absolutely."

"Ah, well!" he said with a sigh. "If you'll just let us have your remaining supply, we'll be on our way. I'll doubtless be in touch with you again."

After their departure I poured myself a large Scotch and sat down to try and sort out my thoughts. To say that I was in a state of shock was a pathetic understatement. I felt as if my whole world had become unpivoted.

The immediate decision which faced me was whether or not to attend the performance of Siegfried the next evening. If I didn't go, it would be quickly assumed that I was in some way connected with Mrs. Sharpe's death. If I did turn up, I was going to be the cynosure of furtive glances and whispered comment, the effect of which not even the power of Wagner's music was likely to erase.

Moreover, I kept on recalling that part of the plot involves a character named Mime trying to induce Siegfried to drink a potion of poison. At least, they didn't have cough lozenges in that mythical era; nevertheless it was hardly conducive to an evening for forgetting one's troubles.

In the event, I did go and found the experience every bit as grim as I had expected. My attendance at *Götterdämmerung* two nights later was not quite as bad, though it was still testing enough. On each occasion I sat staring at the stage with fixed concentration, remaining in my seat during the intervals. Mrs. Sharpe's seat was unoccupied at both performances and Messrs. Fox and Driver regarded me with even greater disdain than previously.

What should have been exhilarating occasions had turned into a ghastly ordeal.

A week passed before I heard anything further. I scanned the local paper each day, but news of the case was soon reduced to a small item on an inside page to the effect that police inquiries were still continuing into the "mystery of the opera-goer's death." Earlier Mr. Sharpe was reported as saying there must be a mad poisoner at large who was prepared to strike indiscriminately as nobody could have had the slightest motive for murdering his wife. I took this to be an arrow shot deliberately in my direction.

I had a great urge to call Detective Chief Inspector Jackley, but refrained from doing so as I feared he might misconstrue my interest in his inquires. I tried to telephone my friend in the box office at Bargewick Park. Three times, in fact. But once he was at a meeting and the other two times I was told he was out, so that, in my slightly paranoid state, I immediately assumed that he was trying to avoid me.

All in all, it was the most nerve-wracking and miserable week of my life. By the end I had almost become a recluse, finding it even an ordeal to be with friends.

I was just sitting down to a lonely cold lunch one day toward the end of the following week when the telephone rang.

"Mr. Mason? Detective Chief Inspector Jackley here. Are you going to be home this afternoon?"

"As far as I know," I said, trying to sound unconcerned and knowing very well that I would be at home.

"Good, I'll drop by about four o'clock."

His tone had told me nothing and I spent the next three hours in wild speculation about the reason for his visit.

He arrived alone and accepted the offer of a cup of tea, both of which I took to be hopeful signs.

"I think we've got the case just about sewn up," he said, as I handed him his tea. He gave me a wry smile. "As far as I was concerned there were only two suspects from the very outset. The husband and you. And the husband was always the more likely. The problem was to establish a motive."

"And you've been able to do that?"

"Yes."

"What was it?"

"Oh, the usual. Another woman. A much younger person."

"Was she involved too?"

He nodded. "She's a research chemist at one of the laboratories. It was she who doctored the fatal cough lozenge. All he then had to do was put it among the others and wait for his wife to consume it. I gather she sucked them all the time, so he wasn't going to have to wait very long. The only uncertainty was when and where, and he made various contingency plans to meet each situation. For instance, if she had died at home he would have immediately destroyed the packet from which the poisoned lozenge came."

"He certainly lost no time in setting me up as the fall guy," I remarked ruefully.

Jackley nodded. "When she returned home that first evening and told him how you'd offered her your lozenges, he quickly saw his opportunity for diverting suspicion. He not only made sure she took her own the next evening, but reduced the number in the packet so that she was bound to reach the fatal one in the course of the performance. Then, unbeknown to her, he put your tin of Buckland's lozenges at the bottom of her bag where it was bound to be discovered later."

"He's told you all this?"

Jackley smiled. "Once we picked up the bit of gossip about his association with the girl, we were able to apply pressure in the right place." He let out a sigh. "Murderers of his class often fail to foresee how they will react after the event. They envisage themselves as made of steel and discover too late that they're frightened jelly babies."

"Fortunately for you," I remarked drily.

"Oh, we have to apply the correct chemistry as well. I believe catalyst is the word. That's us." He finished his tea and rose. "Anyway, I thought you'd be interested to hear the outcome."

"I'm much more than interested. I'm heartily relieved."

He laughed. "I'm afraid we shall need you as a witness at the trial."

"When will that be?"

"Some time next spring I would think."

"I'm going away in April for about ten days."

"Not Wagner again?"

I nodded. "In Vienna."

He shook his head in mock despair. "Some folk never learn, do they?"

The Spy Who Went to the Opera
by Edward D. Hoch

R and was on one of his periodic visits to London when his old chief Hastings took the two tickets from his desk and passed them over. "Do you and Leila ever go to the opera?" he asked.

"I doubt if I've been to one in fifteen years," Rand admitted, "though we sometimes watch one on television."

"Well, here are two good seats for *La Gioconda* at Covent Garden on Friday evening. I'm sure Leila will enjoy it."

Rand hesitated. He'd never known Hastings to be so generous without expecting something in return. Still, he'd helped the man out of a difficult situation last summer and perhaps this was merely Hastings's way of repaying him. "No strings?" he asked with a slight smile.

"Of course not." Hastings shuffled some papers on his desk. "Honestly, Rand, your old department isn't the same since you retired. All these bright young men solving ciphers with their computers. I doubt if one of them ever heard of a Vigenere or a Pigpen."

"I'm sure they get the job done."

"Do you ever think about coming back to us?"

"No." Rand started to put the tickets safely away in his billfold. "Leila and I are quite happy as we are."

"There's so much you could do, even on a part-time basis. Just talking to people, for instance." Hastings paused, averting Rand's gaze, and added, "Like Sergio Guendella."

"Who's Sergio Guendella?"

"I see you really don't keep up with opera. He's singing the role of Barnaba in *La Gioconda*."

"I see." Rand removed the tickets and dropped them back on Hastings' desk.

"Oh, really now, Rand—I'm not asking you to do anything except talk to the man. Go backstage after the performance and tell him how much you enjoyed it."

"How will they allow me backstage?"

"He'll be expecting you. He'll leave word that you and Leila are to be admitted to his dressing room."

"And what do I say to him?" Rand asked, still not retrieving the tickets from the desk.

Hastings leaned back in his chair, trying to appear at ease, as if the little favor he was asking was the most natural thing in the world. "Well, you see, the entire company's leaving for Warsaw soon. We'd like Sergio to contact a friend of ours there, if he's able."

"Since when do you use opera singers as couriers, Hastings?"

"Oh, it's nothing like that. But naturally he'll be entertained by the Polish arts world during his stay. He'll have natural social contact with some dissident factions."

"How would I approach him on this?"

"I don't have to tell you, Rand. Chat with him casually. Make the suggestion obliquely. You know the drill."

"Backstage, after the performance? Won't there be people dropping in?"

"You'll find a way. I have confidence in your abilities." Rand thought he said it with just a twinkle in his eyes. He sighed and picked up the tickets, wondering what Leila would think of all this.

Leila didn't think very much of it. "But Jeffery, you know that's the night of my lecture at the university!" she said. She taught a course in archaeology at nearby Reading and occasionally gave evening lectures on special occasions.

"I forgot," Rand said. "I'll phone Hastings right now and tell him to get someone else. He must have a dozen bright young chaps in the department who'd love a night at the opera."

But he found it was not so easy getting off Hastings's hook. "Oh, come now, Rand, couldn't you go alone?"

"I'd really stand out then, wouldn't I? A lone male going backstage to see Guendella after the show? Who knows? Maybe the Russians are watching the cast, too. They'd spot me in a moment without a wife in tow."

"Very well," Hastings said cheerfully. "I suppose we can supply you with a wife for the night."

Rand had no immediate answer.

It developed that the woman's name was Vesper O'Shea, and as Leila remarked upon hearing it, "Her name alone is enough to make me jealous."

Rand went off to London on the Friday afternoon train, having arranged to meet Vesper O'Shea for a bite to eat before the theater. They dined at an inexpensive restaurant on the Strand, a few blocks from the Royal Opera House at Covent Garden.

Vesper proved to be an attractive young woman in her late twenties who worked as a code clerk in Rand's old Department of Concealed Communications.

"I understand we're to be married for the night," she said with a smile, extending her hand in greeting.

"Only till after the opera, unfortunately," Rand replied, steering her to a table in a far corner of the crowded restaurant. After they'd ordered a drink, he asked, "Are you enjoying Double-C?"

"Oh, yes. I only wish I'd been there when you were in charge. They still talk of you as sort of a grand old man." She grinned at him. "Frankly, I'd expected someone with white hair and a cane."

"Thanks." He raised his drink to her. "How did you happen to get chosen for tonight?"

"Hastings knows I like opera. He thought I could fill you in on the libretto."

"He told you about seeing Sergio Guendella afterward?"

"Yes."

"What do you think?"

She shrugged. "I think it's ironic. Sergio plays a spy in the opera, you know. A man called Barnaba. He's a terrible villain—a spy for the Inquisition in seventeenth-century Venice who plots to destroy a nobleman in love with the title character so he can have her for himself. In the end, Gioconda kills herself rather than submit to him."

"Sounds like a lot of laughs."

"Well, one goes to an opera for the music, not the plot. Actually, La Gioconda is rarely performed in London, though it's had many successful productions in New York. Some of the greatest stars of opera have performed in it—Enrico Caruso, Ezio Pinza, Gladys Swarthout, Richard Tucker, Maria Callas, Eileen Farrell—"

"Did you memorize all that for my benefit?"

She shrugged. "I just have a good memory for facts. It comes in handy in this business." He wondered if she meant spying or the opera.

After dinner, they set off on foot for Covent Garden. When they'd taken their seats on the left side of the orchestra, near the front, Vesper had more facts for him. "The music in La Gioconda is by Ponchielli. He was Puccini's teacher and very famous in Italy, although La Gioconda is the only one of his operas to bring him universal renown. The libretto is by Tobia Gorrio, whose real name was Arrigo Boito. It was based upon a play by Victor Hugo and was first performed at La Scala in Milan on April 8, 1876."

"You even have the date memorized?"

"Well," she confessed, "I just read it here in the program."

The opera was in four acts, and as the curtain rose for the first of them Rand could see he was in for a long evening. The scene was a courtyard of a palace in Venice, where a festival was under way. As the townspeople sang, a tall burly man with a guitar stood off to one side, observing them. "That's Guendella," Vesper whispered. "He's disguised as one of the merrymakers in order to spy on them."

When the courtyard emptied of singers, Guendella as Barnaba took center stage and his powerful baritone filled the theater. He strummed his guitar as he sang, and though Rand could understand very little Italian he found himself marveling at the man's voice. "He's overheard something that tells him where a fugitive from the Inquisition is hiding," Vesper explained. "And he sings of his desire to snare his greatest prize—the street singer, La Gioconda."

As Barnaba finished, Gioconda herself entered with her blind mother. The part was sung by Amanda Faye, a young British soprano who had been getting much press attention because of her role opposite the great Guendella. Gradually, Rand found himself falling under the spell of the opera and he settled back to enjoy it.

But by the third act, he'd grown a bit restless again. Then scene two brought the familiar "Dance of the Hours," with a spectacularly staged masked ball, and his enthusiasm was rekindled. When the curtain finally descended following the death of Gioconda and Barnaba's last lament, Rand was on his feet applauding with everyone else.

"I think we've made an opera fan of you," Vesper announced happily.

"Not quite," Rand said. "But I appreciate good music. Guendella's voice is superb." He helped her squeeze through the crush of the crowd. "We'd better get backstage."

A young stagehand led them to the star's dressing room. Guendella was alone with Amanda Faye, the lovely Gioconda, as they entered. "Your guests are here, Sergio," she said with a smile. "I'll leave you with them and get out of my costume." She hurried out the door.

The baritone rose to greet them. "I couldn't introduce you," he said by way of apology. "The names—"

"I'm Jeffery Rand and this is my wife, Vesper. I wanted to tell you how much we enjoyed your performance."

"Ah, thank you. This is the first time I have done *Gioconda* in London, and the response has been overwhelming."

"I'm sure it will be just as overwhelming in Warsaw."

"Ah! You are a man who comes directly to the point! My manager said it was a matter in the national interest, and though I am not a British citizen I have always felt very close to your country. But you could have come to my hotel."

"It was felt this would seem more casual," Rand explained. "A great many people come backstage after a performance."

Guendella gestured toward his face. "Please—may I remove my makeup as we talk?"

"Certainly."

The baritone sat at the dressing table and smiled in the mirror at Vesper. "You have a charming young wife, Mr. Rand. It is good to have a young wife. It keeps one young in spirit."

Rand remained standing as he spoke. "Your journey to Warsaw could be quite important to us, sir. You will be there for two weeks, and we understand you are to be honored by several groups of Polish intellectuals, including some dissidents."

"That is correct." Guendella was watching Rand in the mirror as he wiped the makeup from his face. "But what do you want me to do? Will I be a spy for you?"

"No—nothing like that. But every country has its dissidents. We have them in England, Lord knows. We want you to speak with them, especially with certain names on a list I'll be giving you, and perhaps ask them a few questions. These are mainly people we've been unable to reach by any other means. It's not exactly a free society over there, you know. Talk to them, ask them questions, and bring us back any information you can about their situation. We especially want to know about the chances of a revolt in the aftermath of the recent unrest. And we want to know what sort of an independent leader the intellectuals would support."

Sergio Guendella nodded. "You want the name of someone acceptable to the West who could—"

They were interrupted by a sudden knock at the door. It opened at once and a youngish bearded man in a bathrobe entered. Rand recognized him as Franc Bougois, the French tenor who'd sung the part of the nobleman Enzo in the evening's performance. "Pardon, Sergio—I did not know you had visitors."

"What is it, Franc?"

"A package was left for you at the stage door. I was passing by and said I'd bring it to you."

"Thank you, Franc." Guendella took it and set it down on his dressing table without a second glance. "A box of candy, no doubt," he told Rand. "An Italian interviewer once printed a story about my love of candy. Now fans send it to me everywhere."

Franc Bougois retreated, closing the door after him. "He's a very good tenor," Vesper commented.

"One of the best," Guendella agreed, rubbing at his face with a moisturized tissue. "But back to the business at hand. You want me to seek out and question Polish dissidents, and bring you a report of what I learn, correct?"

"Correct," Rand said, "though you put it a bit more bluntly than I did."

"You understand that I cannot formally agree to work for you— for British intelligence, if I may use that phrase. But I will do what you wish. Where is this list of names?"

"Here in my pocket. Naturally we'll be happy to reimburse you for any expenses you incur, and to reward you with a small token of our appreciation."

Sergio Guendella held up a hand. "Do not speak of money. I am not in your employ."

"Of course not."

Rand handed him an envelope containing the list of names.

"We leave for Warsaw on the weekend," Guendella said.

Rand nodded and took Vesper's elbow. "The questions are in there, too. Good luck on your trip, and my thanks for a wonderful evening."

The baritone smiled. "*La Gioconda* is always a popular work. I suppose someone in your line can admire its violence and melodrama."

"I have no line of work," Rand said simply. "I'm retired."

He left the dressing room with Vesper, and after a quick drink at a nearby pub they parted. Rand caught the late train back to Reading, assuming incorrectly that the assignment was at an end.

* * *

When he woke up the following morning, the bedroom was bathed with sunlight and Leila was shaking him. "Jeffery, it's Hastings on the telephone from London. He says it's important."

He lifted his head from the pillow. "What time is it?"

"Quarter after eight. Time you were up, anyway."

He put on his slippers and robe and went to the phone. Hastings's voice was brisk and grim. "Rand, how did it go last night?"

"Fine. I thought Vesper would report to you."

"She's not in yet and there's a problem."

Rand sighed. There was always a problem. "What is it?"

"The Russian embassy sent a radio message to Moscow at 1:27 this morning, using their special diplomatic code—the one reserved for urgent dispatches. Do you want to hear it?"

"Not particularly." Still, the fact that Double-C could read the Russian diplomatic texts with such ease certainly interested him. These young chaps with their computers weren't half bad.

"Listen anyway," Hastings said. "It reads: *Guendella contacted by British agent on eve of Warsaw trip. Please instruct what action to take.* The signature is a code name: *Dean Lugel.*"

"Has there been a reply?"

"Unfortunately, we're not quite as skillful at reading the Moscow-to-London messages. Something about the Moscow computer being more sophisticated at generating one-time ciphers. We'll get it in time, but it might take a day or so. I'm worried that Guendella might be in danger."

"Put a guard on him," Rand suggested, wishing he was back in bed.

"It looks as if we'll have to scrub the whole Warsaw mission now. There seems to be a spy in the opera company."

"Perhaps."

"What other explanation could there be?"

Rand didn't answer. Instead he asked, "Have you ever intercepted previous messages from this Dean Lugel?"

"Not that we can find. But he's probably using a changeable code name."

"Or no code name at all, since the entire message was already encoded. I'd suggest you check the university directories to see if there really is a Dean Lugel. And the ecclesiastical directories as well."

"Good idea. We'll get on it." He hesitated. "But, Rand—"

"What is it?"

"I wish you'd come in on this. We think that a warning should be passed to Sergio Guendella. We owe the chap that much."

"All right," Rand decided. "I'll be in as soon as possible."

"I'll look for you."

"One other thing—"

"What's that?"

"Did Vesper know the nature of the mission before last night?"

"Just in general terms, not specifically. Why do you ask?"

"No reason. Just curious."

After he hung up, Rand got out the program for the opera and went over the names of the large cast. There was no Lugel among them, but then he hadn't expected to find one.

When he arrived in London, Rand telephoned the hotel where Sergio Guendella was staying and asked to be put through to his room. When the baritone answered, Rand told him, "This is your friend from backstage last night."

"Oh, yes—how are you?"

"Fine. But there's been a change of plans. The word seems to have gotten out."

"But how could that be?" Guendella asked, genuinely concerned.

"We're wondering the same thing. I called to warn you to be on your guard. We don't know what will happen."

"Who could—?"

"Did you talk to any of the other cast members about it? Amanda Faye or that Frenchman Bougois, for example?"

"Certainly not!"

"There must have been someone, after I left the theater. Did you talk to anyone at all last night?"

"No one but my manager."

"What did you tell him?"

"He knew someone was coming. Your people contacted him first, remember? I said you'd stopped in after the performance and we had a nice chat. I gave him no details."

"What's your manager's name?"

"Hyram Wendel. His office is here in London."

Rand jotted down the address and then, with a final warning to Guendella, hung up.

Twenty minutes later he stepped out of a taxi just off off Fleet Street and made his way up to a second-floor office in an old but well-tended building.

Hyram Wendel was a man in his sixties with an unlit cigar in his mouth. He sounded more American than British as he greeted Rand. "What can I do for you? You want to book Sergio, the world's greatest baritone? Why else come to me on a Saturday?"

"I believe you were contacted regarding his forthcoming journey to Warsaw," Rand began.

"The opera's producers handled all that."

"No, I mean someone here in London asked you if Sergio might be willing to do a little private business while he was there."

"Oh, you're with those guys! Look, I'll tell you, mister, I don't want to know anything about it. I asked Sergio and he said sure, and I passed the word along. That's his own business."

"Who did you tell about it?"

"No one, not even my wife! I know when it's smart to shut up."

He seemed sincere enough, but that proved little. "What about the others in the cast?" Rand asked. "Do you represent any of them?"

"Amanda. I manage Amanda Faye. She and Sergio are close friends, you know what I mean? He wanted her for Gioconda."

"Had she ever sung the role before?"

"Once, a few years back. Opera singers have a wide repertoire. Sometimes the same company will stage two or three different operas on successive nights."

"Do you know anything about Amanda's politics? Does she campaign for leftist causes?"

"No, nothing like that. She sticks to her singing."

"Well, thank you, Mr. Wendel. You've been a great help."

"I hope Sergio isn't in any kind of trouble."

"I hope so, too," Rand said.

When Rand reached his old office overlooking the Thames, he found that Hastings had been called away for a meeting with the Prime Minister. Instead, Vesper O'Shea was awaiting him in the outer office.

"Hastings left a message for you," she reported. "They've been unable to locate any Dean Lugel in church or education records, and he even checked the staff at the Russian embassy. None of them has a name even close to Lugel."

Rand nodded. "It's a code name. I suspected as much from the beginning. It probably changes every day or week, along with the cipher itself. Someone found out we'd contacted Sergio and had the embassy pass the word to Moscow."

"Someone in the opera company?"

"Probably, but not necessarily." He told her about his meeting with Sergio's manager. "I'd suggest we get over to Covent Garden. There's a matinee performance today."

When they were still a few blocks away in Vesper's Fiat, Rand heard the sirens. By the time they'd parked a block away, the area around the opera house was filled with police cars, fire engines, and ambulances.

"What is it?" Rand asked a constable as Vesper flashed her Whitehall identification.

"Looks like a bomb, sir. Backstage."

He allowed them to pass the police line and Rand led the way over fire hoses to the stage door. The dressing-room area was a mass of confusion and they were stopped twice before they managed to reach Sergio Guendella.

He sat dazed in his dressing room while ambulance attendants finished bandaging his hands and arms. "Only powder burns," one of them told Rand, taking him for a police official. "He was lucky."

"A bomb?"

A detective nodded. "But the main charge misfired. There was only a little flare-up when he opened the package."

Vesper tugged at Rand's sleeve, pointing to the scorched wrappings on the floor. "That looks like the package he received last night."

Rand crouched down in front of the dazed baritone and spoke to him. "This is Jeffery Rand. Do you recognize me?"

"Of course."

The detective looked nervous and tried to intervene. "Are you with the official police, sir?"

Vesper showed him her card. "This is a security matter."

"You'd better come with us in the ambulance, sir," the attendant was saying to Sergio. "We should take X-rays and check you over."

Suddenly Amanda Faye was in the room, pushing through the crowd to Guendella's side. "Sergio! What happened? They said there was a bomb!" She glared at Rand and Vesper. "Can't you move back and give him air?"

The baritone was struggling to stand up. "The matinee goes on in an hour—"

"Forget the matinee! Sit down and tell me what happened!"

"The box," he muttered. "The candy box that arrived last night. I unwrapped it and opened it, and it flared up!"

"It's a wonder you weren't killed!" She glanced around. "Where is this box?"

"The bomb squad removed it," someone explained.

Rand bent to pick up the torn wrappings, but other than Sergio's name and the address of the theater there were no markings. "Taking candy from a stranger wouldn't seem like a very good idea under any circumstances," he observed. "Mightn't it have been poisoned or drugged?"

"I am very careful," Sergio replied. "Usually there is a fan letter inside, but this time I found nothing."

Rand spotted the tenor, Franc Bougois, in the doorway. The crowd was thinning out as the firemen folded up the hoses and prepared to depart. "You brought that box to him last night after the performance," Rand said. "We were here at the time."

Bougois bristled at the veiled accusation. "It was left at the stage door. I know nothing of any bomb! Do you think I would harm

Sergio? Without him singing Barnaba, the whole production would shut down and we would all be out of work!"

Someone from the management arrived to announce that they were canceling the afternoon performance. Although Sergio Guendella agreed to go to the hospital, he insisted he would be back for the evening show. He wouldn't allow them to carry him out on a stretcher and insisted on walking to the ambulance.

Rand accompanied him to the stage door. "Forget our conversation of last night," he advised. "I'm sorry we got you into all this."

"My friend, it is not your fault. One attracts enemies at times."

"In the company? A jealous tenor, perhaps?"

Sergio smiled. "You are very perceptive. But bombing would not be his manner."

"He brought you the package. Could anyone else have tampered with it in your dressing room?"

"No. The wrappings were undamaged, and I locked it in my drawer overnight."

"Did you ever hear the name Lugel before?"

Guendella thought about it. "I do not believe so."

"He may be a dean of some sort. Or Dean may be his name."

"No. But one meets so many people—" The ambulance attendants led him to the waiting vehicle as a cheer went up from a crowd of onlookers. Sergio acknowledged the greeting with a wave of his hand and climbed inside.

"We were too late," Vesper observed as the ambulance sped off.

"I've been a great deal later than this on occasion. At least he's not dead or badly injured."

"Hastings said this Lugel sent a message to Moscow. Do you think a reply came back to kill Sergio?"

"I don't know, but I think we should pay a return visit to the opera tonight. Just to make sure the next attempt isn't successful."

Somewhat to Rand's surprise, Hastings decided to accompany them to the evening performance of La Gioconda. "But won't that blow our cover?" Rand argued. "A great many people know you by sight."

"Not so many as you'd think. Government regulations prevent

the press from publishing my name or photograph in connection with my intelligence work. If they know me, chances are they know you as well."

There were three tickets awaiting them at the Covent Garden box office. As they settled into their seats, an announcement was made that Sergio Guendella would be playing the role of Barnaba with bandaged hands as the result of an injury earlier in the day. Rand opened his program and settled back for the overture, a sweeping refrain based upon a theme from one of the first-act songs.

He glanced down at the title page of the program.

And suddenly he knew. It was as clear as that.

He sat through the four acts of the opera with growing impatience, anxious to get backstage. Finally, when Gioconda had once again plunged the dagger into her chest and Barnaba had sung his lament, Rand rose with the others for a standing ovation at the curtain call. Then he told Hastings, "Come on. We have to get backstage."

They hurried down the side aisle, with Vesper trailing along. "What's the rush?" she asked.

"I know who put the bomb in Sergio's candy box, and who sent the message to Moscow."

"This Dean Lugel fellow?" Hastings asked.

"Yes, Dean Lugel."

Then they were inside the dressing room and Rand had introduced Hastings. "Did you enjoy the performance?" Sergio asked him.

"Very much. Until that bomb, I was hoping you could demonstrate for us that you were as good a spy offstage as on."

"I think he's already demonstrated that," Rand said quietly. "How long have you been working for the Russians, Sergio?"

The blood drained from Guendella's face as he sat staring up at Rand. "I do not know what you mean."

"What I mean is that British intelligence tried to recruit you for exactly the same sort of mission you were already performing for the Russians. I imagine you've been contacting dissidents and leftist groups in western Europe and reporting back to Moscow on those that seemed ripe for further contact. You were quite willing to work for us, and I imagine you were just as willing to work for the other side when they approached you."

"You cannot know this!" the baritone protested. Then, turning to Hastings and Vesper, he said, "Do not believe a word of it! I was almost killed by their bomb!"

"The candy box supposedly containing the bomb was delivered to you last night," Rand observed, "hours before the spy's message requesting instructions went off to Moscow. You told me yourself that the wrappings hadn't been tampered with and the box was locked up overnight. So there could have been no bomb in that box when it was delivered—unless we're to believe in the coincidence of some fan with a grudge against you choosing this moment to strike. But such a person would have been far more likely to poison the candy than to rig up a bomb inside the box."

"Why would I risk killing myself with a bomb?" Sergio demanded. "The whole thing is foolishness!"

"There was no risk. You very carefully rigged it so you'd get powder burns on the hands and nothing more. The rest was acting. You *are* a superb actor, after all. As for your reason, when I phoned to tell you the word was out, you saw that you had to protect your own position. You feared we might begin to suspect you'd sent that message to Moscow yourself, so you faked the bombing."

Hastings was still frowning. "You mean Sergio is the mysterious Dean Lugel?"

Rand nodded. "We should have known it at once. This opera he's performing is about a spy, and the libretto is by Tobia Gorrio, whose real name was Arrigo Boito. Vesper told me that after reading the program last night and I was reminded of it when I looked at the program this evening. The author hid his identity with a simple anagram. Isn't it likely that a spy playing the lead in La Gioconda might choose to do the same thing? Dean Lugel is merely an anagram for Guendella."

The fight went out of Sergio, but Rand persisted. "He had the Russian embassy send his message telling Moscow he'd been approached by us, and asking for instructions. Then he faked the bomb attempt to keep us from suspecting him."

"What sort of spy would use a simple anagram to conceal his identity?" Vesper asked.

"A not very good one," Rand admitted. "But keep in mind that the entire message was transmitted in diplomatic code. It probably seemed safe enough to him at the time."

Hastings turned to Sergio Guendella. "How can we let you go back to them? You'll tell them we broke their code."

"Look," Sergio pleaded, holding out his hands. "I only want to sing, not to spy! I agreed to work for the Russians because I thought it would bring peace. That is why I sent the message, to warn them you wished to stir up the Polish dissidents. Maybe I was wrong. Maybe we should talk more. I will do whatever you ask."

Rand decided his work was finished. The rest was for Hastings and Vesper to work out. As he slipped out the stage door and headed for Paddington Station, he was glad to be retired.

The Right to Sing the Blues

by John Lutz

"There's this that you need to know about jazz," Fat Jack McGee told Nudger with a smile. "You don't need to know a thing about it to enjoy it, and that's all you need to know." He tossed back his huge head, jowls quivering, and drained the final sip of brandy from his crystal snifter. "It's feel." He used a white napkin to dab at his lips with a very fat man's peculiar delicacy. "Jazz is pure feel."

"Does Willy Hollister have the feel?" Nudger asked. He pushed his plate away, feeling full to the point of being bloated. The only portion of the gourmet lunch Fat Jack had bought him that remained untouched was the grits.

"Willy Hollister," Fat Jack said, with something like reverence, "plays ultrafine piano."

A white-vested waiter appeared like a native from around a potted palm, carrying chicory coffee on a silver tray, and placed cups before Nudger and Fat Jack. "Then what's your problem with Hollister?" Nudger asked, sipping the thick rich brew. He rated it delicious. "Didn't you hire him to play his best piano at your club?"

"Hey, there's no problem with his music," Fat Jack said. "But first, Nudger, I gotta know if you can hang around New Orleans till you can clear up this matter." Fat Jack's tiny pinkish eyes glittered with mean humor. "For a fat fee, of course."

Nudger knew the fee would be adequate. Fat Jack had a bank account as obese as his body, and he had, in fact, paid Nudger a sizable sum just to travel to New Orleans and sit in the Magnolia Blossom restaurant over lunch and listen while Fat Jack talked. The question Nudger now voiced was: "Why me?"

"Because I know a lady from your fair city." Fat Jack mentioned a name. "She says you're tops at your job; she don't say that about many.

". . . And because of your collection," Fat Jack added. An ebony dribble of coffee dangled in liquid suspension from his triple chin, glittering as he talked. "I hear you collect old jazz records."

"I used to," Nudger said a bit wistfully. "I had Willie the Lion. Duke Ellington and Mary Ann Williams from their Kansas City days."

"How come had?" Fat Jack asked.

"I sold the collection," Nudger said. "To pay the rent one dark month." He gazed beyond green palm fronds, out the window and through filigreed black wrought iron, at the tourists half a block away on Bourbon Street, at the odd combination of French and Spanish architecture and black America and white suits and broiling half-tropical sun that was New Orleans, where jazz lived as in no other place. "Damned rent," he muttered.

"Amen." Fat Jack was kidding not even himself. He hadn't worried about paying the rent in years. The drop of coffee released its grip on his chin, plummeted, and stained his white shirtfront. "So will you stay around town a while?"

Nudger nodded. His social and business calendars weren't exactly booked solid.

"Hey, it's not Hollister himself who worries me," Fat Jack said, "it's Ineida Collins. She's singing at the club now, and if she keeps practicing, someday she'll be mediocre. I'm not digging at her, Nudger; that's an honest assessment."

"Then why did you hire her?"

"Because of David Collins. He owns a lot of the French Quarter. He owns a piece of the highly successful restaurant where we now sit. In every parish in New Orleans, he has more clout than a ton of charge cards. And he's as skinny and ornery as I am fat and nice."

Nudger took another sip of coffee.

"And he asked you to hire Ineida Collins?"

"You're onto it. Ineida is his daughter. She wants to make it as a singer. And she will, if Dad has to buy her a recording studio, at double the fair price. Since David Collins also owns the building my club is in, I thought I'd acquiesce when his daughter auditioned for a job. And Ineida isn't really so bad that she embarrasses anyone but herself. I call it diplomacy."

"I thought you were calling it trouble," Nudger said. "I thought that was why you hired me."

Fat Jack nodded, ample jowls spilling over his white collar. "So it became," he said. "Hollister, you see, is a handsome young dude, and within the first week Ineida was at the club, he put some moves on her. They became fast friends. They've now progressed beyond mere friendship."

"You figure he's attracted to Dad's money?"

"Nothing like that," Fat Jack said. "When I hired Ineida, David Collins insisted I keep her identity a secret. It was part of the deal. So she sings under the stage name Ineida Mann, which most likely is a gem from her dad's advertising department."

"I still don't see your problem," Nudger said.

"Hollister doesn't set right with me, and I don't know exactly why. I do know that if he messes up Ineida in some way, David Collins will see to it that I'm playing jazz on the Butte-Boise-Anchorage circuit."

"Nice cities," Nudger remarked, "but not jazz towns. I see your problem."

"So find out about Willy Hollister for me," Fat Jack implored. "Check him out, declare him pass or fail, but put my mind at ease either way. That's all I want, an easeful mind."

"Even we tough private eye guys want that," Nudger said.

Fat Jack removed his napkin from his lap and raised a languid plump hand. A waiter who had been born just to respond to that signal scampered over with the check. Fat Jack accepted a tiny ballpoint pen and signed with a ponderous yet elegant flourish. Nudger watched him help himself to a mint. It was like watching the grace and dexterity of an elephant picking up a peanut. Huge as Fat Jack was, he moved as if he weighed no more than ten or twelve pounds.

"I gotta get back, Nudger. Do some paperwork, count some money." He stood up, surprisingly tall in his tan slacks and white linen sport coat. Nudger thought it was a neat coat; he decided he might buy one and wear it winter and summer. "Drop around the club about eight o'clock tonight," Fat Jack said. "I'll fill you in on whatever else you need to know, and I'll show you Willy Hollister and Ineida. Maybe you'll get to hear her sing."

"While she's singing," Nudger said, "maybe we can discuss my fee."

Fat Jack grinned, his vast jowls defying gravity grandly. "Hey, you and me're gonna get along fine." He winked and moved away among the tables, tacking toward the door, dwarfing the other diners.

The waiter refilled Nudger's coffee cup. He sat sipping chicory brew and watching Fat Jack McGee walk down the sunny sidewalk toward Bourbon Street. He sure had a jaunty, bouncy kind of walk for a fat man.

Nudger wasn't as anxious about the fee as Fat Jack thought, though the subject was of more than passing interest. Actually, he had readily taken the case because years ago, at a club in St. Louis, he'd heard Fat Jack McGee play clarinet in the manner that had made him something of a jazz legend, and he'd never forgotten. Real jazz fans are hooked forever.

He needed to hear that clarinet again.

Fat Jack's club was on Dexter, half a block off Bourbon Street. Nudger paused at the entrance and looked up at its red and green neon sign. There was a red neon Fat Jack himself, a portly, herky-jerky, illuminated figure that jumped about with the same seeming lightness and jauntiness as the real Fat Jack.

Trumpet music from inside the club was wafting out almost palpably into the hot humid night. People were coming and going, among them a few obvious tourists, making the Bourbon Street rounds. But Nudger got the impression that most of Fat Jack's customers were folks who took their jazz seriously and were there for music, not atmosphere.

The trumpet stairstepped up to an admirable high C and wild applause. Nudger went inside and looked around. Dim, smoky, lots of people at lots of tables, men in suits and in jeans and T-shirts, women in long dresses and in casual slacks. The small stage was empty now; the band was between sets. Customers were milling around, stacking up at the bar along one wall. Waitresses in "Fat Jack's" T-shirts were bustling about with trays of drinks. Near the left of the stage was a polished, dark, upright piano that gleamed like a new car even in the dimness. Fat Jack's was everything a jazz club should be, Nudger decided.

Feeling at home, he made his way to the bar and after a five-minute wait ordered a mug of draft beer. The mug was frosted, the beer ice-flecked.

The lights brightened and dimmed three times, apparently a signal the regulars at Fat Jack's understood, for they began a general movement back toward their tables. Then the lights dimmed considerably, and the stage, with its gleaming piano, was suddenly the only illuminated area in the place. A tall, graceful man in his early thirties walked onstage to the kind of scattered but enthusiastic applause that suggests respect and a common bond between performer and audience. The man smiled faintly at the applause and sat down at the piano. He had pained, haughty features, and blond hair that curled above the collar of his black Fat Jack's shirt. The muscles in his bare arms were corded; his hands appeared elegant yet very strong. He was Willy Hollister, the main gig, the one the paying customers had come to hear. The place got quiet, and he began to play.

The song was a variation of *Good Woman Gone Bad*, an old number originally written for tenor sax. Hollister played it his way, and two bars into it Nudger knew he was better than good and nothing but bad luck could keep him from being great. He was backed by brass and a snare drum, but he didn't need it; he didn't need a thing in this world but that piano and you could tell it just by looking at the rapt expression on his aristocratic face.

"Didn't I tell you it was all there?" Fat Jack said softly beside Nudger. "Whatever else there is about him, the man can play piano."

Nudger nodded silently. Jazz basically is black music, but the fair, blond Hollister played it with all the soul and pain of its genesis. He finished up the number to riotous applause that quieted only when he swung into another, a blues piece. He sang that one while his hands worked the piano. His voice was as black as his music; in his tone, his inflection, there seemed to dwell centuries of suffering.

"I'm impressed," Nudger said, when the applause for the blues number had died down.

"You and everyone else." Fat Jack was sipping absinthe from a gold-rimmed glass. "Hollister won't be playing here much longer before moving up the show business ladder—not for what I'm paying him, and I'm paying him plenty."

"How did you happen to hire him?"

"He came recommended by a club owner in Chicago. Seems he started out in Cleveland playing small rooms, then moved up to better things in Kansas City, then Rush Street in Chicago. All I had to do was hear him play for five minutes to know I wanted to hire him. It's like catching a Ray Charles or a Garner on the way up."

"So what specifically is there about Hollister that bothers you?" Nudger asked. "Why shouldn't he be seeing Ineida Collins?"

Fat Jack scrunched up his padded features, seeking the word that might convey the thought. "His music is . . . uneven."

"That's hardly a crime," Nudger said, "especially if he can play so well when he's right."

"He ain't as right as I've heard him," Fat Jack said. "Believe me, Hollister can be even better than he was tonight. But it's not really his music that concerns me. Hollister acts strange at times, secretive. Sam Judman, the drummer, went by his apartment last week, found the door unlocked, and let himself in to wait for Hollister to get home. When Hollister discovered him there; he beat him up—with his fists. Can you imagine a piano player like Hollister using his hands for that?" Fat Jack looked as if he'd discovered a hair in his drink.

"So he's obsessively secretive. What else?" What am I doing, Nudger asked himself, trying to talk myself out of a job?

But Fat Jack went on. "Hollister has seemed troubled, jumpy and unpredictable, for the last month. He's got problems, and like I told you, if he's seeing Ineida Collins, I got problems. I figure it'd be wise to learn some more about Mr. Hollister."

"The better to know his intentions, as they used to say."

"And in some quarters still say."

The lights did their dimming routine again, the crowd quieted, and Willy Hollister was back at the piano. But this time the center of attention was the tall, dark-haired girl leaning with one hand on the piano, her other hand delicately holding a microphone. Inside her plain navy blue dress was a trim figure. She had nice ankles, a nice smile. Nice was a word that might have been coined for her. A stage name like Ineida Mann didn't fit her at all. She was prom queen and Girl Scouts and PTA and looked as if she'd blush at an off-color joke. But it crossed Nudger's mind that maybe it was simply a role; maybe she was playing for contrast.

Fat Jack knew what Nudger was thinking. "She's as straight and naive as she looks," he said. "But she'd like to be something else, to learn all about life and love in a few easy lessons."

Someone in the backup band had announced Ineida Mann, and she began to sing, the plaintive lyrics of an old blues standard. She had control but no range. Nudger found himself listening to the backup music, which included a smooth clarinet solo. The band liked Ineida and went all out to envelop her in good sound, but the audience at Fat Jack's was too smart for that. Ineida finished to light applause, bowed prettily, and made her exit. Competent but nothing special, and looking as if she'd just wandered in from suburbia. But this was what she wanted and her rich father was getting it for her. Parental love could be as blind as the other kind.

"So how are you going to get started on this thing?" Fat Jack asked. "You want me to introduce you to Hollister and Ineida?"

"Usually I begin a case by discussing my fee and signing a contract," Nudger said.

Fat Jack waved an immaculately manicured, ring-adorned hand.

"Don't worry about the fee," he said. "Hey, let's make it whatever you usually charge plus twenty percent plus expenses. Trust me on that."

That sounded fine to Nudger, all except the trusting part. He reached into his inside coat pocket, withdrew his roll of antacid tablets, thumbed back the aluminum foil, and popped one of the white disks into his mouth, all in one practiced, smooth motion.

"What's that stuff for?" Fat Jack asked.

"Nervous stomach," Nudger explained.

"You oughta try this," Fat Jack said, nodding toward his absinthe. "Eventually it eliminates the stomach altogether."

Nudger winced. "I want to talk with Ineida," he said, "but it would be best if we had our conversation away from the club."

Fat Jack pursed his lips and nodded. "I can give you her address. She doesn't live at home with her father; she's in a little apartment over on Beulah Street. It's all part of the making-it-on-her-own illusion. Anything else?"

"Maybe. Do you still play the clarinet?"

Fat Jack cocked his head and looked curiously at Nudger, one tiny eye squinting through the tobacco smoke that hazed the air around the bar. "Now and again, but only on special occasions."

"Why don't we make the price of this job my usual fee plus only ten percent plus you do a set with the clarinet this Saturday night?"

Fat Jack beamed, then threw back his head and let out a roaring laugh that turned heads and seemed to shake the bottles on the back bar. "Agreed! You're a find, Nudger! First you trust me to pay you without a contract, then you lower your fee and ask for a clarinet solo instead of money. There's no place you can spend a clarinet solo! Hey, I like you, but you're not much of a businessman."

Nudger smiled and sipped his beer. Fat Jack hadn't bothered to find out the amount of Nudger's usual fee, so all this talk about percentages meant nothing. If detectives weren't good businessmen, neither were jazz musicians. He handed Fat Jack a pen and a club matchbook. "How about that address?"

Beulah Street was narrow and crooked, lined with low houses of French-Spanish architecture, an array of arches, pastel stucco, and ornamental wrought iron. The houses had long ago been divided into apartments, each with a separate entrance. Behind each apartment was a small courtyard.

Nudger found Ineida Collins's address. It belonged to a pale yellow structure with a weathered tile roof and a riot of multicolored bougainvillea blooming wild halfway up one cracked and often-patched stucco wall.

He glanced at his wristwatch. Ten o'clock. If Ineida wasn't awake by now, he decided, she should be. He stepped up onto the small red brick front porch and worked the lion's head knocker on a plank door supported by huge black iron hinges.

Ineida came to the door without delay. She didn't appear at all sleepy after her late-night stint at Fat Jack's. Her dark hair was tied back in a French braid. She was wearing slacks and a peach-colored silky blouse. Even the harsh sunlight was kind to her; she looked young, as inexperienced and naive as Fat Jack said she was.

Nudger told her he was a writer doing a piece on Fat Jack's club. "I heard you sing last night," he said. "It really was something to see. I thought it might be a good idea if we talked."

It was impossible for her to turn down what in her mind was a celebrity interview. She lit up bright enough to pale the sunlight and invited Nudger inside.

Her apartment was tastefully but inexpensively furnished. There was an imitation Oriental rug on the hardwood floor, lots of rattan furniture, a Casablanca overhead fan rotating its wide flat blades slowly and casting soothing, flickering shadows. Through sheer beige curtains the apartment's courtyard was visible, well tended and colorful.

"Can I get you a cup of coffee, Mr. Nudger?" Ineida asked.

Nudger told her thanks, watched the switch of her trim hips as she walked into the small kitchen. From where he sat he could see a Mr. Coffee brewer on the sink, its glass pot half full. Ineida poured, returned with two mugs of coffee.

"How old are you, Ineida?" he asked.

"Twenty-three."

"Then you haven't been singing for all that many years."

She sat down, placed her steaming coffee mug on a coaster.

"About five, actually. I sang in school productions, then studied for a while in New York. I've been singing at Fat Jack's for about two months. I love it."

"The crowd there seems to like you," Nudger lied. He watched her smile and figured the lie was a worthy one. He pretended to take notes while he asked her a string of writer-like questions, pumping up her ego. It was an ego that would inflate only so far. Nudger decided that he like Ineida Collins and hoped she would hurry up and realize she wasn't Ineida Mann.

"I'm told that you and Will Hollister are pretty good friends."

Her mood changed abruptly. Suspicion shone in her dark eyes, and the youthful smiling mouth became taut and suddenly ten years older.

"You're not a magazine writer," she said, in a betrayed voice.

Nudger's stomach gave a mule-like kick. "No, I'm not," he admitted.

"Then who are you?"

"Someone concerned about your well-being." Antacid time. He popped one of the white tablets into his mouth and chewed.

"Father sent you."

"No," Nudger said.

"Liar," she told him. "Get out."

"I'd like to talk with you about Willy Hollister," Nudger persisted. In his business persistence paid, one way or the other. He could only hope it wouldn't be the other.

"Get out," Ineida repeated. "Or I'll call the police."

Within half a minute Nudger was outside again on Beulah Street, looking at the uncompromising barrier of Ineida's closed door. Apparently she was touchy on the subject of Willy Hollister. Nudger slipped another antacid between his lips, turned his back to the warming sun, and began walking.

He'd gone half a block when he realized that he was casting three shadows. He stopped. The middle shadow stopped also, but the larger shadows on either side kept advancing. The large bodies that cast those shadows were suddenly standing in front of Nudger, and two very big men were staring down at him. One was smiling, one wasn't. Considering the kind of smile it was, that didn't make much difference.

"We noticed you talking to Miss Mann," the one on the left said. He had wide cheekbones, dark, pockmarked skin, and gray eyes that gave no quarter. "Whatever you said seemed to upset her." His accent was a cross between a southern drawl and clipped French. Nudger recognized it as Cajun. The Cajuns were a tough, predominantly French people who had settled southern Louisiana but never themselves.

Nudger let himself hope and started to walk on. The second man, who was shorter but had a massive neck and shoulders, shuffled forward like a heavyweight boxer, to block his way. Nudger swallowed his antacid tablet.

"You nervous, friend?" the boxer asked in the same rich Cajun accent.

"Habitually."

Pockmarked said, "We have an interest in Miss Mann's welfare. What were you talking to her about?"

"The conversation was private. Do you two fellows mind introducing yourselves?"

"We mind," the boxer said. He was smiling again, nastily. Nudger noticed that the tip of his right eyebrow had turned white where it was crossed by a thin scar.

"Then I'm sorry, but we have nothing to talk about."

Pockmarked shook his head patiently in disagreement. "We have this to talk about, my friend. There are parts of this great state of Looziahna that are vast swampland. Not far from where we stand, the bayou is wild. It's the home of a surprising number of alligators. People go into the bayou, and some of them never come out. Who knows about them? After a while, who cares?" The cold gray eyes had diamond chips in them. "You understand my meaning?"

Nudger nodded. He understood. His stomach understood.

"I think we've made ourselves clear," the boxer said. "We aren't nice men, sir. It's our business not to be nice, and it's our pleasure. So a man like yourself, sir, a reasonable man in good health, should listen to us and stay away from Miss Mann."

"You mean Miss Collins."

"I mean Miss Ineida Mann." He said it with the straight face of a true professional.

"Why don't you tell Willy Hollister to stay away from her?" Nudger asked.

"Mr. Hollister is a nice young man of Miss Mann's own choosing," Pockmarked said with an odd courtliness. "You she obviously doesn't like. You upset her. That upsets us."

"And me and Frick don't like to be upset," the boxer said. He closed a powerful hand on the lapel of Nudger's sport jacket, not pushing or pulling in the slightest, merely squeezing the material. Nudger could feel the vibrant force of the man's strength as if it were electrical current. "Behave yourself," the boxer hissed through his fixed smile.

He abruptly released his grip, and both men turned and walked away.

Nudger looked down at his abused lapel. It was as crimped as if it had been wrinkled in a vise for days. He wondered if the dry cleaners could do anything about it when they pressed the coat.

Then he realized he was shaking. He loathed danger and had no taste for violence. He needed another antacid tablet and then, even though it was early, a drink.

New Orleans was turning out to be an exciting city, but not in the way the travel agencies and the chamber of commerce advertised.

"You're no jazz writer," Willy Hollister said to Nudger, in a small back room of Fat Jack's club. It wasn't exactly a dressing room, though at times it served as such. It was a sort of all-purpose place where quick costume changes were made and breaks were taken between sets. The room's pale green paint was faded and peeling, and a steam pipe jutted from floor to ceiling against one wall. Yellowed show posters featuring jazz greats were taped here and there behind the odd assortment of worn furniture. There were mingled scents of stale booze and tobacco smoke.

"But I am a jazz fan," Nudger said. "Enough of one to know how good you are, and that you play piano in a way that wasn't self-taught." He smiled. "I'll bet you even read music."

"You have to read music," Hollister said rather haughtily, "to graduate from Juilliard."

Even Nudger knew that Juilliard graduates weren't slouches. "So you have a classical background," he said.

"That's nothing rare; lots of jazz musicians have classical roots."

Nudger studied Hollister as the pianist spoke. Offstage, Hollister appeared older. His blond hair was thinning on top and his features were losing their boyishness, becoming craggy. His complexion was an unhealthy yellowish hue. He was a hunter, was this boy. Life's sad wisdom was in his eyes, resting on its haunches and ready to spring.

"How well do you know Ineida Mann?" Nudger asked.

"Well enough to know you've been bothering her," Hollister replied, with a bored yet wary expression. "We don't know what your angle is, but I suggest you stop. Don't bother trying to get any information out of me, either."

"I'm interested in jazz," Nudger said.

"Among other things."

"Like most people, I have more than one interest."

"Not like me, though," Hollister said. "My only interest is my music."

"What about Miss Mann?"

"That's none of your business." Hollister stood up, neatly but ineffectively snubbed out the cigarette he'd been smoking, and seemed to relish leaving it to smolder to death in the ashtray. "I've got a number coming up in a few minutes." He tucked in his Fat Jack's T-shirt and looked severe. "I don't particularly want to see you any more, Nudger. Whoever, whatever you are, it doesn't mean burned grits to me as long as you leave Ineida alone."

"Before you leave," Nudger said, "can I have your autograph?"

Incredibly, far from being insulted by this sarcasm, Hollister scrawled his signature on a nearby folded newspaper and tossed it to him. Nudger took that as a measure of the man's artistic ego, and despite himself he was impressed. All the ingredients of greatness resided in Willy Hollister, along with something else.

Nudger went back out into the club proper. He peered through the throng of jazz lovers and saw Fat Jack leaning against the bar. As Nudger was making his way across the dim room toward him, he spotted Ineida at one of the tables. She was wearing a green sequined blouse that set off her dark hair and eyes, and Nudger regretted that she couldn't sing as well as she looked. She glanced at him, recognized him, and quickly turned away to listen to a graying, bearded man who was one of her party.

"Hey, Nudger," Fat Jack said, when Nudger had reached the bar, "you sure you know what you're doing, old sleuth? You ain't exactly pussyfooting. Ineida asked me about you, said you'd bothered her at home. *Hollister* asked me who you were. The precinct captain asked me the same question."

Nudger's stomach tightened. "A New Orleans police captain?"

Fat Jack nodded. "Captain Marrivale." He smiled broad and bold, took a sip of absinthe. "You make ripples big enough to swamp boats."

"What I'd like to do now," Nudger said, "is take a short trip."

"Lots of folks would like for you to do that."

"I need to go to Cleveland, Kansas City, and Chicago," Nudger said. "A couple of days in each city. I've got to find out more about Willy Hollister. Are you willing to pick up the tab?"

"I don't suppose you could get this information with long-distance phone calls?"

"Not and get it right."

"When do you plan on leaving?"

"As soon as I can. Tonight."

Fat Jack nodded. He produced an alligator-covered checkbook, scribbled in it, tore out a check, and handed it to Nudger. Nudger couldn't make out the amount in the faint light. "If you need more, let me know," Fat Jack said. His smile was luminous in the dimness. "Hey, make it a fast trip, Nudger."

A week later Nudger was back in New Orleans, sitting across from Fat Jack McGee in the club owner's second floor office. "There's a pattern," he said, "sometimes subtle, sometimes strong, but always there, like in a forties Ellington piece."

"So tell me about it," Fat Jack said. "I'm an Ellington fan."

"I did some research," Nudger said, "read some old reviews, went to clubs and musicians' union halls and talked to people in the jazz communities where Willy Hollister played. He always started strong, but his musical career was checkered with flat spots, lapses. During those times, Hollister was just an ordinary performer."

Fat Jack appeared concerned, tucked his chin back into folds of flesh, and said, "That explains why he's falling off here."

"But the man is still making great music," Nudger said.

"Slipping from great to good," Fat Jack said. "Good jazz artists in New Orleans I can hire by the barrelful."

"There's something else about Willy Hollister," Nudger said. "Something that nobody picked up on because it spanned several years and three cities."

Fat Jack looked interested. If his ears hadn't been almost enveloped by overblown flesh, they would have perked up.

"Hollister had a steady girlfriend in each of these cities. All three women disappeared. Two were rumored to have left town on their own, but nobody knows where they went. The girlfriend in Cleveland, the first one, simply disappeared. She's still on the missing persons list."

"Whoo boy!" Fat Jack said. He began to sweat. He pulled a white handkerchief the size of a flag from the pocket of his sport jacket and mopped his brow, just like Satchmo but without the grin and trumpet.

"Sorry," Nudger said. "I didn't mean to make you uncomfortable."

"You're doing your job, is all," Fat Jack assured him. "But that's bad information to lay on me. You think Hollister had anything to do with the disappearances?"

Nudger shrugged. "Maybe the women themselves, and not Hollister, had to do with it. They were all the sort that traveled light and often. Maybe they left town of their own accord. Maybe for some reason they felt they had to get away from Hollister."

"I wish Ineida would want to get away from him," Fat Jack muttered. "But Jeez, not like that. Her old man'd boil me down for axle grease. But then she's not cut from the same mold as those other girls; she's not what she's trying to be and she's strictly local."

"The only thing she and those other women have in common is Willy Hollister."

Fat Jack leaned back, and the desk chair creaked in protest. Nudger, who had been hired to solve a problem, had so far only brought to light the seriousness of that problem. The big man didn't have to ask "What now?" It was written in capital letters on his face.

"You could fire Willy Hollister," Nudger said.

Fat Jack shook his head. "Ineida would follow him, maybe get mad at me and sic her dad on the club."

"And Hollister is still packing customers into the club every night."

"That, too," Fat Jack admitted. Even the loosest businessman could see the profit in Willy Hollister's genius. "For now," he said, "we'll let things slide while you continue to watch." He dabbed at his forehead again with the wadded handkerchief.

"Hollister doesn't know who I am," Nudger said, "but he knows who I'm not and he's worried. My presence might keep him above-board for a while."

"Fine, as long as a change of scenery isn't involved. I can't afford to have her wind up like those other women, Nudger."

"Speaking of winding up," Nudger said, "do you know anything about a couple of muscular robots? One has a scar across his right eyebrow and a face like an ex-pug's. His partner has a dark mustache, sniper's eyes, and is named Frick. Possibly the other is Frack. They both talk with thick Cajun accents."

Fat Jack raised his eyebrows. "Rocko Boudreau and Dwayne Frick," he said, with soft, terror-inspired awe. "They work for David Collins."

"I figured they did. They warned me to stay away from Ineida." Nudger felt his intestines twist into advanced Boy Scout knots. He got out his antacid tablets. "They suggested I might take up post-mortem residence in the swamp." As he recalled his conversation with Frick and Frack, Nudger again felt a dark near-panic well up in him. Maybe it was because he was here in this small office with the huge and terrified Fat Jack McGee; maybe fear actually was contagious. He offered Fat Jack an antacid tablet.

Fat Jack accepted.

"I'm sure their job is to look after Ineida without her knowing it," Nudger said. "Incidentally, they seem to approve of her seeing Willy Hollister."

"That won't help me if anything happens to Ineida that's in any way connected to the club," Fat Jack said.

Nudger stood up. He was tired. His back still ached from sitting in an airline seat that wouldn't recline, and his stomach was still busy trying to digest itself. "I'll phone you if I hear any more good news."

Fat Jack mumbled something unintelligible and nodded, lost in his own dark apprehensions, a ponderous man grappling with ponderous problems. One of his inflated hands floated up in a parting gesture as Nudger left the stifling office. What he hadn't told Fat Jack was that immediately after each woman had disappeared, Hollister had regained his tragic, soulful touch on the piano.

When Nudger got back to his hotel, he was surprised to open the door to his room and see a man sitting in a chair by the window. It was the big blue armchair that belonged near the door.

When Nudger entered, the man turned as if resenting the interruption, as if it were his room and Nudger the interloper. He stood up and smoothed his light tan suit coat. He was a smallish man with a triangular face and very springy red hair that grew in a sharp widow's peak. His eyes were dark and intense. He resembled a fox. With a quick and graceful motion he put a paw into a pocket for a wallet-sized leather folder, flipped it open to reveal a badge.

"Police Captain Marrivale, I presume," Nudger said. He shut the door.

The redheaded man nodded and replaced his badge in his pocket. "I'm Fred Marrivale," he confirmed. "I heard you were back in town. I think we should talk." He shoved the armchair around to face the room instead of the window and sat back down, as familiar as old shoes.

Nudger pulled out the small wooden desk chair and also sat, facing Marrivale. "Are you here on official business, Captain Marri-vale?"

Marrivale smiled. He had tiny sharp teeth behind thin lips. "You know how it is, Nudger, a cop is always a cop."

"Sure. And that's the way it is when we go private," Nudger told him. "A confidential investigator is always that, no matter where he is or whom he's talking to."

"Which is kinda why I'm here," Marrivale said. "It might be better if you were someplace else."

Nudger was incredulous. His nervous stomach believed what he'd just heard, but he didn't. "You're actually telling me to get out of town?"

Marrivale gave a kind of laugh, but there was no glint of amuse-ment in his sharp eyes. "I'm not authorized to tell anyone to get out of town, Nudger. I'm not the sheriff and this isn't Dodge City."

"I'm glad you realize that," Nudger told him, "because I can't leave yet. I've got business here."

"I know about your business."

"Did David Collins send you to talk to me?"

Marrivale had a good face for policework; there was only the slightest change of expression. "We can let that question go by," he said, "and I'll ask you one. Why did Fat Jack McGee hire you?"

"Have you asked him?"

"No."

"He'd rather I kept his reasons confidential," Nudger said.

"You don't have a Louisiana P.I. license," Marrivale pointed out.

Nudger smiled. "I know. Nothing to be revoked."

"There are consequences a lot more serious than having your investigator's license pulled, Nudger. Mr. Collins would prefer that you stay away from Ineida Mann."

"You mean Ineida Collins."

"I mean what I say."

"David Collins already had someone deliver that message to me."

"It's not a message from anyone but me," Marrivale said. "I'm telling you this because I'm concerned about your safety while you're within my jurisdiction. It's part of my job."

Nudger kept a straight face, got up and walked to the door, and opened it. He said, "I appreciate your concern, captain. Right now I've got things to do."

Marrivale smiled with his mean little mouth. He didn't seem rattled by Nudger's impolite invitation to leave; he'd said what needed saying. He got up out of the armchair and adjusted his suit. Nudger noticed that the suit hung on him just right and must have been tailored and expensive. No cop's-salary, J. C. Penney wardrobe for Marrivale.

As he walked past Nudger, Marrivale paused and said, "It'd behoove you to learn to discern friend from enemy, Nudger." He went out and trod lightly down the hall toward the elevators, not looking back.

Nudger shut and locked the door. Then he went over to the bed, removed his shoes, and stretched out on his back on the mattress, his fingers laced behind his head. He studied the faint water stains on the ceiling in the corner above him. They were covered by a thin film of mold. That reminded Nudger of the bayou.

He had to admit that Marrivale had left him with solid parting advice.

Though plenty of interested parties had warned Nudger to stay away from Ineida Collins, everyone seemed to have neglected to tell him to give a wide berth to Willy Hollister. And after breakfast, it was Hollister who claimed Nudger's interest.

Hollister lived on St. Francois, within a few blocks of Ineida Collins's apartment. Their apartments were similar. Hollister's was the end unit of a low tan stucco building that sat almost flush with the sidewalk. What yard there was had to be in the rear. Through the low branches of a huge magnolia tree, Nudger saw some of the raw cedar fencing that sectioned the back premises into private courtyards.

Hollister might be home, sleeping after his late-night gig at Fat Jack's. But whether he was home or not, Nudger decided that his next move would be to knock on Hollister's door.

He rapped on the wooden door three times, casually leaned toward it and listened. He heard no sound from inside. No one in the street seemed to be paying much attention to him, so after a few minutes Nudger idly gave the doorknob a twist.

It rotated all the way, clicked. The door opened about six inches. Nudger pushed the door open farther and stepped quietly inside.

The apartment no doubt came furnished. The furniture was old but not too worn; some of it probably had antique value. The floor was dull hardwood where it showed around the borders of a faded blue carpet. From where he stood, Nudger could see into the bedroom. The bed was unmade but empty.

The living room was dim. The wooden shutters on its windows were closed, allowing slanted light to come in through narrow slits. Most of the illumination in the room came from the bedroom and a short hall that led to a bathroom, then to a small kitchen and sliding glass doors that opened to the courtyard.

To make sure he was alone, Nudger called, "Mr. Hollister? Avon lady!"

No answer. Fine.

Nudger looked around the living room for a few minutes, examining the contents of drawers, picking up some sealed mail that turned out to be an insurance pitch and a utility bill.

He had just entered the bedroom when he heard a sound from outside the curtained window, open about six inches. It was a dull thunking sound that Nudger thought he recognized. He went to the window, parted the breeze-swayed gauzy white curtains, and bent low to peer outside.

The window looked out on the courtyard. What Nudger saw confirmed his guess about the sound. A shovel knifing into soft earth. Willy Hollister was in the courtyard garden, digging. Nudger crouched down so he could see better.

Hollister was planting rosebushes. They were young plants, but they already had red and white roses on them. Hollister had started on the left with the red roses and was alternating colors. He was planting half a dozen bushes and was working on the fifth plant, which lay with its roots wrapped in burlap beside the waiting, freshly dug hole.

Hollister was on both knees on the ground, using his hands to scoop some dirt back into the hole. He was forming a small dome over which to spread the rosebush's soon-to-be-exposed roots. He knew how to plant rosebushes, all right, and he was trying to ensure that these would live.

Nudger's stomach went into a series of spasms as Hollister stood and glanced at the apartment as if he had sensed someone's presence. He drew one of the rolled-up sleeves of his white dress shirt across his perspiring forehead. For a few seconds he seemed to debate about whether to return to the apartment. Then he turned, picked up the shovel, and began digging the sixth and final hole.

Letting out a long breath, Nudger drew back from the open window and stood up straight. He'd go out by the front door and then walk around to the courtyard and call Hollister's name, as if he'd just arrived. He wanted to get Hollister's own version of his past.

As Nudger was leaving the bedroom, he noticed a stack of pale blue envelopes on the dresser, beside a comb and brush set monogrammed with Hollister's initials. The envelopes were held together by a fat rubber band. Nudger saw Hollister's address, saw the Beulah Street return address penned neatly in black ink in a corner of the top envelope. He paused for just a few seconds, picked up the envelopes, and slipped them into his pocket. Then he left Hollister's apartment the same way he'd entered.

There was no point in talking to Hollister now. It would be foolish to place himself in the apartment at the approximate time of the disappearance of the stack of letters written by Ineida Collins.

Nudger walked up St. Francois for several blocks, then took a cab to his hotel. Though the morning hadn't yet heated up, the cab's air conditioner was on high and the interior was near freezing. The letters seemed to grow heavier and heavier in Nudger's jacket pocket, and to glow with a kind of warmth that gave no comfort.

Nudger had room service bring up a plain omelet and a glass of milk. He sat with his early lunch, his customary meal (it had a

soothing effect on a nervous stomach), at the desk in his hotel
room and ate slowly as he read Ineida Collins's letters to Hollister.
He understood now why they had felt warm in his pocket. The
love affair was, from Ineida's point of view at least, as soaring and
serious as such an affair can get. Nudger felt cheapened by his
crass invasion of Ineida's privacy. These were thoughts meant to
be shared by no one but the two of them, thoughts not meant to
be tramped through by a middle-aged detective not under the
spell of love.

On the other hand, Nudger told himself, there was no way for
him to know what the letters contained until he read them and determined that he shouldn't have. This was the sort of professional
quandary he got himself into frequently but never got used to.

The last letter, the one with the latest postmark, was the most
revealing and made the tacky side of Nudger's profession seem
worthwhile. Ineida Collins was planning to run away with Willy
Hollister; he had told her he loved her and that they would be
married. Then, after the fact, they would return to New Orleans and
inform friends and relatives of the blessed union. It all seemed
quaint, Nudger thought, and not very believable unless you happened to be twenty-three and love-struck and had lived Ineida Collins's sheltered existence.

Ineida also referred in the last letter to something important she
had to tell Hollister. Nudger could guess what that important bit of
information was. That she was Ineida Collins and she was David
Collins's daughter and she was rich, and that she was oh so glad
that Hollister hadn't known about her until that moment. Because
that meant he wanted her for her own true self alone. Ah, love! It
made Nudger's business go round.

Nudger refolded the letter, replaced it in its envelope, and
dropped it onto the desk. He tried to finish his omelet but couldn't.
He wasn't really hungry, and his stomach had reached a tolerable
level of comfort. He knew it was time to report to Fat Jack. After
all, the man had hired him to uncover information, but not so
Nudger would keep it to himself.

Nudger slid the rubber band back around the stack of letters, snapped it, and stood up. He considered having the letters placed in the hotel safe, but the security of any hotel safe was questionable. A paper napkin bearing the hotel logo lay next to his half-eaten omelet. He wrapped the envelopes in the napkin and dropped the bundle in the wastebasket by the desk. The maid wasn't due back in the room until tomorrow morning, and it wasn't likely that any-one would think Nudger would throw away such important letters. And the sort of person who would bother to search a wastebasket would search everywhere else and find the letters anyway.

He placed the tray with his dishes on it in the hall outside his door, hung the "Do Not Disturb" sign on the knob, and left to see Fat Jack McGee.

They told Nudger at the club that Fat Jack was out. Nobody was sure when he'd be back; he might not return until this evening when business started picking up, or he might have just strolled over to the Magnolia Blossom for a croissant and coffee and would be back any minute.

Nudger sat at the end of the bar, nursing a beer he didn't really want, and waited.

After an hour, the bartender began blatantly staring at him from time to time. Mid-afternoon or not, Nudger was occupying a bar stool and had an obligation. And maybe the man was right. Nudger was about to give in to the weighty responsibility of earning his place at the bar by ordering another drink he didn't want when Fat Jack appeared through the dimness like a light-footed, obese spirit in a white vested suit.

He saw Nudger, smiled his fat man's beaming smile, and veered toward him, diamond rings and gold jewelry flashing fire beneath pale coat sleeves. There was even a large diamond stickpin in his biblike tie. He was a vision of sartorial immensity.

"We need to talk," Nudger told him.

"That's easy enough," Fat Jack said. "My office, hey?" He led the way, making Nudger feel somewhat like a pilot fish trailing a whale.

When they were settled in Fat Jack's office, Nudger said, "I came across some letters that Ineida wrote to Hollister. She and Hollister plan to run away together, get married."

Fat Jack raised his eyebrows so high Nudger was afraid they might become detached. "Hollister ain't the marrying kind, Nudger."

"What kind is he?"

"I don't want to answer that."

"Maybe Ineida and Hollister will elope and live happily—"

"Stop!" Fat Jack interrupted him. He leaned forward, wide forehead glistening. "When are they planning on leaving?"

"I don't know. The letter didn't say."

"You gotta find out, Nudger!"

"I could ask. But Captain Marrivale wouldn't approve."

"Marrivale has talked with you?"

"In my hotel room. He assured me he had my best interests at heart."

Fat Jack appeared thoughtful. He swiveled in his chair and switched on the auxiliary window air conditioner. Its breeze stirred the papers on the desk, ruffled Fat Jack's graying, gingery hair.

The telephone rang. Fat Jack picked it up, identified himself. His face went as white as his suit. "Yes, sir," he said. His jowls began to quiver; loose flesh beneath his left eye started to dance. Nudger was getting nervous just looking at him. "You can't mean it," Fat Jack said. "Hey, maybe it's a joke. Okay, it ain't a joke." He listened a while longer and then said, "Yes, sir," again and hung up. He didn't say anything else for a long time. Nudger didn't say anything either.

Fat Jack spoke first. "That was David Collins. Ineida's gone. Not home, bed hasn't been slept in."

"Then she and Hollister have left as they planned."

"You mean as Hollister planned. Collins got a note in the mail."

"Note?" Nudger asked. His stomach did a flip; it was way ahead of his brain, reacting to a suspicion not yet fully formed.

"A ransom note," Fat Jack confirmed. "Unsigned, in cutout newspaper words. Collins said Marrivale is on his way over here now to talk to me about Hollister. Hollister's disappeared, too. And his clothes are missing from his closet." Fat Jack's little pink eyes were bulging in his blanched face. "I better not tell Marrivale about the letters."

"Not unless he asks," Nudger said. "And he won't." He stood up.

"Where are you going?"

"I'm leaving," Nudger said, "before Marrivale gets here. There's no sense in making this easy for him."

"Or difficult for you."

"It works out that way, for a change."

Fat Jack nodded, his eyes unfocused yet thoughtful, already rehearsing in his mind the lines he would use on Marrivale. He wasn't a man to bow easily or gracefully to trouble, and he had seen plenty of trouble in his life. He knew a multitude of moves and would use them all.

He didn't seem to notice when Nudger left.

Hollister's apartment was shuttered, and the day's mail delivery sprouted like a white bouquet from the mailbox next to his door. Nudger doubted that David Collins had officially notified the police; his first, his safest, step would be to seek the personal help of Captain Marrivale, who was probably on the Collins payroll already. So it was unlikely that Hollister's apartment was under surveillance, unless by Frick and Frack, who, like Marrivale, probably knew about Ineida's disappearance.

Nudger walked unhesitatingly up to the front door and tried the knob. The door was locked this time. He walked around the corner, toward the back of the building, and unhitched the loop of rope that held shut the high wooden gate to the courtyard.

In the privacy of the fenced courtyard, Nudger quickly forced the sliding glass doors and entered Hollister's apartment.

The place seemed almost exactly as Nudger had left it earlier that day. The matched comb and brush set was still on the dresser, though in a different position. Nudger checked the dresser drawers. They held only a few pairs of undershorts, a wadded dirty shirt, and some socks with holes in the toes. He crossed the bedroom and opened the closet door. The closet's blank back wall stared out at him. Empty. The apartment's kitchen was only lightly stocked with food; the refrigerator held a stick of butter, half a gallon of milk, various half-used condiments, and three cans of beer. It was dirty and needed defrosting. Hollister had been a lousy housekeeper.

The rest of the apartment seemed oddly quiet and in vague disorder, as if getting used to its new state of vacancy. There was definitely a deserted air about the place that suggested its occupant had shunned it and left in a hurry.

Nudger decided that there was nothing to learn here. No matchbooks with messages written inside them, no hastily scrawled, forgotten addresses or revealing ticket stubs. He never got the help that fictional detectives got—well, almost never—though it was always worth seeking.

As he was about to open the courtyard gate and step back into the street, Nudger paused. He stood still, feeling a cold stab of apprehension, of dread knowledge, in the pit of his stomach.

He was staring at the rosebushes that Hollister had planted that morning. At the end of the garden were two newly planted bushes bearing red rosebuds. Hollister hadn't planted them that way. He had alternated the bushes by color, one red one white. Their order now was white, red, white, white, red, red.

Which meant that the bushes had been dug up. Replanted.

Nudger walked to the row of rosebushes. The earth around them was loose, as it had been earlier, but now it seemed more sloppily spread about, and one of the bushes was leaning at an angle. Not the work of a methodical gardener; more the work of someone in a hurry.

As he backed away from the freshly turned soil, Nudger's legs came in contact with a small wrought iron bench. He sat down. He thought for a while, oblivious of the warm sunshine, the colorful geraniums and bougainvillea. He became aware of the frantic chirping of birds on their lifelong hunt for sustenance, of the soft yet vibrant buzzing of insects. Sounds of life, sounds of death. He stood up and got out of there fast, his stomach churning.

When he returned to his hotel room, Nudger found on the floor by the desk the napkin that had been wadded in the bottom of the wastebasket. He checked the wastebasket, but it was only a gesture to confirm what he already knew. The letters that Ineida Collins had written to Willy Hollister were gone.

* * *

Fat Jack was in his office. Marrivale had come and gone hours ago.

Nudger sat down across the desk from Fat Jack and looked appraisingly at the harried club owner. Fat Jack appeared wrung out by worry. The Marrivale visit had taken a lot out of him. Or maybe he'd had another conversation with David Collins. Whatever his problems, Nudger knew that, to paraphrase the great Al Jolson, Fat Jack hadn't seen nothin' yet.

"David Collins just phoned," Fat Jack said. He was visibly uncomfortable, a veritable Niagara of nervous perspiration. "He got a call from the kidnappers. They want half a million in cash by tomorrow night, or Ineida starts being delivered in the mail piece by piece."

Nudger wasn't surprised. He knew where the phone call had originated.

"When I was looking into Hollister's past," he said to Fat Jack, "I happened to discover something that seemed ordinary enough then, but now has gotten kind of interesting." He watched the perspiration flow down Fat Jack's wide forehead.

"So I'm interested," Fat Jack said irritably. He reached behind him and slapped at the air conditioner, as if to coax more cold air despite the frigid thermostat setting.

"There's something about being a fat man, a man as large as you. After a while he takes his size for granted, accepts it as a normal fact of his life. But other people don't. A really fat man is more memorable than he realizes, especially if he's called Fat Jack."

Fat Jack drew his head back into fleshy folds and shot a tortured, wary look at Nudger. "Hey, what are you talking toward, old sleuth?"

"You had a series of failed clubs in the cities where Willy Hollister played his music, and you were there at the times when Hollister's women disappeared."

"That ain't unusual, Nudger. Jazz is a tight little world."

"I said people remember you," Nudger told him. "And they remember you knowing Willy Hollister. But you told me you saw him for the first time when he came here to play in your club. And when I went to see Ineida for the first time, she knew my name.

She bought the idea that I was a magazine writer; it fell right into place and it took her a while to get uncooperative. Then she assumed I was working for her father—as you knew she would."

Fat Jack stood halfway up, then decided he hadn't the energy for the total effort and sat back down in his groaning chair. "You missed a beat, Nudger. Are you saying I'm in on this kidnapping with Hollister? If that's true, why would I have hired you?"

"You needed someone like me to substantiate Hollister's involvement with Ineida, to find out about Hollister's missing women. It would help you to set him up. You knew him better than you pretended. You knew that he murdered those three women to add some insane, tragic dimension to his music—the sound that made him great. You knew what he had planned for Ineida."

"He didn't even know who she really was!" Fat Jack sputtered.

"But you knew from the time you hired her that she was David Collins's daughter. You schemed from the beginning to use Hollister as the fall guy in your kidnapping plan."

"Hollister is a killer—you said so yourself. I wouldn't want to get involved in any kind of scam with him."

"He didn't know you were involved," Nudger explained. "When you'd used me to make it clear that Hollister was the natural suspect, you kidnapped Ineida and demanded the ransom, figuring Hollister's past and his disappearance would divert the law's attention away from you."

Fat Jack's wide face was a study in agitation, but it was relatively calm compared to what must have been going on inside his head. His body was squirming uncontrollably, and the pain in his eyes was difficult to look into. He didn't want to ask the question, but he had to and he knew it. "If all this is true," he moaned, "where is Hollister?"

"I did a little digging in his garden," Nudger said. "He's under his roses, where he thought Ineida was going to wind up, but where you had space for him reserved all along."

Fat Jack's head dropped. His suit suddenly seemed to get two sizes too large. As his body trembled, tears joined the perspiration on his quivering cheeks. "When did you know?" he asked.

"When I got back to my hotel and found the letters from Ineida to Hollister missing. You were the only one other than myself who knew about them." Nudger leaned over the desk to look Fat Jack in the eye. "Where is Ineida?" he asked.

"She's still alive," was Fat Jack's only answer. Crushed as he was, he was still too wily to reveal his hole card. It was as if his fat were a kind of rubber, lending inexhaustible resilience to body and mind.

"It's negotiation time," Nudger told him, "and we don't have very long to reach an agreement. While we're sitting here talking, the police are digging in the dirt I replaced in Hollister's garden."

"You called them?"

"I did. But right now, they expect to find Ineida. When they find Hollister, they'll put all the pieces together the way I did and get the same puzzle-picture of you."

Fat Jack nodded sadly, seeing the truth in that prognosis. "So what's your proposition?"

"You release Ineida, and I keep quiet until tomorrow morning. That'll give you a reasonable head start on the law. The police don't know who phoned them about the body in Hollister's garden, so I can stall them for at least that long without arousing suspicion."

Fat Jack didn't deliberate for more than a few seconds. He nodded again, then stood up, supporting his ponderous weight with both hands on the desk. "What about money?" he whined. "I can't run far without money."

"I've got nothing to lend you," Nudger said. "Not even the fee I'm not going to get from you."

"All right," Fat Jack sighed.

"I'm going to phone David Collins in one hour," Nudger told him. "If Ineida isn't there, I'll put down the receiver and dial the number of the New Orleans police department."

"She'll be there," Fat Jack said. He tucked in his sweat-plastered shirt beneath his huge stomach paunch, buttoned his suit coat, and without a backward glance at Nudger glided majestically from the room. He would have his old jaunty stride back in no time.

Nudger glanced at his watch. He sipped Fat Jack's best whisky from the club's private stock while he waited for an hour to pass.

Then he phoned David Collins, and from the tone of Collins's voice he guessed the answer to his question even before he asked it.

Ineida was home.

When Nudger answered the knock on his hotel room door early the next morning, he wasn't really surprised to find Frick and Frack looming in the hall. They pushed into the room without being invited. There was a sneer on Frick's pockmarked face. Frack gave his boxer's nifty little shuffle and stood between Nudger and the door, smiling politely.

"We brought you something from Mr. Collins," Frick said, reaching into an inside pocket of his pale green sport jacket. It just about matched Nudger's complexion.

All Frick brought out, though, was an envelope. Nudger was surprised to see that his hands were steady as he opened it.

The envelope contained an airline ticket for a noon flight to St. Louis.

"You did okay, my friend," Frick said. "You did what was right for Ineida. Mr. Collins appreciates that."

"What about Fat Jack?" Nudger asked. Frack's polite smile changed subtly. It became a dreamy, unpleasant sort of smile.

"Where Fat Jack is now," Frack said, "most of his friends are alligators."

"After Fat Jack talked to you," said Frick, "he went to Mr. Collins. He couldn't make himself walk out on all that possible money; some guys just have to play all their cards. He told Mr. Collins that for a certain amount of cash he would reveal Ineida's whereabouts, but it all had to be done in a hurry." Now Frick also smiled. "He revealed her whereabouts in a hurry, all right, and for free. In fact, he kept talking till nobody was listening, till he couldn't talk any more."

Nudger swallowed dryly. He forgot about breakfast. Fat Jack had been a bad businessman to the end, dealing in desperation instead of distance. Maybe he'd had too much of the easy life; maybe he couldn't picture going on without it. That was no problem for him now.

When Nudger got home, he found a flat, padded package with a

New Orleans postmark waiting for him. He placed it on his desk and cautiously opened it. The package contained two items: A check from David Collins made out to Nudger for more than twice the amount of Fat Jack's uncollectable fee. And an old jazz record in its original wrapper, a fifties rendition of *You Got the Reach but Not the Grasp*.

It featured Fat Jack McGee on clarinet.

The Family Rose

by Charlotte Hinger

Maybelle Rose's eyes swept across the girl with contempt, but she reached for the autograph book and signed it with a quick flourish. The fan was a ratty little thing, wearing a faded jean jacket and a gauze blouse tucked into a three-tiered calico skirt. Her long blond hair crinkled down her back and she had puppy-trust blue eyes. Clearly nobody.

But on the other hand, they weren't exactly lined up at her concerts nowadays. Tiredly, Maybelle tried to remember just when was the last time a real somebody had asked for her autograph. It was what came from being the opening act for newer, brighter stars with brassier sounds.

"You don't know how much this means to me," the girl said fervently. "I've loved the Family Rose all my life. There just ain't no other group like them. And you're my favorite of all."

"What's your name, honey?" asked Maybelle, quickly deciding she'd misjudged her.

"June," she said softly. "June Jones."

"Well, June, let's me and you have a little talk about the Family Rose."

"Oh, I wouldn't feel right," said June reverently, "taking up your time and everything."

"No bother. After all—if it weren't for our fans! Besides, we're short on help here and I could use a hand in wrestling some of these props back into the van."

June scurried back and forth looking as if she were trying out for a job at McDonald's, smiling and nodding at Maybelle all the while she packed boxes and cartons and instruments. Maybelle watched, shrewdly evaluating June's tireless energy.

The high lonesome sound of pure bluegrass had its own loyal following, and God knew, not so long ago, ten, well maybe fifteen years, she had been on top and she would be again. At one time, she was one of the high-flying fussed-over members of the Family Rose.

She winced as she recalled the reviewer who had just recently referred to her as the "last rose of summer."

Momma and Maybelle and her two sisters had been like a sweet bouquet of country wildflowers, picking and singing their little hearts out.

"And when I die," Momma'd said, "one of you is going to get the family rose. If one of you is worthy by then."

Every time she'd said this, Maybelle and Lulu and Winona would stare wistfully at Momma's guitar—which had an elaborate cloisonné rose inlaid on the polished mahogany case. It was very old and a wonder of workmanship. It had been made by the husband of the slave woman who gave Momma's great-great-grandmother the medicine bundle, and they could only guess at how the man had managed to bring the tiny lengths of rare woods out of Africa.

The daughters' guitars all looked like hers. It required a trained eye to discern that the woods used to shade the petals on Momma's were cocobolo and purpleheart and teak whereas the girls' were merely mahogany and birch with a smattering of maple.

It was a family ritual for Momma to begin each concert by telling folks the history of the guitar—slyly working in their aristocratic Southern background. Then she delicately extended the guitar as if she were inviting them to partake of a sacrament, and Maybelle and Lulu and Winona would walk forward and reverently touch the center of the family rose. Their fans loved the sight of the three lovely daughters paying homage to Momma Rose's abilities.

Momma reminded them often that only one daughter would receive her guitar—the family rose—along with the blessing and the medicine bundle as they had been handed down to her from generations of women.

There were two things Maybelle had wanted more than anything in the world: the family rose—and Momma's medicine bundle.

"You've got a mean streak to you, child," Momma had said once, eyeing Maybelle suspiciously when she urged Momma to choose her inheritor before it was too late. "Don't seem right to give the family rose to the one with the tiniest heart. And as to the medicine bundle! That's to be buried with me. None of you care a fig about being a Wise Woman. It would be misused."

Maybelle's mouth twisted with bitterness as she watched June work. Momma had up and died without naming her successor or writing down her wishes, and Maybelle had them both: the family rose and the medicine bundle. But a lot of good it did her! She had acquired the guitar without the blessing and now she simply could not bring herself to play it.

After all, if she did have a mean streak, she had gotten it from Momma. It would be just like the old witch to curse her from beyond the grave.

But the guitar was there at every concert, propped up on a little stand with a spotlight trained on it. And before she sang she would reverently step forward and touch the center of the family rose and say, "This one's for you, Momma," and the crowd would go crazy.

After Momma died, Maybelle's sisters wanted to break up the act.

"You can't *mean* that," Maybelle had protested. "We're a family group. A tradition."

"Without Momma, we ain't nothing, kiddo," Lulu had said flatly. "Without Momma, we can't even carry a tune."

"She died without passing down the gift," said Winona. "We might as well face it."

"That's not true," stammered Maybelle, "and I'm going to prove it."

Well, she had been ten, maybe fifteen years proving it, and now she had nothing to show for it, except a collection of satiny skirts and blouses and callouses on the tips of her fingers and a few ratty old run-down pitiful fans like this poor pathetic little old June Jones. The girl was a worker though. She could say that for her.

"That's it, kid. Thanks a bunch. Now put Momma's guitar back in the case."

"Oh, I couldn't," June said passionately. "I'm not worthy. I'm just a poor homeless orphan girl without kith or kin. I could never, never bring myself to touch Momma Rose's guitar."

"Well, as I live and breathe," drawled Maybelle, "a true believer. Where you staying, kid?"

"Nowhere," she mumbled. "I'm just kind of hanging around the parks. I'm sorta between jobs right now. I'm not a hooker," she blurted suddenly. "Don't want you to think that."

"It never entered my mind, darlin'. Tell you what, I'm a little down on my luck too, right now. Had a little spat with the boys. They got a little impatient over some money they claimed I owed them. No loyalty from anyone nowadays. I could use a little help setting up and taking things down, so why don't you throw in with me."

June's face lit up like a child's at Christmas.

"Oh, thank you, thank you, thank you. I just want you to know I'll do *anything* for you."

"Except touch Momma's guitar," Maybelle teased lightly.

June lowered her eyes and dug the toe of her old shoe around and around in the dust.

"Ma'am, there's some things I'd rather you didn't tease me about. And the feelings I have for Momma Rose's guitar is one of them. It's kind of like you're making fun of Jesus or something. Growing up in an orphanage was hard. Harder than you'll ever know, and music—especially your family's music—was the only thing that kept me from going crazy."

Maybelle rolled her eyes and examined her nails, but she shut her mouth.

They took off for Nashville, with June driving and Maybelle talking a blue streak as she sipped on a Budweiser.

June worked steadily setting up the stage at a minor open-air concert which Maybelle assured her was not typical of the bookings she ordinarily got, but just one of her little charity obligations she did out of the goodness of her heart.

"You know how to see if everything is hooked up right, kid?"

June nodded. "We had a little group at the orphanage."

"Great. I'll go catch twenty winks. Need my beauty sleep. Then after you sweep everything up, come get me in about an hour—and have some lunch ready."

June nodded and picked up one of the two guitars besides Momma Rose's that they had hooked up to the amps. She strummed the first one, then seeing that all the wires were in working order, she crossed to the second guitar, picked it up, and began to sing.

Maybelle Rose froze in her tracks. Stopped cold dead still. The child had a rare pure voice that sent chills down her spine.

"Stop that caterwauling," she said quickly, needing time to think. "Just strum." She did not want anyone else to hear that voice.

"Sorry, ma'am," said June, her voice quivering with shame. "Guess I just got plumb carried away, I miss my old group so much."

"Never mind, darlin'," said Maybelle, "I forgive you. Shucks, child, with a little coaching from me—your voice is untrained, of course—maybe you could sing backup for me."

June paled with wonder and she looked down at her feet.

"That would be my idea of going to heaven. Truly it would ma'am."

Maybelle switched off the amplifier and asked June to sing "Wildwood Flower." Her eyes misted. The kid had It. That illusive quality that made critics spin circles. It was the sound that had been missing ever since Momma died. In fact, there was a quality of the voice that brought Momma to mind. If she closed her eyes, Maybelle could see Momma Rose standing there.

"Darlin', do you know the words to all the songs I'm going to be singing tonight?"

June nodded.

"I want you to sing right out. Not overpowering, but confident. Understand?"

"Oh yes, ma'am." The girl's eyes shone.

That night, Maybelle sang and swayed and for the first time in two years, she could see the audience responding in kind. They liked her. Liked her a lot. Pity she was just a simple warm-up act instead of getting top billing. Then after two weeks of studying and stewing, she began fiddling with the sound systems, and in a moment of superb inspiration she tried switching the mikes and amps and sound systems around until it sounded as if June's voice was coming from her mike. And it worked.

By the next stop she had coached June to give the appearance of just swaying modestly and only moving a little, while she was actually belting out the lead using the whole range of her extraordinary voice. Maybelle was actually doing the modest backup, but through hopping, dipping, swaying, and passionately mouthing the words, she appeared to be the one really singing.

"Guess you know," said Maybelle sullenly, after one concert when they had been called back for five encores, "that you don't get to touch the family rose, kid. It's an honor that's reserved for our family."

"I wouldn't think of it," said June. "I told you that right off."

"Just don't want you getting a swelled head. Forgetting who's the actual star around here," said Maybelle.

"About that," said June timidly. "Is what we're doing really right? After all, you're the one all those good folks are paying to see."

The night before the Merle Watson Memorial Concert, they were one of several groups checking their equipment. The patriarch of bluegrass guitar, Doc Watson, blind since childhood, was being led from group to group. He had a legendary sense of sound and had been known to stop a number stone cold dead to holler out instructions to a bewildered technician.

"That bass is too bright, son," he would snap, and listen keenly, with an ear cocked to one side, as minute adjustments were made in the balance of tweeters and woofers. Despite all his efforts to sound gentle, nothing softened his underlying irritability with inept musicians. He simply could not tolerate them. He had an august, dignified, white-headed physical presence, further augmented by the fans' awareness of the pain he had borne throughout his life.

Old now, and mourning the tragic death of his son, Merle Watson, his awesome stature as the World Champion Flat Guitar Picker unsettled many of the musicians who appeared at this star-studded annual memorial concert. Seasoned guitarists dropped their picks and fiddlers' fingers fumbled on the frets. Cloggers stepped on each other's toes and little starlets squeaked on the high notes until the kindly old man settled them down with a tolerant chuckle. Doc Watson had become art, and the epitome of tragedy borne with dignity.

He stopped before June and Maybelle where they were rehearsing on the porch of the cabin. A setting where the lesser solar system of stars performed. He listened keenly, then turned and spoke sharply to his assistant. The man looked blankly at the arrangement of the sound systems. Hastily Maybelle stepped forward.

"As I live and breathe," she gushed, standing directly in front of the grand old man, "I'm Maybelle Rose, sir. And I believe you knew Momma. I'm so proud to meet you. I'm sorry that you've had to listen in before we get things set up right."

"I'd like to meet your backup singer," Doc Watson said quietly.

She studied his face, then spun around and asked June to step forward.

She did, but she could barely blurt out a hello. She dipped her head.

"It's an honor," she murmured.

Doc Watson changed color and he was deathly still.

He knows, Maybelle thought wildly. He knows.

He walked off without saying another word to either of them.

Feverishly Maybelle paced the floor that night. The old man knew! His temper was well known. Sickened, she tried to imagine what he would do or say. Would he expose her right off? Ruin her? Her big chance was becoming a living nightmare.

By morning she had made up her mind. Never in a hundred years would she allow June to take her place. Never.

Calmly, she sent a note to Doc Watson's assistant. "Please inform Doc Watson that my first two songs will introduce my backup singer, June Jones, a young lady of exceptional voice."

She pulled on her rubber gloves and trembled as she loosened the leather tie on her medicine bundle. The substance she wanted was in a golden locket molded around a tiny vial. Gingerly she unscrewed the stopper and dipped a pin inside. Then she carefully dropped a pinpoint of liquid onto the center of the rose on Momma's guitar.

There were poisons which would have acted faster. But a long, loving, extravagant introduction would set well with Doc Watson. Maybelle savored the idea of folks talking about how generous and unselfish she'd been. Besides, the first song would not show off the spectacular range of June's voice.

"Ready, kid?" asked Maybelle, just before they were ready to go on.

June nodded, her eyes filled with tears.

"I have a surprise for you, Maybelle."

"Well, I have a surprise for you too, kid," said Maybelle coldly.

"But I want to tell you something," begged June.

Maybelle brushed past her and walked out of the cabin.

"Come on," she hissed back at June. "My fans are waiting."

"Thank you. Thank you." Maybelle smiled brightly at the applause.

"And now, as many of our fans know, before we begin a concert, I always thank Momma Rose. We owe it all to her."

The applause was deafening. She respectfully dipped her head and walked over to Momma's guitar.

"Be with us, Momma," she said slowly. She reached for the rose, but her fingers stopped short by a quarter of an inch.

Then June stepped forward and imitated Maybelle. Her fingers connected, resonating on the soundboard with a soft muffled thump. Then, standing side by side, they gave a slight bow and went to the front and picked up their guitars.

"My little backup singer knows I have a surprise for her, but she doesn't know what," said Maybelle coyly. "As you all know, it has long been the tradition of the Family Rose to support new talent."

She swallowed hard, nearly choking on the words. "And today, making her debut solo performance is my own little ol' backup, June Jones."

June gasped and stepped forward.

"I can't," she stammered. "I can't possibly."

"I insist," hissed Maybelle. "Give it all you've got."

June stepped forward as if she were waking from a dream. At first she kept her head bowed, then when the warmth of the audience reached her, the rhythm began pulsing through her body. She finished the first song to deafening applause and then started on her second number. The one that would demonstrate her incredible range.

Horrified, Maybelle watched. Her throat constricted in protest. She shouldn't be able to carry on. Now everyone would know it had been June's voice all along. Everyone would know.

June's eyes glittered with excitement and she became lost in the high sweet tones, her fingers flying across the guitar.

Maybelle's heart beat faster and faster. The audience rose to its feet and was swaying—clearly loving, adoring June Jones. Maybelle's blood rushed to her head. It wasn't working. She gave a little squeal before she fell writhing to the floor of the stage.

June got to her first.

"No, no, no," she cried frantically. "Please!" She turned to Doc Watson's assistant, who had rushed onto the stage. "Get an ambulance."

"Maybelle, you're the only family I've got. You're going to be a star." June cradled Maybelle in her arms. Tears streamed down her face.

"Maybelle. Listen to me. I tried to tell you. It's your time. Momma came to me in a dream last night and said so. She told me it was time that you had her guitar. You were playing her guitar, sweet darlin' Maybelle. Momma said it was time to hand you the family rose."

Concerto for Violence and Orchestra

by William Bankier

People will steal anything. The police could open their files and show you cases of a ship being stolen, or lead from a church roof, or a herd of cattle. Countries even try to steal other countries—we read about it in the papers every day. These thoughts cross my mind as I remember what happened between me and Carlotta Teddington and Leonard Zolf. Perhaps I should begin in the traditional way.

Once upon a time there was a man who tried to steal a dance band.

The band in question is The Bones Cornfield Quintet and I am the leader. The nickname suits me. I weigh 190 pounds but it is spread thin over a six-foot-four-inch frame. A sadistic guitar player once told me that when I am asleep it is easy to imagine what I will look like when I've been dead a few years.

The quintet is a semipro band. We play once a week at a pub in southwest London. The money is minimal but the management is enlightened. He charges no admission, so we always have a full house of beer drinkers who like the forties swing we play.

Some of us have regular jobs. Carlotta, our vocalist, teaches school in Wandsworth. Muir Levy, our piano player, sells cut-price Asian holidays to homesick Pakistanis. That may be the beginning of a lyric. Clay Braithwaite, our reed player, drives a Number 93 bus for London Transport. Pat Manta, the drummer, paints houses occasionally and collects social security regularly. And I play double bass when I'm not pulling pints on the morning shift at the Rose and Crown.

Quintet, you say, counting on your fingers. Quintet?

I'm coming to the fifth member of the band (sorry girls, we don't count the female vocalist). He is the man I mentioned earlier, Leonard Zolf, trumpeter. Leonard used to be with the National Westminster amateur jazz band till the bank fired him. Now he sells used cars. When we ask why the bank gave him the sack, Zolf inflates like a pigeon, tugs at the points of his red waistcoat, smooths his pale thinning hair with both hands, and changes the subject.

It was shortly after Zolf joined the band that the trouble started. We had finished our Tuesday night rehearsal in the back room at St. Stephen's Church hall. The vicar lets us use the room free because the band plays for nothing at his annual summer fête. I was inviting Carlotta to join me for coffee when we heard Zolf's voice rising in that locust drone of his.

"Terrible to be playing this out-of-date music when we could be making money." He was not talking to anybody in particular. Zolf has a way of soliloquizing, scattering words like a fisherman flinging bait on the water, confident that sooner or later something will surface. "We should be playing disco. That's where the money is."

"The bank is where the money is," Braithwaite said. Braithwaite is from the West Indies. When he plays soprano sax, he sounds like Sidney Bechet. "You never told us why you left the bank."

Zolf ignored the probe. "I know the man who books the Aladdin Disco. We could get in there twice a week on a standard contract."

Nobody said anything. Muir Levy played a progression of Shearing-esque chords. His eyes were on me. So were those of the other sidemen. Their heads were raised, their movements frozen, like antelopes around the water hole checking out their leader to see if it was time to run.

I followed rules one and two of my emergency procedure used

whenever I am threatened by events. I said nothing and I did nothing. Later, as Carlotta was helping me load my double bass into the back of the minivan, she said, "Zolf is deliberately making waves."

"I felt them lapping around my ankles."

"How long are you going to wait? Till your nostrils get wet?"

"It's only talk."

"That's how palace revolutions begin. Talk. He's trying to steal your band."

She got behind the wheel and I sat in calmly beside her, a good man, a harmless man, everybody likes me. "Never trust a musician who wears rimless glasses," Carlotta warned.

Our weekly Thursday night gig at the pub was a great success. We went through our modified arrangements of big-band standards and the crowd ate it up. Carlotta was in good voice. She sings like June Christie used to do with Stan Kenton, in a pure, clear, almost childlike voice. But whereas Christie was a blond beauty, Carlotta Teddington's appearance suggests gypsy ancestors. Her long black hair falls over one shoulder in a braid thick enough to moor one end of the QE2. Her broad face maintains a tan even under the random English sun and those pale green eyes announce that no phonies need apply.

When we stopped playing at 10:30 and the crowd dispersed in deference to English drink-licensing laws, the manager, a shaggy man named Shep, shuffled over to the bandstand. "Good news and bad news," he said. "Which do you want first?"

"No news," Manta the drummer said.

"Means good news," Shep concluded. "Okay, the good news is I can't afford to pay you any more."

"Thank goodness the money is so bad we won't miss it," Braithwaite said.

"I can always paint a house," Manta said.

I joined in the mood of levity. "I can always move back to Nottingham and resume my job dragging the rain covers on and off the cricket field. At least it's steady work."

Muir Levy played a heavy fanfare on the piano. "And now for the bad news."

"The bad news," Shep said, "is that I want you to keep on playing for me. You're sounding better all the time. *Take the A Train* was really super tonight."

"I think we've just been told we're loved," I said.

"Is that what you call it?" Zolf muttered. "I call it rape."

Before we left, I reassured the pub owner that we would continue showing up on Thursday nights. The following week, on Monday at half past seven, I took a bus to Carlotta's school. She gives a bunch of the older girls a class in voice production after which I collect her and we go for a tandoori chicken dinner at the Bombay Paradise Take-Away Café. Yes, that could become another lyric.

I was early but the girls were leaving and there was no sign of Carlotta. "She had to go," one of them told me. "Something about a special band meeting at the church hall."

I sprang for a taxi, spending my now-redundant tandoori money. At the church hall there was no music being played. It was more like a conference at the bank. Carlotta interpreted the expression on my face. It told her there had been activity from the Zolf department of treachery, Doublecross Division. "I thought you knew about this," she whispered. "I expected you to be here."

"And here I am," I said, giving Zolf one of my nice-guy smiles. Everybody likes me, that's why I'm the leader.

"This is about the disco gig," Zolf said in my direction. "I thought you weren't interested."

"Rimless glasses," Carlotta murmured.

"I'm interested in whatever affects The Bones Cornfield Quintet," I said. "Carry on."

It seemed Zolf had been negotiating with the manager of the Aladdin Disco. When Shep announced he could no longer pay us, the former bank employee rubbed the magic lamp. The result was an offer for us to play not one but two nights a week at the Aladdin for a fee which, if not exactly handsome, was certainly not as homely as the amount we had been getting from Shep.

At the end of Zolf's explanation the band members turned and looked at me. "What do you say, boss?" Braithwaite asked.

"I don't like discos," I said. "I hate disco music. In my opinion it is to popular music what sausages are to food. I would hate to see The Bones Cornfield Quintet playing in a disco."

"That's another thing," Zolf said. "I don't think that's a persua-sive name for a disco band. We should call ourselves something like Zodiac or Starsounds."

This opened the door to a fifteen-minute creative session as every-body suggested names for a disco band. It proved my point about the sterile disco scene: say any word that comes into your head and it can be the name of one of their pseudo-bands. Paperclip. Blinding Headache. Desk Lamp. It's the same with race horses. You can call a race horse anything and you can call a disco band anything.

I began to realize the other four were ready to try this enterprise. The money appealed to them. So did two nights a week. The Bones Cornfield Quintet was not as holy an institution to them as it was to me, Bones Cornfield.

"There's something else," I argued. "The Aladdin has a bad rep-utation. The kids pour out into the street when the dance is over and they have gang fights. Punks against mods. They vandalize the bus shelters, intimidate people walking their dogs. It's a bad scene."

"I don't see what that has to do with the band," Zolf said, dis-missing me as if I was a teenager asking for a loan. "How many of you want to give it a try?"

Diabolical sonofagun, how could anybody object to giving some-thing a try? Up went the hands of Manta, Levy, and Braithwaite. Carlotta and I felt the ship going down beneath us.

"As for your old-style double bass," Zolf said to me, "I'd rather have an electric bass for this gig. I know a guy. And no hard feelings, Carlotta," he said, filling the room with feelings as hard as anthra-cite, "but we don't need a vocalist for the music we'll be playing."

No question about it, the band was being stolen from under my nose.

I wanted to yell, "Arrest that man!" Instead I said, "Don't count me out, Len. I can borrow a Fender bass from a friend of mine. And I'll know the fingering by the time we play."

"And I'll shake a tambourine and look sexy on stage," Carlotta said. "This is my band, too."

One rehearsal was all the quintet needed to master the tedious music played to accompany the gymnastics of the disco crowd. After an evening's work the group was ready with a program to be performed in half-hour chunks alternating with recorded music supervised by a DJ with a professional vocabulary of thirty-five words.

I brought a few tins of beer to Carlotta's flat the night before the first gig and we conducted a premortem, sitting in deck chairs on her back roof, watching strips of lighted train windows flowing past on the overhead tracks a mile away, listening to a tape of my old favorites that included the Dinning Sisters singing *Don't Blame Me*.

"I found out why Zolf was kicked out of the bank," Carlotta told me.

"How did you do that?"

"A friend of mine works at the Wandsworth branch. She'd never heard of Leonard Zolf but she asked some questions."

"What were the answers?"

"He took it upon himself. The loans manager was away for a week and during that time Zolf granted loans and overdrafts to several people who should not have had them. He did it because it made him feel important."

"That's our Zolf."

"He takes it upon himself," Carlotta repeated as she opened two more beers and passed one to me.

"Whatever happened to our nice band?" I asked more or less rhetorically. "And how is it all going to end?"

"Nothing stays the same," was Carlotta's defeatist reply.

"I'll tell you something that stays the same," I said, listening to the pure voices on the tape blending like silver chimes. "Sweet harmony stays the same. Good sounds."

Carlotta picked me up and drove me to the Aladdin. As we went inside, I saw the band's new name on a sign near the door. Zolf the banker had been at work—the group was now called Overdraft.

The experience was as boring and as threatening as I knew it would be. We played our first set all in one chunk, not even bothering to change keys. Zolf repeated a monotonous riff on the trumpet, stepping to the microphone every now and then to cry, "Get down!" and sometimes he blew a blast on a referee's whistle. What it had to do with music was beyond me.

The kids lurked in groups and might have been in communication except when they danced. Then it was zombie time. I suppose they were all imagining themselves to be John Revolting or Trivia Neu-tron-Bomb. I remembered the old days when a dance meant arms around each other and heads together, sweet kisses and whispered promises.

When closing time rolled around, the kids were turned out into the street, and we soon heard the sounds of combat. We went to the doorway. There were a dozen lads fighting and a hundred watch-ing, screaming them on. I saw boys on the ground covering up, the boot going in, lots of spit and cursing. One thing struck me—not much physical damage was being done. It was like a ritual; they did it because it was expected of them. We used to have the home Waltz and today they have a punch-up.

A bus went by and wisely refused to stop. Some boys and girls ran after it flinging bottles which smashed in the street. "Is this what we're doing two nights a week from now on?" I said to no-body in particular.

Zolf picked it up. "Nothing to do with us." He had a fistful of money. "Come on inside," he announced. "It's payday."

That was the Tuesday fiasco. We had another scheduled for Friday. On Thursday, Carlotta came to my place and I put on the album of Charlie Parker with Strings. Eventually we would wander down the road for fish and chips. For now we were talking and sipping rosé and getting hungry.

"I don't think I can face the Aladdin any more," I said.

"Nobody really likes it except Leonard."

"Then why are we doing it?"

"Because it's been sold to us."

"Same reason the kids go, I suppose. They've been told this is the thing to do."

"And a lot of hustlers in the record business are making a fortune merchandising schlock."

"Well, I'm not buying any more. Let Zolf get his friend to play bass."

Carlotta punished me with half a minute of disapproving silence. Then she said, "Do you know all that is needed for the triumph of evil?"

I completed the axiom. "That good men do nothing."

"Right. This is your band, Bones. We're going through a bad patch, you can't desert us now. Stay and fight."

The thought of confronting Zolf, of taking him on for control of the band, was very upsetting. Zolf loved contention, the threat of violence fueled his engine. I wanted peace at any price, almost. Even now I felt the tension, a frightening anger boiling up inside me.

Then the stylus slid into the next track on the record and Charlie Parker began to blow *April in Paris*. As the string section laid down a fabric of lush chords, Bird's alto poured out notes like hard, bright diamonds tumbling from a velvet sack. I felt my tension evaporating.

"Carlotta," I said, "I think I have an idea." I told her what I had in mind.

"That's more like it," she said, and she gave me an approving kiss.

"That's more like it," I said.

The Friday disco was a photocopy of the one before. I suspected they would all be the same until the kids died of boredom at seventeen. During one of our breaks, while the DJ was plugging the top ten and Zolf was in the manager's office counting the take, I had a word with the other members of the group. They needed no long explanation—they were with me immediately.

The only problem would be getting rid of Zolf at the crucial time. Carlotta said she would take care of it.

As we began our final set, she went to Zolf and said, "I was just out in the parking lot having a breath of air. Your car is gone."

Zolf put down his trumpet and left on the run. "Is his car really gone?" I asked.

"Sure is," Carlotta said. "I sneaked the keys from his coat and moved it during intermission. It's on the next street. He'll be a good half hour talking to the police."

The band played two more identical numbers and then I stopped the sausage machine. I went to the mike and said, "Okay, kids, a change in mood. We're going to close with something different. We call this a time to get to know your partner."

I counted a slow four and the band began to play one of our

romantic medleys. We started with *Sentimental Journey*, segued into *Harlem Nocturn*, then ended with *Dream*. Carlotta sang the final number in that clear voice of hers, no pretense, just an intelligent concentration on the meaning of the words.

". . . *Things never are as bad as they seem . . .*"

The crowd applauded when the set ended, the first human response I have ever heard from a disco floor. As they drifted out of the hall, Zolf appeared with a livid face. "All right," he said, "which one of you cretins moved my car?"

"Guilty, and proud of it," Carlotta said.

"Acting on my instructions," I put in. "We needed you gone so we could change the program."

"Yes, I heard that Mickey Mouse music from the outside. What's going on?"

"Follow me and I'll show you."

I led the group to the front door and we stepped outside into a calm summer evening. The kids were drifting away, some of them queueing for a bus. There was a certain amount of exuberant teen-aged shouting, but not a clenched fist anywhere.

"What we did was soothe a lot of savage breasts and ennoble a few hearts," I said. "We charmed these kids with our music."

"That isn't the idea," Zolf fumed. "Disco music turns people on, it strings them out. Man, we are paid to establish a 'high' and sustain it. No way are you going to change this lucrative gig into your square old failure of a band concert. That was the first and last time you alter my program."

Zolf turned and headed inside. I glanced at Carlotta; she was watching me. So were the other members of the quintet. Carlotta nodded but said nothing. Words were unnecessary. I knew this was a perfect example of the bad guy winning unless the good guy is willing to take action. "Hey, Zolf," I called, stopping him at the door.

"Yeah?"

"I take exception to everything you just said."

"So?"

I approached him, took the rimless glasses off his nose, and handed them to Carlotta. "So this," I said and planted one on his jaw. He sat down on the pavement and looked up at me. "The band now goes back to being The Bones Cornfield Quintet," I said. "We'll keep the disco job. But we'll play a balanced program, the frenetic stuff interspersed with standards that don't all sound the same. All right?"

I'm not sure whether Zolf replied because the response from the boys was immediate and loud. "Yeah! That's right, boss. That's what we're going to do."

Driving home with Carlotta, I said, "That felt good. It really did. One punch on the chops gave me more satisfaction than saying all the right things in a ten-minute argument."

"That's why they invented violence," she said. "It's like making love. It feels good." The car rolled to a stop in front of her house. "And you were terrific," she added, putting her arms around me. "I like the way you took charge." She kissed me so hard my teeth hurt.

"Which was that?" I asked. "Love or violence?"

"Take your choice," she said. "It's a fine line."

And I think that's a fine line to end on.